Ria Alice & Jessica May

ISBN: 9781036916718

To all the girls who fantasise over fan edits of the hottest celebrities in the world.

Playlist

"Accidentally in Love"- New Found Glory
"Guilty Pleasure" - Chappell Roan
"bad idea" - Ariana Grande
"Stop The World I Wanna Get Off With You" - Arctic Monkeys
"Please Please Please" - Sabrina Carpenter
"Dangerous Hands" - Austin Giorgio
"Bad for Business" - Sabrina Carpenter
"Flawless" - The Neighbourhood
"Come Back...Be Here (Taylor's Version)" - Taylor Swift
"PILLOWTALK" - ZAYN
"Take a Bow" - Leona Lewis
"vampire" - Olivia Rodrigo
"Ghost Town" - Benson Boone
"Normal Thing" - Gracie Abrams
"What A Time" - Julia Michaels, Niall Horan
"Daylight" - Taylor Swift

CONTENT NOTES

This story contains explicit sexual content, profanity and topics that some readers may find sensitive including: sexual harassment and mild violence.

AUTHOR'S NOTES

This story follows the production of a film. Please note, certain details about the length of time a movie takes to be filmed and the process itself have been modified for the purposes of the storyline. We are not professional filmmakers so please forgive any incorrect information!

1

VERITY

"Happy birthday!"

I blew out the candles on the homemade chocolate cake that my best friend, Lilah, had baked, as the clock struck midnight. The flames extinguished and I looked around at the happy faces of my closest friends, dressed in casual attire. The four of us were crammed into my tiny kitchen as Lilah set the plate down on the counter and the sound of fireworks bursting in the distance began.

"And happy flat warming!" Jacob exclaimed, as he popped a bottle of prosecco and began pouring the bubbles into four mismatched vessels. I took the mug of sparkling wine from him and raised it in a cheers.

"And happy new year!" I added. 1st of January, what a crap day for a birthday.

"Ah that's the least important thing that's happening right now." Amelia joked as she clinked her wine glass against the ceramic of my cup, whilst the faint sound of Auld Lang Syne from the flat below echoed into the room.

I smiled inwardly as I reflected over the past twelve hours. We were all in tracksuits, hair scraped back and had a thin sheen of sweat across our brows from the physical activity of the day. I had finally picked up the keys for my new Shoreditch flat that morning and my friends had been kind enough to give up their New Year's Eve plans to help me lug numerous boxes of belongings up three flights of stairs - thanks to the lift conveniently being out of order.

"Thanks again guys, I really appreciate you helping me today - well yesterday now." I grinned warmly.

"No where else we'd rather be, V!" Lilah said, wrapping me up in a huge hug, her auburn hair getting in my face as she squeezed me tightly. Lilah and I had been best friends since we were kids and had been there for each other through the good and bad times over the years.

"Was Zane okay with you abandoning him this evening?" I queried.

"He'll get over it." She shrugged jovially. "Anyway, he's out with Theo, so I'm sure he's having a good time." As if on cue her phone began to vibrate with an incoming call.

"Speak of the devil." Jacob laughed, noticing Zane's contact pop up on Lilah's device.

"Hey," Lilah answered the phone, waving off Jacob's comment as she excused herself to the corner of the room.

Zane was Lilah's boss turned boyfriend. It had been a pretty whirlwind few months for the pair after Lilah had started working back at Moreno Jewellery, the company Zane owned, helping to get everything ready for their anticipated Valentine's launch. She had also recently moved into Zane's swanky townhouse which was a mansion in comparison to my box flat.

"What about Josh, what's he up to tonight?" I asked Amelia.

"Oh, he's out too. I'm not sure of his plans exactly, I haven't heard from him since this morning." She replied, shrugging her shoulders. Her phone pinged and her brown eyes lit up. She tapped the screen, as it illuminated, her expression dimmed and a downcast look spread across her face.

"Wow, I'm manifesting your boyfriends contacting you!" I giggled.

"It was just a friend." Amelia replied, forcing a fake laugh, as she tried to hide her disappointment.

"Babe, can you manifest me a boyfriend please?" Jacob joked, bringing a real smile to Amelia's face.

"Sorry, my powers aren't *that* strong." I tapped him on the shoulder in jest, as *his* phone began to blow up with notifications. "Doesn't sound like you need any help in that department anyway, Jake."

"Oh you know me, hun, I like to keep my options open." He winked, turning over the phone. "You know the saying, treat 'em mean."

I met Amelia and Jacob last Summer when Lilah was going through a hard time and needed her support system. The three friends had met at Moreno Jewellery when Lilah started working there last Spring and they kindly welcomed me into the friendship group with open arms, when I declared I was moving to London for an upcoming work opportunity.

"And before anyone asks, I haven't had any messages," I held up the evidence of my silent phone, before the device betrayed me with a notification. "Ah, I tell a lie Gregg's messaged me!"

"Who's Gregg?" Lilah asked, returning to the group.

"The bakery," I laughed, "I've got a free birthday sausage roll I can claim!" I waved the text in the air as laughter erupted from my friends.

"Well, I suppose you have to keep yourself available for Mr Axel Ford." Jacob exclaimed, fanning himself dramatically.

"This is my first big film role. I can assure you I'll be keeping it professional. I won't be mixing work and pleasure." I looked in Lilah's direction, "unlike some people I know."

"Don't knock it 'till you've tried it. It worked out well for me." She shrugged.

"Yeah, I'd shag my boss too if it was on the cards!" Jacob took a sip out of his plastic cup.

"Jacob?!" Amelia burst out, looking towards Lilah who was choking on a mouthful of prosecco.

"Um, that's my boyfriend you're talking about." Lilah complained, light-heartedly.

"And good for you hun, I've been very open about how fit I've found your man from day one, you should be thankful he's straight," he smirked, "well, regardless of whether you really fuck Axel, at least you get to pretend to. I've read that book and I know there are some pretty smutty scenes, you lucky girl." He nudged me, raising his eyebrows suggestively.

It had been my dream for as long as I could remember, to be an actor. I had followed all the steps: go to a performing arts university, sign with an agent, work temp jobs until I hit the big time, but the best I had achieved so far were some toothpaste adverts and minor extra work on period dramas which were totally uncredited. However, I had surprisingly booked the female lead in an upcoming movie, *Accidentally in Love*. A big-budget, highly anticipated adaptation of the number one New York Times bestselling romance novel from Claudia Winslow. Imagine if *Fifty Shades* and *Gilmore Girls* had a baby, they would have birthed this story. It was complimentary coffees and cakes rather than contracts and boardrooms but there was still *plenty* of spice!

The book had been taking the charts by storm ever since its release last year and everyone had been waiting to see who would be cast as the romantic leads, Rosie and Tyler.

They set up an open casting to find the perfect Rosie, which drew in thousands of blonde-haired novices to audition for the leading lady and by some miracle I was chosen! Thankfully when it was announced that an unknown person had been selected, I'd received very little complaints.

However, Axel Ford had been fancast as the American bad boy from the get-go and luckily for the admirers of the book, he had accepted the role when offered - which was a step in a different creative direction for him.

Axel was the current biggest actor in Hollywood, known for his superstar good looks, serious, alternative movie roles and fuckboy demeanour. I was equal parts surprised, thrilled and anxious at having to get into close quarters with him. So far, our communication had been via Zoom calls only, during script reads which we couldn't do in person, as Axel was finishing up another job on the other side of the world. Even just hearing his husky, Brooklyn accent, through a crackly speaker, set my nerves alight. Next week, I would be meeting him in the flesh, the man who my sister and I had ogled on screen since we were pre-teens and I hoped that some of the news stories I'd read about him being an arsehole had been dramatised for clickbait.

Diva co-star aside, my dreams of being on a real blockbuster film set were finally coming true and as I began my twenty-seventh year, I couldn't deny the feeling of excitement I felt for the twelve months ahead.

Good friends, good job, what could possibly go wrong?

2

VERITY

I woke up to the familiar sound of purring and the surprisingly painful pressure of four paws padding across my chest.

"Morning, Misto," I yawned, peeling my eyes open and scratching the black and white fur of my tuxedo cat, Mr Mistoffolees, named after the character from my favourite musical. I had rescued him from a cat sanctuary two years ago and after a lot of convincing, I had been able to keep him at my parents' house until I finally found my own place for us. To be honest, I hadn't planned on living at home for quite so long but between unsteady acting jobs and temporary admin work at local corporate companies, the timeline had shifted on a bit further than initially intended. "Someone's finally feeling more at home!" He had been hiding behind the sofa for the past week, only coming out when coaxed by his favourite treats. "Let's get you some breakfast."

I checked the time on my phone, 7am, an hour to go until the car would be picking me up. I threw the covers off and padded to the kitchen, Misto wound his way through my legs and meowed hungrily as I filled his bowl.

I headed to the bathroom and splashed cold water on my face to wake myself up fully and centre my thoughts for the big day ahead.

Today was the day!

First day on a film set, first day as Rosie with the team and most nerve wracking, the first day meeting Axel Ford. I stared at the reflection in the mirror and lost myself in a daydream.

I vividly recalled getting the call from my agent last year telling me I had gotten the role. I swear time stood still as she relayed the details to me.

The casting director loved you, you not only perfectly fit the description physically but the way you portrayed the innocence and naivety of Rosie's character won you the job!

I took a deep breath in a poor attempt to settle my nerves as I brushed my long blonde hair before tying it up loosely with a scrunchie and applying minimal make up in classic Rosie style.

Although no actual filming was taking place today, I wanted to feel the part for our first official table read. I decided on a pair of dark blue denim mom jeans and a cropped, knitted baby pink jumper that complimented my blue eyes.

I grabbed my annotated script, tucking it neatly into my canvas tote, checking I had everything I needed for the day. Slipping on my Converse, I slung my bag over my shoulder and headed down to meet my driver.

Movie star perks!

"Good morning, Miss Sloan." A well-dressed man in his fifties, greeted when I reached the road, opening the door of the black town car.

"Hello," I replied as I slid into the backseat and the door closed behind me.

"I'm Clive. I'll be your driver over the next few months of filming. Anything you need, just give me a call and I'll be there in a jiffy." He advised, smiling warmly at me in the reflection of the rear-view mirror as he got back into the car and started the ignition.

"Nice to meet you and please, call me Verity." I replied, clicking my seatbelt into place. The car pulled out of the space and I looked out the window as we started the journey to set. My nerves began to creep in as I fiddled with my nails, trying to resist reaching for my script.

"How are you feeling on your first day?" Clive asked, glancing at me.

"Erm, I'm okay." I responded, not wanting to show the true level of my anxiety. He had probably met some of the biggest stars and the last thing I'm sure he would want is a newcomer crippled with self doubt in his backseat.

"Everyone's nervous on their first day, Miss Sloan. I bet you'll be great!"

"Thank you Clive and it's Verity remember?" I laughed, feeling grateful for this stranger's words of encouragement. "Do you know any of the other cast or crew? Any advice? Who to avoid in the mornings until they've had a coffee? Who's easily offended?" I word vomited.

"Okay let me see. On the whole, this crew is a lovely one but you can always butter up the runners with pastries when it's a particularly early call time."

"Okay noted…what about Axel Ford? Are the rumours true?" I enquired, unable to stop myself from asking the burning question.

"I've never worked directly with Mr Ford and I'm not one to gossip, but I have heard from other drivers in the trade, that they have had to wait hours for him to arrive at pick up locations and he's not been particularly polite or friendly when he has finally shown up. Although, that was a year or so ago, so hopefully he's grown up a bit now." He informed me. I pondered his words. I had hoped to be reassured that the countless stories of him turning up to studios late after evening escapades might have been exaggerated for the media but hearing of his tardiness and inflated ego towards staff, it didn't sound as though we'd be friends any time soon.

"Ah well, he's in his late thirties now, so I'm sure he's gained some manners." I said. Clive smiled reassuringly at me although, there was a certain look in his eye that seemed he didn't share my optimism.

"Here we are, Miss Sloan." Clive announced, pulling into the busy car park of the studio a little while later. "Have a good day and I'll be back to pick you up tonight!"

"Thanks, see you later!" I called, letting his formal address go, getting out of the vehicle. I fumbled in my bag for the pass I had been sent earlier in the week and walked towards the large warehouse style buildings ahead of me. When I reached the tall iron fence, I tapped my card against the reader and was relieved that it granted me access. There was a part of me that still thought this whole thing could've been a prank and that I hadn't actually gotten this role. I half expected a camera crew from a reality show to jump out at me when the pass was proven to be fake - thankfully, that wasn't the case!

Closing the heavy gate behind me, I checked my phone for the location to head to.

Studio 2, Room 3A.

I looked around my vast surroundings, until I spotted a map and quickly read the information before walking in the direction of the meeting.

When I arrived at the destination, I tentatively knocked on the door, nerves fully consuming me. After a minute, no one had answered, so I slowly pushed it open to reveal a conference style white room. On the right side of the space were numerous tables lined up to form a large square with chairs lining the perimeter. Bottles of water and place cards were stationed at each seat, highlighting the actor's name and the character they were playing or the job they had on set. The earlier apprehension was replaced with pure excitement as the realisation sunk in, that I was on an actual table read!

"Miss Sloan, lovely to meet you. Welcome to the first day on set of *Accidentally in Love*, ah, so exciting!

Would you like a drink? Breakfast? Can I get you anything?" An overexcited brunette bounced over to me. "I'm Grace, I'll be your assistant on set." She held out her hand and enthusiastically shook mine as I returned the gesture.

"Hi Grace, I'm Verity. I'm okay for the moment thank you, but maybe in a bit." I smiled, before taking a shaky breath.

"You're gonna smash it by the way! I can't wait to see Rosie come to life." Grace said reassuringly, sensing my nerves as she placed a soft hand on my arm.

"Thanks," I lowered my voice to a whisper, "to be honest with you, I'm shitting myself a bit but gotta fake it till you make it right?"

"Exactly! You've got this, girl." She encouraged, "and if you ever want to escape and find a room to scream into a pillow, track me down and I'll join you."

"That sounds great but I'm more of a drown-my-worries-in-alcohol kinda girl, so maybe let's hit a bar instead?" I suggested, in an open invitation. My nerves disappeared almost entirely around her bubbly personality.

"I'd love to!" She replied as her eyes lit up. "Follow me, I'll properly introduce you to the rest of the team!" I recognised the majority of the people in the room from virtual introductions as most of the crew were from overseas.

She took my coat off me and hung it on a peg on the wall, before guiding me towards the group chatting on the sofas, on the left hand side of the room.

I spent the next twenty minutes introducing myself to various members of the cast and crew, my cheeks hurt from smiling so much. Grace led me towards the final two people in the room who I hadn't spoken to yet. Nora Black, the Director, and Claudia Winslow, the Author of the book, stood before me.

"Nora, Claudia, this is Verity - our wonderful Rosie Woods," Grace introduced me, for what felt like the hundredth time that morning. Nora, a striking brunette, exuded sophistication in a white t-shirt, sharp black blazer and tailored trousers. She gave me a polite, professional smile. Claudia, on the other hand, radiated warmth, with her wavy mousy brown hair and mismatched attire, exactly how you would picture an author to look. When I held my hand out towards Claudia to shake, I was surprised when she instead, enveloped me in an all-encompassing hug.

"Thank you for bringing Rosie to life, you look exactly how I pictured her and I know she's in safe hands with you." She declared, holding me by the tops of my arms and leaning back to take in my appearance. A genuine smile spread across her face and I returned the look, the pressure of doing her beloved character justice on screen was still there but her approval calmed my nerves tenfold.

"Welcome Verity, we're excited to have you with us and kick off the project! Great to finally meet you in person," Nora greeted. As expected, she had been heavily involved in the casting process but like many others, had been tied up completing other projects so reviewed my auditions virtually, "speaking of, has anyone seen Axel yet?"

"Not that I've been made aware of Nora, let me chase up and I'll get back with some info asap." Grace stated before disappearing off, tapping away on her phone. The lively woman from earlier, now replaced with a straight professional.

"Well, whilst we wait for Mr Ford to grace us with his presence, why don't we start working out some clothing options for our Rosie. Colin, can you take Verity to wardrobe please?" A bald man, with thick black rimmed glasses appeared beside me, out of nowhere. I double took, this man was the twin of Stanley Tucci's character from *The Devil Wears Prada*. I was almost certain I was dreaming and that Miranda Priestly was going to pop out and berate me over a cerulean jumper!

"Certainly Nora, Verity dear, come this way."

For the next hour or so, I felt like a Barbie playing dress up as we flipped through various brightly coloured, patterned fabric swatches and clothing pieces that fashion houses had sent to the set to dress me in. One thing about Rosie Woods, the girl was not afraid of standing out.

"He's pulling up outside everyone!" A member of the crew called through to announce Axel's impending arrival. My heart began to thud with anticipation. It was as if a member of the Royal Family was about to appear. Should I curtsy when he entered? Refer to him as Your Majesty? I didn't consider myself the fangirl type but I'd never met a celebrity of his calibre before, let alone the biggest star on Planet Earth so my nerves were off the chart.

"If everyone can take their seats, we will begin as soon as he arrives." Nora clapped her hands together authoritatively as the room became a buzz with chatter and movement.

Sitting down in the chair that Grace had shown me earlier, I was relieved to find Claudia sat across from me. There was something overwhelmingly cosy about her. The oversized knit cardigan draped over her petite frame and her round, orange-framed glasses balanced at the tip of her nose. She scrunched up her face in excitement, her expression brimming with kindness as she gave me an enthusiastic double thumbs up. Despite the anxious knots twisting in my stomach, I couldn't help but grin back at her. I glanced to my left and saw the empty seat, quickly checking the name on the place card.

Of course, it's *him*.

Get it together, Verity. You're just sitting next to each other, that's all.

I knew I had to get comfortable being around him and fast if I was going to survive this shoot. I had to kiss him. Multiple times. With our clothes off, for God's sake, but I would have to worry about that later.

Right now, the hottest person in the world was headed this way and would be spending the next six hours a few inches away from me.

The door swung open and I could have sworn the air changed as the man of the hour walked into the room. There he was. Axel bloody Ford, all six foot two of him. I had seen hundreds of photos of the man over the years, but *nothing* could have prepared me for the vision he was in person.

His whole aura screamed megastar. He was dressed in distressed black jeans coupled with a vintage t-shirt and an oversized black leather jacket. His face was hidden behind dark aviator glasses however his chiselled jawline was hard to miss. He stood there oblivious to the number of people in the room, a large percentage of which were gawking at him, whilst he scrolled absentmindedly on his phone.

"Pleasure of you to join us, Axel." Nora called in his direction, seemingly breaking him out of his daydream.

"The pleasure's all mine, Ms Black." He drawled in his American accent, sauntering towards the only empty seat at the table. My hands shook nervously as he walked towards me and I wished that the name card had been placed in the wrong position. Just before he took his seat, I clasped my hands together to steady them and gave myself an internal pep talk.

He's just a man. An insanely attractive man. But a man no less.

As he took his seat, a cloud of his cologne flooded my senses. I immediately recognised it as Tobacco Vanille. I gulped, trying to dislodge the lump in my throat, as I built up the courage to introduce myself.

"Hi, I'm Verity, I'm playing Rosie. I'm looking forward to working with you." I smiled sweetly, trying to make my voice sound calm and confident as he removed his sunglasses. He looked directly into my eyes and I froze.

Holy fuck. His grey eyes bored into my literal soul and I was overwhelmed by his beauty. I attempted to pull myself together to shake his hand, however before I had a chance to hold mine out, he merely looked me up and down and turned his body back towards the table.

Okay then. I guess those rumours may have been true after all. He shrugged off his jacket and hung it over the chair. I tried with all my self control, not to look, but my eyes were drawn to his now exposed bulging arm muscles which were inked with faded tattoos.

"Let's get started then, shall we?" Nora announced, beginning to read out loud the stage directions from the script. I quickly took a sip of my water as my mouth had become as dry as the Sahara Desert.

I took a deep breath and began to speak my first line

3

AXEL

"That's a wrap on the first full table read of *Accidentally in Love* everyone!" Nora declared as the room erupted into obnoxious clapping.

Thank God that's over. I wouldn't call myself a snob but this wasn't exactly my usual genre. I had spent years building up a respectable repertoire of thought provoking works that went beyond the surface level. The deepest thing about *Accidentally in Love*, was the grande cup in Rosie's coffee shop for fuck's sake. Don't get me wrong, it was easy money and an easy gig, the most Tyler did was smile charmingly, fawning after Rosie as she dreamed of expanding her caffeine empire.

How original!

I was thirty seven and feeling very out of place as I recited the twee romantic lines dripping in caffeine and baked goods related humour. But sitting there, I reminded myself why I had agreed to take on this role in the first place.

I'd had it on good authority that my favourite Director, Gus Kensington, was in the process of casting his next upcoming project, *Requiem*. A film noir centred around a serial killer and the police force that were unsuccessfully tracking him down. Think Fincher's *Seven* but thirty years on.

I was desperate to be cast as the lead detective in the movie and work with a hero of mine, but when discussing the opportunity with my agent, Sarah, she had informed me of the level of press I had received around my so-called 'unprofessionalism' and how Gus was a serious man who didn't take lightly to negative media attention being associated with his sets or the talent.

We had brainstormed for a while over ways to secure the role and all roads had led back to good publicity, hence why I now found myself sitting around the table, reading girly, softcore porn. Sarah had looked into the role further when she had been contacted by the casting director. They had told her that fans of the book were desperate to see me as the leading man, so we agreed with the amount of eyes on the project and the opportunity for squeaky clean exposure, it was too great to miss.

How much trouble could I really get up to on a rom com set?

The sound of rustling paper broke me out of my thoughts as Verity collected her plethora of notes.

I had to stop myself from physically rolling my eyes at the action. God, what a teacher's pet. Sure, she was a pretty girl, with that blonde hair, blue eyed thing going on, but her clear eagerness to please was totally off putting. I could tell that these next few months were going to be filled with high levels of irritation and impatience for the film to be wrapped.

Her whole demeanour screamed naivety. I didn't know for certain, but I'd put money on the fact that this was her first role from the deer-in-headlights expression alone.

Bless her, that light in her eyes will dim over time.

4

VERITY

Ping!

Thank God for chef Mike after a long day at the studio. I took out my steaming ready meal from the microwave and carefully peeled off the plastic before pouring the molten pasta onto a plate.

I carried the food across the room to my sofa, placing it on my lap. I leant across to pick up the remote to turn on Netflix and find a comfort show to watch. Just as I was deciding between *The Office* and *Miranda*, my phone started to ring.

I sighed as I saw 'Mum' flash up on the screen. I'd been in this flat for nearly a fortnight and this was the first time I'd heard from her.

This wasn't going to do anything to reduce my stress levels. "Hello?" I answered apprehensively.

"Good evening, Verity, I hope I'm not interrupting." My mother, Eleanor, said feigning regard for my plans. "I wanted to call you to let you know some exciting family news."

Of course she wasn't calling to check in on her youngest daughter who had moved to London and out of the family home for the first time. Silly me!

"I'm all ears." I said flatly, clicking the call to speaker before setting the phone down beside me.

"Our Charlotte has been made partner at the law firm she's been working at. How amazing! What an incredible feat at such a young age and when she's only been working there a year or so. We are so proud!" She exclaimed excitedly. *Our Charlotte.* As in my sister, who was two years older than me and the apple of my parents' eyes.

To them she had everything I didn't. A stable, highly salaried job, a devoted husband and a work ethic that meant she completely burned herself out on cases to the detriment of her wellbeing but that, to my parents, was the sign of a hard worker. Whereas I was, in Mum's words 'an unemployed layabout with unrealistic dreams beyond my capabilities,' not to mention very much single and not on the lookout to provide grandchildren any time soon.

"That's great."

"Oh and Dominic has been working tirelessly to open his new surgery. We expect it to be up and running by the end of the month." My mother gloated like she was reciting achievements to show off to the ladies in her book club.

"Well done, Dominic." I interjected, trying to keep the sarcasm out of my voice. She continued to boast about her wonderkid and perfect doctor son-in-law whilst I daydreamed, twirling my pasta absentmindedly, making interested noises at suitable intervals.

My mind drifted back to today's table read. The room had buzzed with the same nervous excitement as the day before as we worked through the script for the second time. I had started to find my rhythm, feeling more confident delivering my lines in front of the group. My day one nerves had dissipated and I was settling into the role of Rosie! Lunch had been enjoyable too - I'd spent it with a few of the other actors and Claudia, the five of us laughed and chatted as if we'd known each other longer than just a day and a half.

My only grievance at the moment was Mr Ford. Yes, his good looks were impossible to ignore but so was his arsehole attitude. Throughout the entire read, he hadn't said a word to me. Not a hello, not even a glance in my direction, he was completely indifferent to my entire existence. I had tried to convince myself that maybe this was part of his process, not to exchange basic niceties with his co-stars so as to not detract from the relationship on screen. But as more time went on, the more it became apparent that Axel was just self-centred rather than an overly deep thespian.

Rosie and Tyler seemed to get on quite nicely however, my character poured her heart out and Axel delivered his lines like a true professional, each phrase coated with emotion that made the entire room hang off his every word. But the moment the scene ended; any lingering chemistry vanished!

I tried to focus on my lines but my attention kept drifting and I couldn't help sneaking glances to my side. As if he wasn't distracting enough already, halfway through act two, he casually slid on a pair of reading glasses. I nearly passed out. Just when I had thought the man couldn't get any sexier!

"Verity, are you still there?" Eleanor questioned as I must have missed reacting to a *fascinating* part of her speech.

"Yes, sorry Mum, I'm just tired from a long day at the studio." I replied, shaking myself out of the memory.

"Oh yes, how could I forget, how's the little film going?" She asked, I rolled my eyes at her belittling statement. I'd hardly call a £25M budget movie a 'little film'.

"Not bad, thanks, we start shooting next week." I stated unemotionally, knowing it was futile to go into the details too heavily.

"The rest of the week off then? You really should look at getting a second job on the side, Verity." I hummed in mock agreement, there was no point fighting my corner. I was hardly getting paid pennies for this role but I wasn't in the mood to divulge my personal finances tonight. "I suppose it is strange not having you lazing about on our sofa." My mother continued, in what was, I think, supposed to be a compliment?

"Yeah, it is odd not being home. But the flat is really nice." I lied, looking around at the tiny apartment. My eyes caught on the peeling wallpaper, wonky floorboards and a suspiciously damp-looking patch on the ceiling above me. Safe to say, I wouldn't be having my family round to visit any time soon…

"I'm sure it is, Verity. Oh, Charlotte's calling me. I've got to go. Speak to you soon."

"Goodnight, Mu-" The sound of the call ending cut me off.

I grabbed the previously abandoned TV remote and clicked on the first show that appeared. As I sat in my box flat, chowing down on my Tesco carbonara, I tried hard to keep the insecurity at bay as thoughts of Charlotte's successes threatened to creep into my mind. Snap out of it Verity! I should have been excited and proud of myself for landing such a sought-after role, not crippling myself with self-doubt because my perfect big sister had impressed our parents yet again. That was hardly a new phenomenon.

My phone lit up with a text from Lilah which instantly shook me out of my funk.

> How were the table reads superstar? Still can't believe you're officially a big time actor!

She was right. I wasn't going to let Eleanor Sloan; President of the Verity-Could-Do-Better fan club get me down! I was settling into my own rented London apartment, working on the most anticipated movie of the year and living my dream! No one was going to rain on my parade today.

5

AXEL

The first day of filming had officially arrived and as much as I hadn't been chomping at the bit to kick off the project, getting started at least meant it would be one day closer to this all being over.

I walked through the studio doors and was immediately pulled into hair and makeup. As I relaxed into the black swivel chair, I flung my bag onto the counter and proceeded to flick through my phone whilst the team of professionals got to work. For the next hour, they massaged my face, prepped my skin for the cameras, including covering my plethora of tattoos and smoothed down my usually unruly dark brown hair. Within minutes of the artists completing, I had been whisked straight into wardrobe where I was met with racks upon racks of the drabbest clothes I had ever seen.

Don't get me wrong, over my well-versed career, I'd played some characters with very questionable fashion tastes but my God, Tyler Burke's wardrobe really took the cake.

Standing in front of the full length mirror, I was stunned speechless at the man before me. It was official there was no edge to Tyler, no personality, he was a total beige person. Nondescript blue faded jeans, brown tan boots and a green checked flannel shirt; I could have walked into an Old Navy store and been mistaken for a mannequin if I'd stood still for long enough.

I put on a red trucker cap to complete the character's signature look, rolled up my script and tucked it under my arm.

Let's get this over with, shall we?

As I meandered towards the sound stage, my Agent, Sarah caught my eye, standing in the doorway of an office she must have acquired for her unexpected visit. She gestured at me to join her and then disappeared back into the room.

"Well, this is a surprise, Sarah." I said calmly, as I walked into the office, shutting the door behind me before leaning against the wall. Sarah was based back in my home state of New York and I hadn't been expecting her arrival. "I hope you come bearing good news?"

"And good morning to you too, Axel." Sarah replied flatly, her ginger hair pulled back tightly into a sleek bun which gave her a permanently astonished look, "take a seat." She directed, pointing at a vacant chair. I released a deep breath before walking over to one of the velvet armchairs, opposite the desk, she was now sitting behind.

"Have you heard from Gus Kensington? Is it confirmed that I have the role?" I blurted out, wanting to get to the point of this spontaneous meeting.

"I wish I could say it was that easy. Unfortunately, as we've discussed before, Gus is a stickler for a clean set and signing onto a romcom isn't enough to convince him that having the notorious party boy, Axel Ford, involved in his project will ensure good publicity." Sarah said, tapping a pen she was holding rhythmically against the wood. "So, until he is reassured, the part is off the table."

"For fuck's sake. Then what am I even doing here?" I scrubbed my stubble on my chin with my hand, exasperated. "You told me taking on this job would guarantee *Requiem* and if that's not the case, why am I sitting in this poor man's lumberjack outfit about to spout off some drivel opposite a kiss ass rookie?"

"Come on, Axel, let's not throw a strop, these things take time. Have I helped you become the number one star on the planet by accepting 'no' the first time I hear it? No! We pivot." She said determined. "If Gus wants squeaky clean, good boy Axel, then that's exactly what we'll give him. No more late nights out with your boys, no more pictures with different girls on your arm after parties and no more public feuds."

"Christ Sarah, are you telling me I've gotta be locked in my apartment, doing crosswords until Gus deems me worthy? I'll go fucking insane!" I put my head in my hands. I knew I was acting like a petulant toddler but I couldn't help it. *Requiem* was my dream role and

Kensington was my hero. I always imagined one day I would try my hand at directing and I admired his cinematography and storytelling greatly. The fact I was within reach of working with him, but my personal reputation could jeopardise it, drove me mad.

"Now now, I have a plan B in mind already. You won't be holed up alone, you're going to be with your girlfriend." She clicked her fingers towards me, her eyes glistening with mischief.

"Come again? Who the fuck is that?" I bit back, flinging my hand in the air in question, she knew full well I was single.

"Well, your fresh faced ingénue out there of course. This is her first major role, no prior scandals in the papers and nothing salacious flagged up on the background check I ran."

"Blondie? You've got to be joking? She seems like the most boring person ever. She's highlighted her script in about five different colours, for God's sake! She's such a goody two shoes. It's bad enough I have to spend so much time on set with her, let alone in my own personal time too." I ran my fingers through my hair, messing up Tyler's carefully constructed quiff in the process. The thought of spending even more unnecessary time with Verity made me shudder, the last thing I wanted was for her to invade what little alone time I had during this filming process.

"Oh perfect, she sounds like an even better fit than I first anticipated." Sarah clapped her hands together, beaming with pride that her little plan was coming together. I sat in silence for a few minutes, staring off into space, tapping my foot as I mentally ran through whatever I may have had in my arsenal to avoid this and counter it, but fell short. I heard one of the producers make the five minute call to set and knew my time for negotiation was up. Dejected, I looked across the desk to Sarah.

"And you really think this will win me the part?" I breathed out, accepting my fate.

"Absolutely. It's simple Axel. Be a good employee, a good boyfriend and only garner positive press and you'll be stepping onto that Kensington set before you know it. We'll tell Verity at the next break."

Slowly, I stood up and nodded in a silent agreement. If this was the key to unlock my next big career step, then I'd be an idiot not to give it a try. Was it possible that I'd sold out? Perhaps, was I going to live to regret giving up my precious free time to spend it with my complete opposite? Most certainly.

But how difficult would a few months of pretending to enjoy her company and smiling for the cameras be. It was acting and I was pretty damn stellar at that. I'd just think of it as my next role.

The hopelessly in love, doting, perfect boyfriend. Easy.

6

VERITY

Nora shouted 'cut' and signalled the first break of the day. My stomach growled as I realised how hungry I was. I wasn't usually one to skip meals, however with the early call time I received today and the fact it was the first day of filming, my nerves won out. I also wasn't expecting to have to go such a long time before I could go to craft services.

I meandered to the catering truck, intrigued to discover what delicious options awaited me and reflected on my morning on an official film set.

Despite the disgusting sound of my alarm ringing at the ungodly hour of 4am, the excitement of filming made me bounce out of bed and into the waiting town car before the sun had risen.

Call me a typical girl but I'd always enjoyed being pampered so I was looking forward to getting moulded into my character. Although this wasn't going to be my usual style, as Rosie had that whole 'no makeup-makeup' thing going on whereas my signature feel-my-best look was often completed with a bold lip, I couldn't wait to get in the chair!

My nerves diminished as the professionals worked their magic to transform me into Rosie. I always found that although I studied my characters inside and out and felt like I knew them like the back of my hand, having my hair done and putting their clothes on, was always the finishing touch in getting me ready to perform.

This morning's scene wasn't a particularly challenging one. It was a scene where my character was deep cleaning the bakery she had bought. By the end of the numerous takes, the counter was positively gleaming - I was certain I could see my reflection perfectly with how much I had buffed it.

As I reached the truck, I pursued the options. It was the usual breakfast items: sausage, bacon, eggs. A greasy roll had never smelt so appealing. Taking a bite of the bap, I started to head back towards my trailer when a shrill voice called over.

"Verity!" I looked over to see a tall, slim woman in a power suit and a tight ginger bun, standing in a doorway. "A moment please," she clicked, ordering me to follow her. I subconsciously did as I was told, heading towards the mysterious room. Although I didn't have any clue as to who this person was, she certainly didn't seem like someone to disobey.

Upon entering the room, I was surprised to find Axel, casually lounging, with one leg crossed at an angle over the other, on one of two blue velvet armchairs. The poor chair looked like it could give out from the sheer magnitude of the man sitting on it. Dressed in what I assumed were Tyler's clothes, stripped back of his movie star aesthetic, he was still as breathtaking as the first time I saw him.

Before either of them spoke, my heart pounded with anxiety. I knew Axel and I were yet to really communicate and hadn't formed the best relationship yet, but would he really have filed a complaint this early on? Given his status and power on set, one word from him and I'd be a goner!

"Please sit, Verity." The unknown woman commanded. Sheepishly, I sunk into the seat beside Axel. "I'm Sarah, Axel's Agent, I wanted to have a little chat. How's the first day going?" She smiled, although it looked as though it pained her to do so.

"Fine, thank you." I quickly responded.

Oh God, oh God, what does she know that I don't?

"Excellent." Sarah sat down, into the chair, behind the wooden desk, "and how are you feeling about working with Axel?" She gestured to the man beside me who was deeply engrossed in his phone and didn't appear at all phased by this conversation.

Aah! Why are we talking like he's not in the room!

"Good, we've not had any scenes together yet but I'm looking forward to it."

The sound of Axel scoffing, to my right, made me jump. I turned my head towards him, but was met with the side of his face, his eyeline still locked on his device. My cheeks warmed with embarrassment at my lick arse comment.

"Yes, it's all very exciting isn't it!" Her patronising voice was saturated with artificial kindness. "Whilst we're on the topic of you and Axel, we have a proposition for you."

My mind blanked.

"You're new in the biz and I know what it's like for us women, always having to work harder to be seen." Sarah leant forward, onto clasped hands.

Where was she going with this?

"And I'm sure you, like us, want as many people to be excited about this film as possible."

"Of course." I agreed, tentatively.

"Headlines drum up interest, wouldn't you agree?" I must have looked like an idiot with the vacant expression plastered on my face. "It's all part of the appeal. Would the *Twilight* series have blown up as much if Rob and Kristen weren't emulating Bella and Edward's chemistry offscreen too? Just look at Tom and Zendaya; Zac and Vanessa," she counted on her fingers as she listed the celeb couples. With each example my pulse quickened at what she might've been suggesting…"Axel and Verity." She concluded, gesturing to the two of us, stars gleaming in her eyes. Panic washed over me. "What do you think?" She prodded after a beat of silence.

"Are you suggesting what I think you are?" I threw a look at Axel, expecting him to have a similar bewildered reaction but he was still buried in that bloody phone. "Do you not have anything to say about this?"

I reached across the short distance between us and tapped him on his ridiculously hard bicep. I almost jolted back from the bolt of electricity I received at the contact. He tipped his head and looked up at me from under his brow, unbothered.

"Verity, a lot of actors have a successful film under their belt, but not a lot have a second, or third. Trust me, hitching your wagon to Axel's star power will guarantee you success after this little rom com." She waved off our current film dismissively.

"I-I-I'm going to have to think about this." I stammered, a million thoughts swirling around my head.

"I'm not that bad am I, Dollface?" The mute finally spoke. I turned to look at him, perplexed by his beauty and the ridiculous nickname that rolled off his tongue.

"Are you honestly not fazed by this in the slightest? You've never even spoken to me." I protested to the seemingly unaffected party. I had really tried to put up with Axel's attitude on set but I didn't know if I'd be able to deal with it in my personal life too.

"We don't need to speak to have a public love affair." He smirked. His reaction proved to me that this wouldn't be his first stunt relationship.

"And they say romance is dead…" I rolled my eyes and pushed onto the arms of the chair to stand, turning back towards Sarah. "I'll get back to you."

"Great, although Verity, I'll only be in London for another twenty-four hours, so don't take long." She shot me a wink before I left the room.

****

Although I was relieved to be back home with Mistoffelees after a long day of filming, the conversation from earlier with Sarah and Axel, still rattled in my brain.

After pouring myself a large glass of red, I settled onto the sofa to mull over my options. Misto curled onto my lap, clearly sensing my inner turmoil. I began to stroke him with my left hand, the glass balancing between the fingers of my right.

"Oh Misty, what am I going to do?" I pondered, scratching behind his ears. "Am I really selling out on my first film?"

Misto meowed up at me.

"Yeah, you're right, I guess it does happen a lot in Hollywood," I took a huge swig of wine, "but he's so rude to me."

Meow.

"You're so right, once again, he's gorgeous. That just makes him harder to be around."

As I finished the glass, I couldn't help but wonder what he was getting out of this.

What could *I* possibly do to help *his* career?

I made my way to the comfort of my bed, deciding I'd thought enough about Axel for one day. I flopped onto the covers and began to doom scroll. After the fourth cooking video in a row, I flicked onto the next post, only to be met by a fucking Axel Ford thirst trap, for God's sake.

As the song *Cuffing Season* played for a third time, and I'd subconsciously memorised every clip of Axel in various movie roles, looking devastatingly handsome, it was clear I'd made up my mind.

Fuck it!

7

VERITY

Walking on set, I immediately tried to locate Axel. I spotted him lounging on one of the bakery cafe chairs between takes.

"Do you have five mins?" He looked up at me, surprised, "well?" Axel nodded, running his fingers through his dark, thick hair, before standing up. His height eclipsed me, causing my mouth to dry.

"Let's go." He agreed gruffly. I hurriedly walked towards Sarah's office, certain that if I turned to look at Axel following behind, I would wimp out.

When I reached the door, I knocked rapidly,

"What are you waiting for?" Axel questioned, having caught up. I turned only to find him standing overbearingly close.

"She hasn't called us in yet." *Obviously.*

"Pfft." He reached above me to push the door open. My heart stuttered as his spicy, woody scent overwhelmed my senses.

"Ahh Axel darlin- Oh, hello Verity. What a surprise to see you this morning." Sarah greeted from behind her desk, though the look on her face seemed as though she had, in fact, been expecting me.

"Hello Sarah, I won't take up much of your time." I said, trying to sound confident. "After much consideration, I've decided, I'll do it." I blurted, keeping my eyes fixed on Sarah so as not to see Axel's reaction.

What seemed like a genuine smile spread across her face.

"Anyway, I'm due on set soon, so I best be off." I announced, turning quickly to leave.

"Whoa, Verity, sit down, there's much to discuss." She called, stopping me in my tracks, flapping her hands towards the seats. As Axel and I sat in the same chairs as yesterday, she produced two thick files and slid them across the table to us. My eyes widened at the words 'nondisclosure agreement' on the front page. She'd created those quickly!

"Didn't take you long to draw these up, Sarah." Axel commented, a slight surprised edge to his husky voice.

"I like to be prepared, I knew our girl wouldn't be able to resist you, she's only human after all." She shot Axel a wink, which made my stomach turn and a blush spread across my cheeks. I hated how predictable I was.

Damn hormones.

"The contract would run from today until the first week of the film's release in November, then you will be free to stage a breakup and move on with your lives." I tried to concentrate on Sarah's words as I looked down at the paperwork before me. "Don't worry, Verity. Axel's solicitor has read over this and there's nothing untoward." She reassured, sensing my reluctance. Charlotte would have a heart attack if she knew I was considering signing this without seeking my own legal advice. I saw Axel scribble his signature along the dotted line, nonchalantly and reached for the pen in front of me. He had a lot more to lose than I did. I sucked in a deep breath and signed the next nine months of my life away.

"Now the legalities are in order, let's chat ground rules. Firstly, no dating other people unless you can one hundred percent guarantee it's private. Secondly, no talking to the press unless I've vetted the questions *and* the answers first." She emphasised, clearly proving I had lost not only my dignity but also my free speech. "And thirdly, it's by no means a part of the contract, but if you do end up having sex, by God use protection. We want the publicity but not a scandal. I can see the headline now!" She exclaimed, shaking her head as if picturing the front pages.

"I don't think we'll need to worry about that." I assured, half to myself.

"You're damn right. It's definitely not on my agenda." Axel agreed firmly. Although I was aware that there was no physical aspect to this fake relationship, I couldn't deny the sense of rejection I felt at his harsh words. There was no need for his attitude.

"Well, that's agreed then. Great news!" Sarah declared, clearly chuffed with herself as she collected up our signed contracts. "Your first public appearance will be Valentine's, so only a few weeks to plan. I'll be in touch with the details shortly. I am travelling back to the States later today but can be back as required or hop on a Zoom to chat whenever needed."

I nodded along, before glancing at Axel sheepishly and heading for the door. "Oh and Verity, you'll be under the biggest microscope once this goes public, so a word of advice, keep the tracksuits in the drawer." Sarah said pointedly. I looked down at the matching velour co-ord I had thrown on to travel into set today and my heart sank slightly.

The sound of Axel laughing beside me, caught my attention before he tapped me, patronisingly on the shoulder.

"Welcome to Hollywood, Doll."

8

AXEL

I smiled through gritted teeth as we started the first take of Rosie and Tyler's meeting. In this scene, my character had stumbled across the 'quaint, quintessentially British cosy coffee shop, Cobblestone Cafe, nestled between the banks of London City,' in his search for the best Americano. I thought back over the description from the script and the sugary sweet words threatened to give me diabetes.

"Action!"

I opened the fake cafe door and pretended to take in the gaudy surroundings: picture frame clad walls, eclectic mix of seating and the round tables with crocheted covers. The whole thing looked as if it had jumped straight out of a Hallmark movie. I proceeded to walk towards the counter to my mark and mindlessly perused the array of cakes, made of God knows what so they wouldn't perish, whilst I awaited my cue.

"Bye Colin! See you tomorrow." Verity trilled. There it was. I spun on my heels and crashed into her carrying a tray of empty crockery.

We both bent down to begin gathering up the scattered items, following the steps we had rehearsed.

"I'm so sorry," I apologised, placing a teaspoon back onto the tray.

"No, don't be sorry, it was my fault!" She replied, actively trying not to make eye contact with me in line with the awkward traits of her character.

We both reached for the last cup, our hands touching and eyes locking for the first time in the movie, in the most generic meet-cute possible. As 'Rosie' gazed up at me with surprised appreciation, I took in Verity's doe-eyed expression. Her natural beauty was impossible to deny. Long golden hair, bright blue eyes and a dimple that appeared on her right cheek when she smiled that I hadn't previously noticed. *I guess she wasn't exactly happy when we were around each other!* It was a real shame that I knew how much of an irritatingly annoying, goody-two-shoes she was, otherwise I'd be finding it hard not to drag her back to my trailer and ruin her.

Verity pulled back her hand and sheepishly tucked a strand of hair behind her ear.

"Here," I passed her the mug, before we both stood to face each other, my height towering over her petite frame.

"Thank you," 'Rosie' flustered, licking her lips nervously, catching my attention momentarily. "What did you want? Whatever it is, it's on the house."

I began to protest.

"I insist." She smiled warmly at me, walking round to the never-before-used coffee machine.

"Americano, thanks," I winked in character and internally cringed as the soppy scene ended.

"Cut! Reset the stage." Nora directed. I sauntered back to the outside of the fake shop, ready for take two. After a few more run throughs, Nora broke us for lunch.

As I made my way to craft services to pick up my food, I was looking forward to some peace and quiet back at my trailer.

"Axel, wait up!" I stopped and turned to face the owner of the voice. "Do you wanna get lunch?" Verity questioned, looking up at me, almost anxiously.

"Why?"

"Well, you are my boyfriend now!" She nudged me playfully, before turning serious once met with my stoic expression. *What's with this kid?* "Come on, I don't even know your middle name." She pleaded, a pout pulling at her full lips.

"Google it, Doll. Everything anyone wants to know about me is on the internet." I replied as I carried on walking.

"Well, I wanna hear it from you." She persisted, trying to keep up with my strides.

"Ugh, fine." I yielded; it was clear that she wasn't going to take no for an answer. "But we've gotta eat here. Sarah's still ironing out the finer details of our launch into the world, so nowhere with paps. And I don't want people seeing me invite you back to my trailer."

"Don't worry I'm not asking you out on a real date, Big Shot!" She muttered under her breath sarcastically, however the crimson blush spreading across her cheeks gave her attraction to me away. I rolled my eyes, not caring to hide the fact that I didn't want to do this. I would usually spend my lunch alone, running lines or trying to stay in the emotion of my character however, I suppose it was hardly strenuous to snap into Tyler's lovesick puppy persona. He was a very surface level kinda guy. So maybe giving up this lunch break wasn't such a big deal to my artistic process, but it wasn't going to be relaxing with Verity yapping on at me.

We grabbed our chosen food options and settled onto a table in the corner of the communal cafeteria. I began to eat in silence.

"So, what *is* your middle name then?" Verity asked, smiling, picking through her salad.

"James."

"Is that a family name?" She pried. I didn't dignify her with an answer. "Changing the topic, what's your coffee order? Considering we're going to be spending a lot of time in a cafe. Well, a fake one but nevertheless." She word vomited. "Mine's an oat milk latte with a shot of pistachio." *Course it fucking is, trust this girl not to have a straightforward order!*

"What is this? A fucking interview?" I threw my hands up in frustration. Not in the mood to be probed for information.

"I'm just interested to learn more about you. We're going to spend a lot of time together." She said, a hint of apprehension coating her words.

"Yeah, as Rosie and Tyler. You don't need to know about my personal life." I took a bite of my sandwich.

"*And* as 'girlfriend and boyfriend'." She added, making finger quotations.

"God, has anyone ever told you how annoying you are?" I bit out, exasperated. She blinked a few times, obviously taken aback by my no-bullshit attitude, but I couldn't stand to fuel this girl's clear infatuation with me. This wasn't the first time I'd been the object of a co-star's desires and I wouldn't put up with it this time, especially considering our complicated 'relationship'.

"Do you know what, I give up. Eat alone." She stood up huffing, picking up her plate of food.

"Thanks, that's exactly what I wanted." She threw a scowl in my direction before turning to leave me in blissful silence.

9

VERITY

14th February.

Relationship launch day.

Our first date.

I stared up at the dress hung on my wardrobe door. A present from Sarah. A note accompanied it, suggesting it was my decision whether to wear it or not, but we both knew I had no choice. Although I didn't like being dictated to, I had to admit that Sarah had good fashion sense!

I slid on the strapless, silky, red mini dress which had a large bow detail on the back, before applying my signature bold lipstick, to match the colour. My hair fell in perfectly styled ringlets which framed my face. Checking the time on my phone, I had ten minutes until my taxi would arrive. I slipped on a pair of fake black Louboutin's and headed into the kitchen for some Dutch courage.

"Oh Misto, I'm nervous!" I said to my furry friend, pouring a large glass of red wine, whilst he nuzzled the side of my leg. My phone vibrated in my hand.

Jake

Happy V day gorgeous gals!

Jake

What are everyone's plans tonight?

Jacob messaged in the group chat, my stomach flipped as I watched my friends' responses come through, contemplating my own answer.

Lilah

I just found out we're jetting off in the next half hour to have dinner near Notre-Dame, just call me Lilah In Paris!

Jake

God, I forget your boyfriend is literally a billionaire sometimes. Bring me back a baguette.

Lilah

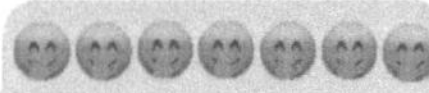

Lilah

What are you doing?

Jake

Got a first date! I know I know, pressure! But better than sitting in on my own.

Jake

NERVOUS!!!

Yeah, you and me both, Jake.

My mind raced as I thought over what I could tell my best friends. I didn't want to lie to them; however, I didn't know if I was even contractually allowed to divulge the truth until we were officially launched this evening!

A cold sweat washed over me at the prospect of Jake wanting to hang out and me not having a good excuse to turn him down!

My phone buzzed, this time with a notification informing me the taxi had arrived. I downed the remainder of my drink and headed for the door.

"Wish me luck, Misty!"

****

Ten minutes late and counting. What a fucking surprise! It would appear he didn't just have bad time keeping at work. I was really starting to regret my horny decision to give this stunt relationship a go. Seemed I was thinking with my clit at the time…

As I contemplated leaving, the sound of screaming and camera shutters clicking outside alerted me to Axel's arrival.

I kept my eyes fixed on the menu in front of me, not wanting to turn around and see him too early. The feeling of a large, masculine hand on my bare, upper back made me jolt, heat searing at his touch. His vanilla scent flooded my senses as Axel leant dangerously close to me, his lips brushing the shell of my ear.

"Remember, they're watching, Doll." He whispered, his breath ghosting over my neck, leaving goosebumps as a shiver ran down my spine. He placed a kiss on my cheek before pulling away and taking the seat opposite me. "Good evening, Verity."

"Good evening, Axel." I echoed his words, unable to form an original thought.

My God, he looked incredible.

His dark brown hair fell in short messy curls, it looked as though he'd been running his hands through it. Something I was jealous of. He was wearing a silk black shirt, unbuttoned down to expose his broad chest with the sleeves partially rolled up, highlighting his decorated, muscled forearms. The front of his shirt was tucked into tailored trousers of the same hue - did this man own anything colourful? Thank fuck Tyler didn't dress like this as I'd be in trouble!

Axel glanced towards the well positioned paparazzi on the pavement who had a perfect view of the scene, which I was certain was no coincidence, before taking my hand in his. It was clear to see why he was the most famous actor in the world, he was even beginning to convince me at this point!

The waiter appeared to take our food and drink orders before disappearing off, leaving the two of us alone once more.

"How did you know I wasn't a vegetarian?" I joked, referencing the chicken dish that he'd ordered for me.

"Lucky guess." He shrugged, letting go of my hand.

"Well thank you, it sounds delicious." I said, taking a sip of the white wine that had just arrived. "So, how was your day today?"

Axel and I hadn't filmed together for the past couple of weeks. We had been ticking off a lot of the solo scenes that our characters had which I had been thankful for to be honest, after the embarrassing lunch we had shared.

The waiter arrived carrying two plates of chicken ballotine with sides of dauphinoise potatoes and asparagus. The two of us dug in.

"Well?" I probed, after not getting a response. Axel glanced up at me whilst cutting the meat.

"Look Verity, let's get one thing straight. I don't want to talk. I don't want to get to know you. I don't care about this date. I don't care about *you*. So, if you can just stop going on and keep looking pretty, that would be perfect." I waited gobsmacked for Axel to finish his speech. His harsh words cut through me like a knife shattering the illusion. All I'd done over the past month was act cordial and civil towards him and all I'd had in return was monosyllabic responses and rude remarks. I'd been trying my best to be positive and forgiving of his diva attitude, for the sake of a calm work environment but Axel was pure toxicity. I couldn't believe I was subjecting myself to months 'dating' this arsehole.

"You are so full of it. How dare yo-"

"Now, now Verity, we are supposed to be a happy couple on our first date. Time to put your acting skills to the test." He cut me off, in reference to my obvious anger, grinning condescendingly.

"You were the one who asked me to agree to this and you're the one who's acting like a prick." I spat back at him, plastering a thousand kilowatt smile on my face to keep up the charade.

"Just because I asked for this, doesn't mean I have to be happy about it." He countered, matching my overly positive expression.

"I don't understand you, Axel." I said, my smile slipping slightly. I waved my hand in frustration before he caught it with his own, placing it firmly on the table and intertwining his fingers with mine. Giving me a pointed look. I wanted to rip his touch off me. "If you don't want to do this, why suggest it?" I said, my voice dripping with fake sweetness.

He paused for a moment in obvious thought. "Like Sarah said, publicity."

"As if *you* need extra publicity. You being involved in this film alone is publicity enough."

"You're right, so really, I'm doing *you* a favour. You're welcome." He narrowed his eyes. My blood boiled in my veins; I'd never been a violent person, but he was asking for a slap.

"You're impossible." I concluded, admitting defeat. I went back to eating my main, trying not to show the bubbling rage to the gathering crowd outside.

After we'd finished our food and it had been cleared away, the waiter returned with another menu.

"Any desserts?" He asked politely.

"No-"

"Yes." We responded simultaneously. "I would love the chocolate cake, please." I said, looking straight at Axel.

"And for you, Sir?"

"Nothing thanks." He replied, gruffly. The waiter collected our menus, "why are you longing this out more than we need to?" Axel whispered once they were out of earshot.

"I don't want to hang out with you any longer than necessary, but I'd like to enjoy *something* on this date." I explained.

The best-looking slice of cake was presented to me and I couldn't wait to tuck in! At least the night hadn't been a total waste. I looked out at the cameras, still flashing away, totally engrossed in our newsworthy romance. "Would you like a bite, lover boy?" I asked sarcastically, batting my eyelashes as I offered out a spoon of the chocolatey goodness.

Axel raised an eyebrow, analysing my suspicious kindness, "why not?" He resigned, reaching out for my spoon.

"Open wide," I smirked. He rolled his eyes before opening his mouth for me.

I leant across seductively, pressing my chest against the table, unintentionally emphasising my cleavage. I noticed his attention dart to the bare skin, threatening to spill over the top of my dress. Ah ha, so there's one thing he didn't hate - or should I say two!

"Enjoy, dickhead." I insulted, sliding the spoon into his mouth aggressively, hitting the back off his throat. He began choking on the contents, glaring at me angrily.

"Time to put your acting skills to the test, Big Shot!" I mirrored his earlier sarcastic comment, sitting back in my chair and folding my arms across my chest triumphantly. I watched as he composed himself before requesting the bill.

I had tried playing this the nice way but if he wanted to make it difficult, game on.

10

AXEL

After yesterday's Valentine's 'date', I was glad to be rid of Verity for the weekend. What a fucking psycho! Note to self, don't agree to be spoon fed by a woman that you've just pissed off.

I appreciate I could have been better company, but friendliness wasn't a part of the contract. Unfortunately for her, she wasn't signing up for an actual boyfriend. Maybe I'd have to remind her of this fact. I saw the way her body reacted to my touch, when I was performing to the cameras.

"I've got four beers, lads." A British voice cut through the crowd in the bar. I turned to see my friend, Aaron, placing down a tray of drinks on the wooden table. He handed them to the other two people at our booth, Brad and George. These three guys were my go-to contacts whenever I was in the UK and needed to wind down. All of them were actors, with varying levels of success, who I had met along my own acting journey.

"So, I got a call about that dad role for the new Hawkins horror movie today." Brad said, swigging his Moretti.

"Oh, so did I! May the best man win." Aaron replied, raising his glass bottle in a cheers. The pair of them were often in competition for the same part, given their matching blonde hair, broad statures and similar heights.

"Ha dad, that's gotta suck. Especially when our boy Axel is in his late thirties and still getting the lead roles." George laughed, nudging my arm.

"Yeah, in a schlocky romance." I grumbled quietly, picking off the label on my beer bottle.

"It still is quite a main role actually." Brad continued, defending his movie and missing my comment.

"Ah mate, you know what I mean. You're basically a scream queen and Axel's drowning in pussy." George retorted. I rolled my eyes. Although I wasn't short on offers from the opposite sex, it was unlikely that I would be living up to my inflated playboy image, especially with Verity to factor in.

"Fuck off mate." Brad laughed, shaking his head.

"Excuse me, are you Axel Ford? Can I get a picture please?" A pretty brunette who looked to be in her twenties asked me nervously as she approached the table.

"Yeah, I am, sure." I said, trying my best to fake enthusiasm. "Aaron, can you take it?" I asked, sliding off the chair. Taking my place next to the fan, I put my arm around her shoulders as her's slinked tightly around my waist, and we smiled for the camera.

"Thanks so much! Bye!" She giggled, turning a shade of red, before she returned to her friends who had excitedly watched the scene.

"I thought you said I wouldn't be bothered here?" I huffed, sitting back down, taking a sip of my beer.

"Sorry mate, I've never had an issue. It's always just other celebs or businessmen here." Aaron defended.

"Yeah, but you're hardly Axel fucking Ford fella." Brad chimed in, gesturing to me like I was a trophy.

The boys had brought me to a high-profile spot in London, the Gilded Cage. A dark, moody bar that was clad in wood and velvet and was heaving with revellers on that Saturday night. Given how much I was used to travelling around with my work, all I wanted was a beer and some undisturbed time with friends regardless of the location. Generally, I would have no issue with someone approaching me for a chat or a photo and I was happy to stop whatever I was doing to speak to fans. However, there was a time and a place, and a late night outing with the boys wasn't it. I'd had many an evening ruined by hordes of people swarming to get a moment with me, so I was always apprehensive to agree, to avoid the floodgates opening. But tonight, it would appear I was feeling charitable.

"Ah mate, I don't know what you're complaining about. She's fit and so are her friends! We should have invited them over." George piped up from beside me, peering over at the group of young girls.

"Not on the cards, haven't you heard boys? I have a girlfriend." I declared to the group now that my 'relationship' had officially gone public.

"Yeah, I saw! The bird from your new movie. How'd you score her? She looks too innocent for you, are you planning on corrupting her?" Aaron replied.

My mind wandered to the image of a dolled up Verity, sitting across from me, lit by candlelight. Dressed in the outfit I'm sure Sarah would have sent; it was hard to deny how sexy she looked in it. The red silk clung to her petite frame perfectly and the neckline was just low enough to catch my attention. She looked like a present, with that bow on the back, just waiting to be unwrapped. *Fuck.*

"Trust me, I'm not going to corrupt her." I assured, finishing my drink to clear my head of any thoughts of my unbearable co-star. "I'm going to get another round."

11

VERITY

Entering the Gilded Cage, we queued to get some cocktails before shuffling through the growing crowd in the swanky bar, to find some seats. Luckily enough, we found a booth tucked away at the back that provided just enough quiet for us to continue our conversations.

Lilah, Jacob and I had spent the evening at Gino's, our favourite Italian restaurant, discussing the success of the Moreno Jewellery Valentine's launch, which Lilah had designed the limited edition product for. She had told us that the sales had surpassed all expectations and that they were now working on a new range together, the Emerald Hart collection, which would feature ten unique jewellery pieces all created from Lilah's sketches. It was due to hit the shelves in the next few weeks.

"That's so amazing, Lilah and not long until it's out now." I gushed, sipping my cosmo. "I can't believe you've kept it a secret for so long!"

"I wanted to tell you sooner, but I was so nervous something would go wrong, I didn't want to jinx it!" She laughed.

"Trust me it's been hard to keep my lips locked too. It's been so fun to work on a project together babe!" Jacob added, excitedly. The pair of them giggled like school children.

"Well, congrats to you, Lils," I raised my glass to the others, as my friends collectively clinked theirs to mine. "It's a shame Amelia isn't here to celebrate."

"I'm just happy things seem to be better between her and Josh at the moment to be honest." Lilah replied as Jake nodded along in agreement.

Ping!

The sound of Jake's phone receiving a notification, cut through our conversation. He picked it up to see who the message was from. As he read the text on the screen, his eyes widened.

"Erm, what the fuck is this, Verity?" He shouted dramatically, before turning the phone over and putting the device in my face. "Tell me why, StarBuzzDaily's Insta has a photo of you and Axel Ford holding hands at dinner last night?!" *Oh fuck.*

"Sorry what? Let me see that!" Lilah snatched the phone from Jake's hand, gasping as she flicked through the photos.

"I can explain." I babbled, my face flushing with panic.

"On Valentine's night?!" Jake blurted. "So much for your solo wine night!"

"He's kissing you on the cheek in this one!" Lilah exclaimed as my friend's spoke animatedly over each other, "start talking, Sloan."

It felt like my heart was going to beat out of my chest, I hated lying to my friends but if there was ever a time to put my acting skills to the test, this was it.

"It's early days. We're getting to know each other and I didn't want to freak you guys out." I lied, nonchalantly.

"Well colour me freaked girl. You're dating the HOTTEST guy in the world." Jake emphasised, his eyes sparkling with the prospect of juicy gossip.

"Tell us everything. How did it start?" Lilah asked, tugging my arm, trying to shake the information out of me.

"Oh, I don't know, it just kind of happened…" I shrugged flustered. I really should have gotten my story straight before seeing these two.

"Okay, keep the details to yourself then, but I need to know…what's he packing?" Jake wiggled his eyebrows suggestively.

Your guess is as good as mine, Jacob.

"I need more drinks for this conversation." I laughed nervously, as I stood up from my seat. I turned towards the bar and slammed directly into another person. I looked up to apologise and was met with two piercing grey eyes. Oh my fucking God.

"What are you doing here?" We questioned in unison.

"I'm with my friends." I responded.

"Me too."

We stood in silence staring awkwardly at one another, as I realised I was partially in his arms. I flinched instinctively as his touch burned my skin before remembering that Lilah and Jake were right beside us. That must have looked so strange. I jumped back towards 'my boyfriend' to appear less like I hated him.

"If you wanted a cuddle, Verity, you could have just asked." He stated sarcastically. I darted my eyes in the direction of my table in close proximity.

"My friends." I said pointedly, hoping he got the message to keep up the facade. Axel looked around me to be met with two deer in headlights sitting under a metre away. He smiled politely, to his credit.

"Go on mate, give her a kiss!" A male voice shouted over from the other side of us, a couple of booths down. I furrowed my brow at Axel.

"*My* friends." He confirmed, as he released his grip, ignoring their heckle. "I was going to,"

"The bar, yeah me too."

We walked in silence. The crowd of people parted like the Red Sea for him. Within seconds, Axel was being served.

"Four Birra Morettis." He knocked on the wood rhythmically.

"And three cosmos please!" I interjected, leaning on the bar next to Axel. He turned to me, surprised, as the bartender began mixing the cocktails.

"Oh, I must have missed when I offered to buy you and your friends' drinks, Doll."

"It wouldn't look good if my superstar boyfriend *didn't* buy us drinks now, would it?" I batted my eyelashes at him mockingly.

"You're welcome then." He scoffed. I couldn't work out if he was irritated or impressed by my ballsy action. Axel paid and all seven drinks were given to us on the same tray.

"Are you going to take yours?" Axel queried, pointing at the three pink drinks.

"I've only got two hands." I said jokingly, holding them up in evidence, "be a gentleman." I winked, trying to make him feel as uncomfortable as I did.

"Fuck's sake, you really are a pain in my ass you know. Come on then." He ordered, gesturing to the table. I followed closely behind as he carried the beverages through the horde until we reached my friends. I lifted them off the tray and set down the cocktails.

"Axel bought us all bevvys." I trilled.

"Oh, wow, thanks so much Mr Ford." Jake smirked and I internally face palmed at the cringey response. "Care to join us?"

Panic shot through me as I prayed that Axel hadn't had a personality transplant overnight and become interested in my life.

"Gotta get back to my friends," he thankfully declined, same old Axel, thank God, "but enjoy."

He stood holding the tray of beers next to me as we avoided eye contact.

"Bye then." I stated, tapping him twice on the shoulder.

"See ya." He nodded his head in response before disappearing back to his own table. I released the breath I didn't know I was holding and sat back down.

"Well…that was fucking weird." Lilah said, confused, taking a sip of the pink liquid, cutting through the awkward tension.

She was right, that *was* fucking weird. Why did I tap him on the shoulder like I was petting a dog?!

"He just doesn't like PDA. You know, paps and that." I replied curtly, praying she didn't dig further.

"Yeah sure." She narrowed her eyes suspiciously. She could read me like a book.

"Fair enough but if he was my boyfriend, I would be climbing him like a goddamn tree." Jake sighed wistfully. The three of us burst into fits of laughter. "I'm not kidding, you'd have to pry me off him with a crowbar." He insisted.

"Just be quiet and enjoy your free drink, you tart." I snorted.

I had completely underestimated what it would be like to lie to my best friends about such an important part of my life and I certainly wouldn't be rushing back into a group scenario anytime soon!

12

AXEL

"Cut!" Nora's exasperated voice stopped the filming. I groaned, my eyes flicking towards Verity's flushed face, "let's take five and try again," the director instructed as the team reset the scene.

Verity grabbed her script, from behind a cushion, on a sofa in the bakery and frantically started refreshing herself on the dialogue. I walked over and stood closely beside her, she was oblivious to my presence, as she tried to take the information in.

"Maybe if you spent less time drinking with your friends and more time learning your lines, we would have gotten through this scene by now." I whispered, causing her to jump at my sudden proximity.

"You were out too." She jabbed back, turning to look at me with thunder in her eyes.

"Correct, but I'm not the one messing up my lines, Doll." I smirked sardonically.

"Fuck off, Axel." She grumbled, her attention turning back to the paper she was holding.

"Noted. I'll leave you to it." I said, flicking the top of her overly annotated script, before heading back to my mark, to await Nora's next direction.

I was trying my best to look like the supportive boyfriend I was supposed to be, but Jesus she was making it difficult. It wasn't even a challenging scene! After our launch into the public eye, the news was officially out and everyone on set was aware of our relationship - which to them, was one hundred percent real, meaning I couldn't blow up and complain about the lacklustre performance happening in front of me.

"Right, let's try this again, shall we? Places!" Nora announced. The minimal crew shuffled behind the cameras, as Verity quickly stuffed the script back into its hiding place and stood behind the counter. I took an internal deep breath to settle my frustration. As I heard the word "action," I pushed open the fake door and began walking towards her.

"Morning Rosie, what a lovely day it is! The usual please." 'Tyler' said cheerily, reaching the counter and resting my arm onto it.

"Hello! Of course, Americano, cheese and ham toastie and a synonym swirl. Coming right up!"

Synonym?! Is she for real?

I heard sighs and stifled groans from the crew as she fucked up her line *again*.

"Verity babe, cin-na-mon." I sounded out phonetically, trying to hide the bitterness in my voice.

"Yeah thanks, Axel," she glared.

"We can call it for now, Verity, let's go from the next line." Nora called over from the director's chair in a reassuring tone.

"No, no it's fine, let's do it again, please." Verity responded, shaking her hands in the air. As if that was going to help her pronounce fucking cinnamon!

Nora nodded. "Places."

I swear to God, if I have to walk through this front door again, I will lose my mind.

I retraced my steps through the entranceway to the counter and delivered my line perfectly for the fifth time.

"Hello! Of course, Americano, cheese and ham toastie and a cina-synim-aah!"

"Fuck's sake! Get it together!" I met Verity's surprised look, before realising the crew sported the same uncomfortable expression.

Whoops, that was *not* an internal thought!

I pictured Sarah's scowling face as I threatened to expose our sham of a relationship, to the entire set. I walked around the counter and wrapped an arm around Verity's shoulder.

"I'm sorry Babygirl, I'm just tired today." I said in a sickly-sweet voice, before kissing her softly on the cheek, "it's not a big deal, we can run lines at lunch if you like."

Hatred burned in her eyes at my condescending words. I winked at her knowing that she couldn't retaliate without giving the game away.

As much as I didn't enjoy her company and my stress levels had hit a new high today, it was undeniable that I got a sadistic kick out of toying with her.

13

VERITY

Despite the nightmare scene that occurred on Monday, the rest of the week had been plain sailing, as far as work was concerned. Unfortunately, the same couldn't be said about mine and Axel's relationship.

It was like he had a vendetta against me and was always waiting to spot any tiny sign of weakness to attack. Although I tried to play it down to avoid giving him the satisfaction, it was something I was used to from my family, so I had to admit it struck a nerve.

Thankfully, it was Friday now and I had the weekend off which meant two lie ins and an Axel-free forty eight hours ahead - hallelujah!

Honestly, that man had been on one I swear. Tuesday, we were filming a scene on location, a date in a local park, so had a chance to get out of the studio. It was a beautifully crisp, sunny February day and I was feeling in good spirits, hoping the fresh air would clear my mind, after the mess I had made of my words the day before. However, it seemed like Axel was not going to let me forget it. From the moment I had seen him, it was endless jabs and snotty comments.

"Have you been practising your lines or will we be treated to a repeat performance?" He mocked with a shit-eating grin.

"Oh, will you give it a rest, Axel?" I said, not rising to him.

"Hey, I just want to make sure we won't all be having our time wasted today." He tapped me patronisingly on the top of my head before swanning off.

Wednesday, we were back in the studio and I had the unfortunate pleasure of bumping into Mr Ford at the gate to the lot.

"Be a doll and beep us in." He gestured to the keycard hung over my cleavage.

I narrowed my eyes, "why don't you do it yourself?"

"As you wish." He reached out to me and grabbed a hold of the plastic. With one swift movement, he yanked the card, breaking the clasp on the cord, freeing the lanyard from my neck.

My breath caught in my throat.

He beeped the card to the lock on the gate and held it open with his foot. Pushing the key back against my chest. I prayed that he couldn't feel the pounding of my heart where his fingers brushed against my skin.

I caught it as he released his grip and walked into the gate failing to hold it open, leaving me hot and bothered. Surprisingly, I found his arrogant action mildly attractive but as I realised that I had been left on the other side of the gate by the arsehole, that flame quickly extinguished. I shook my head to rid any unwanted thoughts and let myself in to start the day.

Thankfully, Axel had a day off yesterday, so I had been free from ridicule. However, I didn't escape judgement for too long as my mother blessed me with a phone call.

I took a deep breath, answering the phone, as I braced myself for the impending criticism.

"Verity darling, I see you have a boyfriend that you had failed to mention?" Her voice was surprisingly less critical than usual. My irritation spiked at the thought that my connection to Axel was impressive to her, when my real achievements never seemed to meet the mark.

"Yes, Mum." I answered curtly, not wanting to go into detail with her on this.

"Tell me all about this superstar then." She pried, interest coating her words.

"Anything you want to know is on the internet." Axel's prior comment tumbled from my mouth.

"Oh of course I've already Googled him. He seems to be doing very well for himself," she paused, "for an actor." I held back a giggle. Even the great Axel Ford couldn't meet my mother's sky-high standards! "Enjoy it while it lasts Verity. You won't be his shiny new toy forever." *There's that cutting tone!* "You don't want to be left picking up the pieces once he's done with you." Although my mother didn't know the truth of the agreement, it hurt that this was her view on my seemingly good relationship. Of course she didn't think I was worthy of that kind of love.

"I'm being called to set. Bye Mum." I lied, hanging up and tucking my phone deep into my bag, as if burying the device also suppressed the negative feelings brought on by her words.

Lastly, today, we had thirty minutes until freedom and when I didn't think Axel had any jibes left in him, he surprised me yet again.

"What are your weekend plans?" Jason, who played Rosie's coworker, asked inquisitively.

"Nothing. I'm looking forward to laying on the sofa with my cat and not moving." I laughed, as Nora and the crew reviewed the previous take of the scene, we had just filmed.

"Sounds great! But if you happen to fancy some fresh air, I know about this great free exhibit at the V&A." Jason offered with a friendly smile.

"Oh cool, that sounds interesting, I'll let you know!" I matched his expression, knowing full well I had no intention in taking him up on the offer.

"Awesome, I'm gonna get a drink, back in a mo!" He walked away, only to reveal Axel, leaning against the counter that Jason had just been standing in front of.

"Tryna make me jealous, Doll?" The thick Brooklyn accent sent shivers down my spine - not the good kind!

"Didn't know you cared, Axel." I sighed, mockingly placing my hand over my heart.

"I'm your boyfriend, of *course* I care." He responded sarcastically.

"So, I can't have male friends now?" I said, exasperated at this point.

"Not in public, no, and a V&A trip sounds awfully like a date to me." He suggested, subtly reminding me that all my actions were being analysed by the outside world.

Before I had a chance to speak, Jason walked back over to the two of us.

"See you after work, Babygirl." Axel lied, keeping up appearances, booping me on the nose.

Back at my apartment, I poured myself a *huge* glass of wine, to begin my wind down after reflecting on a week of feeling dejected and belittled. My mum's words replayed in my head about being left sad and alone and I felt a weird confidence that I would be proving her wrong for once. You can't have your heart broken from a fake relationship.

As the night came to a close, there was one silver lining to it all. This arrangement wouldn't last forever, one day I would be free from the torment of Axel Ford.

14

AXEL

I stared at myself in the grainy webcam, dressed ready for my scene, as I waited for Sarah to join the meeting. *God, I look ridiculous, only a couple more months until I can hang up Tyler's dorky flannels.*

"Axel, darling!" Sarah cooed as she appeared on screen, "you're looking great, you should bring more orange into your offscreen wardrobe!" I rolled my eyes as she buttered me up. Although our meetings were scheduled to occur weekly, I was always apprehensive to hear what hair brained plan she had in mind next.

"Afternoon, or should I say morning for you." I greeted, remembering the time difference as she called from her New York office.

"Just a quick one this time, Axel, I won't keep you long." She reassured me, clapping her hands together, leaning uncomfortably close to the camera. I raised my eyebrows for her to continue. "How is your lovely girlfriend?"

"Fine." I shrugged.

"Yes, well the Valentine's date looked very romantic and the tension between you both was clear to see," *not that kind of tension*, "however, you've not been seen publicly together in nearly two weeks. If you're not careful, people will think it's just another meaningless fling - which is exactly the perception we are trying to avoid."

"What do you suggest then?" I asked, running a stressed hand through my hair.

"Well, if she really was your girlfriend, what would you be doing?"

"We wouldn't be leaving the apartment, let's be honest." I muttered under my breath; flashes of ruining Verity's crimson lipstick momentarily crossed my mind before I shook my head to rid the image.

"Exactly, Axel." Sarah clicked, "invite the girl round, the paps need to see her going in and out of your apartment."

Fuck's sake, it was hard enough seeing Verity at work and having to keep up appearances there. Let alone, having her invade my private space.

"Come on, Ax," I cringed at the overly friendly nickname. "Once she's inside, the cameras won't be watching, so you don't need to make friendship bracelets and braid each other's hair. She just needs to be seen going in." She continued, sternly, making it clear I did not have any other options.

"Fine. When does this need to happen?" I asked, leaning back on my chair and folding my hands behind my head, as I released an exasperated breath.

"Well, it's not up to me to dictate your personal life," I scoffed at the ironic comment, "but I'd suggest tonight."

"Noted." I said sarcastically, saluting my manager/dictator with two fingers.

"Anyway, got to dash, enjoy your date later." Before I had a chance to respond, Sarah had disconnected from the call, leaving me faced once again with my plain, awkward reflection.

I sat for a moment, thoughts swirling as I scrubbed my stubble with my hand. I knew I had agreed to this but I couldn't deny it was harder work than I had anticipated.

A couple of dinner dates here and there was manageable, but I didn't even consider welcoming her into my home and having to keep her entertained for hours!

I mulled over the idea of giving up my well deserved free time for a few minutes.

Sarah was right about one thing. There would be no eyes on us once the front door closed, so maybe this would be easier than a public outing.

I stood quickly, interlocking my hands and stretching my arms out ahead of me. A renewed sense of optimism coursed through my veins as I went to find Verity.

She stood off set, giggling along to Jason. I was almost certain whatever he was yammering on about hadn't been *that* funny. I strode over to the pair, sliding my arm around her shoulders when I reached her.

"Hey, Babygirl," I purred, Verity turned to me, I could see the vitriol in her eyes despite the fake smile plastered on her face, "hi Jason." I greeted, nonplussed.

"Hi Axel," Jason responded, "I'm going to get a snack." He disappeared towards crafts services sheepishly. I could see the way he looked at Verity, it was plain as day that he wanted her. Even though she wasn't my real girlfriend, *he* didn't know that! If I cared more, I'd be having words with him about his blatant disrespect.

"What do you want, Axel?" Verity sighed, her expression souring as I removed my arm from her.

"You're coming over tonight, Doll. Sarah will send my address, be there for eight." I informed her.

"Oh wow, what an invitation, and to what do I owe the pleasure?" She asked, arching an eyebrow.

"The public need to think we are in the early stages of a relationship; they need to see you entering my apartment. You know, portray the image of the honeymoon phase." I didn't want her to get any wrong ideas and think I was inviting her round out of anything other than necessity.

"I'm honoured." She crossed her arms.

"Perfect, it's a date." I smiled sweetly and booped her on the nose again, as I was certain it irritated her the first time.

"Can't wait." Verity mumbled flatly as I walked away.

15

VERITY

"Verity, Verity, look over here,"

"Give us a smile, love."

"Movie night with your boyfriend?" The paparazzi heckled from the street, as I buzzed the intercom to Axel's penthouse apartment.

"Coming." Axel stated quickly through the crackly speaker before appearing at the door a few minutes later. Even though he was in much slouchier clothes than I was used to seeing him in, he still gave off that rugged movie star vibe in a simple pair of black tracksuit bottoms and a t-shirt. I stood awkwardly in front of him, giving a 'what do we do now?' look.

Effortlessly, he swept me into a hug, wrapping one strong arm around my neck and placing a kiss to my forehead, as if the movement was ingrained in his muscle memory. I cringed knowing this wasn't anything out of the ordinary to him. As quickly as possible, I went to step back out of his unwanted grip, but it tightened like a vice.

"Not yet Doll, make sure they've got the shot." He whispered into my ear, holding me prisoner. His warm breath ghosted against my skin. It was funny how thousands of women would have killed to be in my position right now and all I wanted was to get far away.

After what felt like a lifetime, I was finally free and we entered the building. The elevator doors opened immediately when Axel pressed the button on the wall and we rode in uncomfortable silence to the top floor.

"Welcome to my humble abode." He said sarcastically, as he unlocked his front door and pushed it open.

I was flabbergasted. This apartment was easily five times bigger than my own! As we walked into the open living room and kitchen area, lined with floor to ceiling windows, my attention was caught by Tower Bridge lit up in all its glory along the Thames below us.

"What? You've never seen that before?" He asked, referring to my dumbfounded expression.

"I've seen the bridge you idiot, just not from such an amazing viewpoint." Of course Axel Ford would take this scenery for granted. The man had been in the industry since before I was in school and had the net worth to prove it.

"Well, if you sit in that seat over there, you'll be able to gawk shamelessly at it all night." He mocked, pointing to the far corner of the large U-shaped sofa.

I rolled my eyes before making myself at home, in the spot he recommended, whilst I waited for him to join me. This was the last place I would have wanted to be on a Monday night, especially before a busy shoot day tomorrow but I was trying my best to think positively. Maybe an uninterrupted evening together, would help us to build some sort of friendship or at least, respect for one another after the tormenting last week.

He sat down on the opposite side, swinging his legs onto the sofa in front of him. He folded his arm behind his head, accentuating his inked tricep and settled into the cushions, beginning to scroll through his phone.

"What are we doing for food?" I queried, as my stomach grumbled. In hindsight, maybe I should have eaten beforehand…

"I hadn't thought about it. Order what you want." He said, not taking his eyes off his device. He dug his card out of his pocket and flung it in my general direction.

"Talk about being wined and dined…" I started, snatching up the plastic that had fallen beside me.

"What did you expect, a candlelit dinner and a dozen roses?" He scoffed, flicking his eyes towards me, momentarily.

"Obviously not but forgive me for thinking my host might have thought about my basic human needs." The usual feeling of anger that arose in Axel's presence threatened to spill over now there was no reason to play house.

"Maybe you need reminding, but I am not hosting you." He put his phone down and turned to face me head on, from the opposite side of the sofa, "this was an obligation, not a heartfelt invitation."

The hatred burned in his eyes as he glared at me, like I was an out-of-control fangirl that needed to be put in her place. My heart began to beat furiously, as my composure snapped.

"I'm well aware of that, Axel," I crossed my arms, "but that doesn't mean there can't be some common decency." He ran his hand through his hair, frustrated.

"It's adorable that you thought we were actually going to have a date night. Did you pick out your sexiest pyjamas to seduce me with, Doll?" He smirked, with a tensed jaw. I felt my cheeks flush with equal parts anger and embarrassment.

"I'm sure you're used to women throwing themselves at you but that doesn't mean I'm going to. I'm not here by choice either." As my rage increased so did the volume of my voice.

"Oh come on, we both know a rookie like you wasn't going to pass up the opportunity to be seen with me and it's a just bonus it boosts your career too."

That self obsessed, arrogant, conceited prick. How could he possibly think I wanted anything to do with him after the way he'd been treating me.

Fuck civil.

"You've got to be fucking stupid, if you think that I would willingly come here to spend my evening basking in the glory of Axel Ford's glowing personality."

"I didn't think you wanted to get to know my *personality*. I'm used to people using me for more than just my status. There's nothing I hate more than young industry newbies. You're all the same." He waved his hand dismissively in my direction. "This isn't my first rodeo with clout chasers, you're not the first and you certainly won't be the last."

The weight of his insult hit with full force, stunning me.

"Do you know what? I don't have to sit here and listen to you insulting me." I grabbed my belongings and headed for the exit as adrenaline rushed through me. My body shook with anger and my fingers trembled as I began to pull the handle. A firm hand slammed the door shut from above me, holding me hostage. All I wanted was to get away from this incorrigible arsehole!

"Sit down. You can't leave yet." He ordered, his voice like gravel. I whipped around to face my captor, my back pressed against the door. "Paparazzi." Words died on my tongue as I looked up at the giant fencing me in. His grey eyes stared so intensely into mine, that I was frozen in place, his sweet tobacco scent enveloped me. My breathing became shallow with frustration, my whole body flushed with heat that rushed through my veins and pooled between my legs. The anger mingling with a fierce, uninvited want. Although his expression was stern, I could see the challenge on his face. I couldn't make sense of the fire licking at my insides. Axel clenched his jaw, bringing my attention to his lips. I held my breath as an image of him breaking the small distance between us and crashing his mouth to mine momentarily played in my mind. His eyes darkened as if he could read my thoughts.

"Save it for the cameras, Doll." He purred, dropping his arm and walking back to his previous seat.

I finally breathed.

****

Twelve hours since whatever the fuck that was at Axel's flat last night and although my hormones betrayed me momentarily, I had never been more sure of my hatred for that man. For the remainder of the night, we sat in silence while we focussed on our own interests. I watched a couple of episodes of *Miranda* on my phone whilst Axel read *The Count of Monte Cristo*. I internally cursed myself out when I watched him put on his pair of black rimmed glasses and the hot, unwanted feeling swirled in my lower abdomen once again.

His Grace finally allowed me to leave after four agonising hours. I'd never been so relieved to be back in the comfort of my own flat, only to wake up to the horrifying realisation that today we were filming Tyler and Rosie's first kiss.

As I arrived on set, I had a quick scan of the immediate area. Phew, no Axel. I rushed to my trailer to brush my teeth. As much as I wasn't excited about kissing him, I at least didn't want bad breath.

Not only was this going to be our first kiss, when we'd rather have throttled each other, it was also my first onscreen kiss ever!

Opening the squeaky door, I froze at the sight of Axel lounging on my trailer sofa, his body taking up the whole space, feet dangling off the edge of the arm rest.

"What do you want?" I sighed, not in the mood for an argument. I walked in, leaving the door open behind me.

"An olive branch," he smiled sweetly. Maybe he'd realised his dickish ways overnight after our bust up and was actually accepting fault.

"Okay," I answered warily, waiting for him to continue.

"Hold out your hands," standing, he walked towards me as I did as he asked. He stopped a few inches away, towering over my small frame, my eyes locked onto his once again. "Close your eyes." I obliged before he dropped a cylindrical object into my palms.

"Are you fucking kidding me?" I questioned, opening them to find a fresh pack of Polo mints. I looked up at him as a smug smile pulled at his lips.

"I wanted to make sure you're prepared, Verity." He shrugged, an expression of fake innocence spread across his face. "I've got to make this somewhat bearable." I couldn't think of anything coherent to say, this man was trying to get under my skin and annoyingly, he was succeeding. He ruffled my hair and walked to the open exit, turning to look back over his shoulder. "See you out there, Doll." He winked before disappearing, leaving me flustered and ten times more nervous for the scene ahead. Arsehole.

An hour later and the time had arrived to lock lips with the enemy. The set looked incredible. A beautiful autumnal park scene had been recreated with the utmost detail. If it hadn't been for the ceiling of fluorescent lights beating 'sunshine' onto us, I would have been convinced I was actually in Hyde Park, in October.

Five minutes passed, then another five. With each added second, my anxieties increased, turning me into a jittery wreck as I played with the pockets of my character's trench coat. Not only did we need to make this convincing for the film, but everyone on set also believed Axel and I were in the throes of the honeymoon period, so a lacklustre kiss was out of the question. Nora was frantically checking her watch and querying where the superstar was until he eventually swanned in, wearing his usual flannel but this time paired with a grey beanie, his dark curls poking out from the edge.

Nonchalantly, he sauntered to take his place beside me on the makeshift pathway.

"Thought you got cold feet." I said flatly, not looking directly at him.

"Thought I'd prolong the tension, good things come to those who wait, Verity." He mocked in a hushed tone.

"Let's just get this over with." I stated, matching his volume to avoid anyone overhearing.

"Action." Nora announced, as the sound of a clapperboard signalled the start of the first take.

We instinctively locked hands in character, meandering down the leaf strewn pavement, reciting the dialogue until it was time for Axel to stop in his tracks.

"...I guess what I'm trying to say is I'm falling in love with you, Rosie." He pulled on the lapels of my tan coat, bringing my body against his broad frame. Air snagged in my throat at the motion that I was fairly certain wasn't in the script, before he snaked a hand over my hair, to cup the back of my head. His grey eyes stared deeply into mine, with the same intensity that he had possessed last night.

I released a shaky breath.

Before I inhaled again, his mouth found mine. He kissed how I'd imagined. Hot, heavy and all encompassing. I almost forgot the crew were only metres away as Axel's hand moved to the small of my back, pulling me closer to him as he nipped at my bottom lip. That was *definitely* off script!

I responded with equal fervour, running my hands down the front of his chest, feeling the ripple of his sculpted abs through his shirt. God, I was a mess. How could something feel so wrong but also so right? There seemed to be some wires crossed between my body and my brain, my mind was screaming at me to abort but I found myself dissolving at his touch.

Axel broke the kiss but kept me in his arms, gazing at me with pure admiration. I narrowed my eyes slightly in confusion before panic set in. It was my line! *What* was my line?

"I-I love you too." I stuttered, my mind a blur. Axel's soft expression hardened immediately as I fluffed my line, the arsehole returning.

"Cut!" Nora shouted. Axel released me from his grip and stepped away, the air around me colder now I wasn't pressed against his firm body. He turned to face the director as she gave us feedback. "Firstly guys, the lust was palpable and that's great for some of our saucier scenes but this is their first romantic kiss. It's awkward, it's soft, it's careful. It's not snogging each other's faces off until your lips go numb!" She laughed, I felt a blush growing on my cheeks. "Let's tone it down, but don't forget that passion for when the time comes."

"Do you need to practise your line before we go again? I don't want another synonym situation just so you can kiss me more, Doll." Axel prodded, in a statement only audible to me. I wanted to slap the smug look off of his face despite the pounding between my legs that I was desperately trying to ignore.

I rubbed a hand across my face letting out a deep sigh as I prepared myself for take two of this dreaded scene.

16

AXEL

Popping off the cap of my beer, I took a hearty swig as I checked my Rolex. Not long now and Verity would be back at my apartment and simultaneously under my skin!

This would be the fourth time I'd have to endure her. However, today was only a fleeting visit as I had been roped into attending a jewellery launch for some girl she knew.

I had to admit that the last couple of apartment visits had been slightly more bearable, since she had mortified herself the first time. The effect my proximity had on her wasn't lost on me. Despite her tantrum about how she was so unlike the other girls and not into me, it didn't take much to prove she wasn't as unique as she had argued.

Standing in the doorway, as my height encompassed her, I watched her pupils dilate and her breath become shallow the more I toyed with her. I knew how much she wanted me to kiss her. To close the gap and corrupt her innocence but unfortunately for her, that wasn't and wouldn't ever be on the cards.

Since that moment, we seemed to have come to an unspoken agreement. I would meet her at the front door, have our obligatory hug in front of the cameras and then split into our separate hobbies when we had returned upstairs. Generally, we would sit in silence, on opposite sides of the sofa, focussed on our respective books. I had noticed that whilst I was akin to the classics, she opted for more colourful, cartoony front covers with a generic couple staring lovingly at each other, and some comical title. I hadn't gone to the effort of searching the plotlines, but my immediate guess was that they were low brow in comparison to the literature I was reading. But if it kept her quiet, then I wasn't going to complain.

Right on time, the doorbell rang. Showtime! When I reached the ground level, I saw her through the glass exterior door trying to avoid looking in the direction of the paparazzi. For a split second, I didn't recognise her. Wearing a champagne sequin dress, she looked worlds away from how I'd seen her before, even Valentine's when she was all dressed up, I knew that was curated by an outside influence. It was interesting to see a glimpse of the person that I had spent so much time with but barely knew.

Her attention turned to me, as I opened the door.

"Evening, Doll," I said, wrapping an arm around her and placing a rehearsed kiss to the side of her head.

"Took you long enough." She muttered quietly, pulling away from me slightly.

"Shall we go?" I ignored her dig, taking her hand in mine and walking towards the waiting car. I opened the door for her, putting on a show for the onlookers.

Gotta keep up the fake chivalry.

"Thanks Clive, onto the Natural History Museum, please." Verity instructed, shuffling into her seat as I took my place beside her.

We settled into our usual silence. I flicked through my phone until I noticed Verity pull out her lipstick and begin to reapply it over her already rouge lips. The colour deepened with each swipe and I was unwittingly entranced as I recalled what they felt like.

The day we filmed our first kiss, I had been caught off guard with my sudden improvisation. I'm unsure if it was the way in which I knew I was in control or the way her body reacted to my touch, but I'd let myself slip. If Nora hadn't called cut, I wouldn't have known when I would have stopped or if I would have continued to give in to the primal urges. It seemed the hostility I felt towards Verity was rearing its head as a different kind of frustration. Looking at her now, I could understand why I had gotten carried away. Her golden hair was curled effortlessly, the lights reflected in her sea blue eyes and the shadows fell along the profile of her face accentuating her delicate features, as we drove past the amber streetlights. She was clearly beautiful. I hated to say it but I was fighting the urge to smudge that lipstick.

"Ugh, I hate being late." She tutted, a clear poke at me. Fantasy, ruined.

"I'm sure you won't miss much. How much entertainment is there going to be at a jewellery launch." I snorted.

"It's basic manners, Axel. Not that I expect you to know anything about that." She sneered, turning to face me directly, narrowing her eyes.

"Excuse me Miss Sloan, we're here." Clive coughed, breaking the tension, as we pulled up outside the iron gates of the Museum.

"Oh thank you Clive. Sorry about that, long day." I saw the blush tainting Verity's cheeks as she tried to brush off our 'argument.' I shook my head at her blatant obsession with seeking validation from others.

"No apology necessary. Call me when you're ready to be picked up, I won't be far." Clive replied.

She smiled before we slid out of the vehicle, reassuming our previous position, holding hands. I could feel the animosity between us, it was tangible, as we walked towards the grand building.

We entered the large double doors to the party. Hundreds of revellers chatted under the enormous whale skeleton, dressed to the nines in sequins, perfectly following the 'sparkles' theme that had been set. How original!

"What are their names again?" I whispered in Verity's ear.

"Are you serious?" I looked back at her plainly, as she scowled, "Lilah and Zane."

"And what do they do?"

"You've got to be fucking joking?" She looked like she wanted to rip my balls off.

"Calm down, I'm not that stupid." I responded, rolling my eyes. "How many meaningless events do you think I've been to, I know how to schmooze, Doll." I winked.

"Let's go, I need a drink." She said flatly, leading us towards the temporary bar.

"VERITY!" I heard bellowing across the room. I turned to see a flash of red bounding towards us as Verity released her grip. The stranger reached us and Verity pulled her in for a hug. The pair of them screeched into each other's faces, threatening to trigger my fight or flight.

"Thank you so much for coming! I can't wait for you to see everything." The woman gushed, holding Verity at arm's length.

"I wouldn't have missed it for the world."

"And hi, Axel. We briefly met at the Gilded Cage. Thanks for the drink!" She joked, nudging me with her elbow. I smiled politely in return.

I thought for a moment, *who is this person?* "Oh don't mention it. Anytime." I blagged.

"This is my best friend, Lilah. The woman of the hour!" Verity introduced, clearly realising I had no recollection of this woman. "And Zane, how lucky are you to have another amazing collection under your belt." She congratulated, looking to the side of me. I nearly jumped when I realised a six-foot tanned man had managed to sneak up on me.

"This is all her." He smiled, wrapping an arm around Lilah's waist and placing a kiss on her cheek. The redhead looked up at him with hearts in her eyes, it was clear to see the love between them.

Okay, so this is Zane and Lilah!

"Congratulations to the both of you on the," I glanced around the large room hoping for a miracle, as I spotted a poster detailing the event, "Emerald Hart collection." Verity cast a warning look as I nearly fumbled the name.

"Thanks, it's so exciting!" Lilah vibrated with giddiness.

"Thank you for coming, we've heard a lot about you." Zane responded, holding out his hand to shake. I returned the gesture.

"Only good things I hope?" I laughed, looking at Verity who I could see was hiding a glare. "Now I think about it, she's not actually said that much." Lilah said, giving me an inquisitive look, like she was analysing me. "Break her heart and I'll kill you, Axel Ford." She waved a finger in my face, threateningly. Zane gave me a pointed look that she wasn't joking.

Ooo, I'm so scared. "She's in safe hands, I promise." I tapped Verity on the shoulder.

"Oh my God, Axel Ford! Welcome to the gang." A blonde scruffy haired man appeared, holding a tray of champagne flutes.

"Hi, thanks." I said, taking a glass from who I assumed was a waiter.

"Oh babe, does my Tom Ford sequin suit not set me apart from the staff? Jake. Nice to see you again." The man chuckled.

"Oh shit," I started. *Great, another person I've supposedly met!*

"It's fine hun, I'll let you off. You're lucky you're good looking." He placed the tray down on the round bar table beside us, as he handed out the remaining drinks.

"Don't inflate his ego, Jake!" Verity interjected jokingly, although I could sense the bitter undertone.

"*Mi Joya*, we better continue mingling." Zane said, squeezing Lilah's shoulder.

"Okay, we'll see you all soon! Enjoy the free booze." She waved as they turned towards the rest of the crowd.

"So Axel, huge fan. I feel weird to ask given the circumstances," he waved in Verity's direction, "but can I get a picture please?"

God fucking help me, I didn't know I'd come to a meet and greet.

"Course." I agreed, barely covering my bored facial expression as I stood next to him and he lifted his phone to take the selfie. I smiled through gritted teeth.

"Cheers, this is going to blow up my Insta." He laughed, "how's filming going? I'm looking forward to the movie!"

"Good, thanks." Verity and I said in unison, I watched her cringe at how rehearsed that sounded.

"Great! I can't wait to see chapter thirty-two on the big screen." He wiggled his eyebrows suggestively as I stared back blankly. "Their spiciest scene." He said, noting my oblivion.

"Oh, I've never read the book." I responded. Verity subtly nudged me with the side of her body. "But I've read the script and you're in for a treat."

"Awesome, don't forget to score me premiere tickets, V!" He shot finger guns towards her, with a wink.

"Of course, you're already on the guest list - all of you are." She laughed, causing that sickly sweet dimple to appear on her cheek.

I spent the next two hours, painfully caught in an awkward triangle as the 'besties' spoke animatedly, sinking countless drinks while I nursed mine. I had to admit it seemed my acting skills were beginning to slip as I was finding it more and more difficult to pretend to care about what the pair were discussing.

"Come on, let's get you home, *V*." I said, as it neared midnight. I hoped the use of Jake's nickname for her, in my mouth, would wind her up.

"Don't let me stop you love birds; don't do anything I wouldn't do." Jake laughed, slurring from the alcohol in his system before making his way back into the crowd. *Trust me I won't be doing anything.*

As we left the event, we were handed two white goody bags. When we were out of view of the event, I let go of her until we reached the waiting vehicle.

"Good night?" Clive asked with a smile, as we took our seats in the back of the black town car.

"Super. Can we have some privacy please, Clive?" Verity said with little emotion. Clive nodded and shut the partition.

"You may as well have this." I offered, carelessly chucking my goody bag in her direction.

"How thoughtful." She snapped, looking out of the window.

"What's got your panties in a twist?" I prodded.

"You're so rude." She stated, keeping her attention fixed on the darkness outside.

"Me? I was the perfect gentleman." I said, placing a hand to my heart, mockingly.

"Oh give over." She whipped her head around to shoot daggers at me. "Outwardly you might have been but believe it or not, I know when you're being a prick."

"Come on, I could have been a lot worse. I made the best of a bad situation." I defended.

"Well, you weren't the top choice to be my plus one but when Sarah caught wind of it, there was no escaping." She continued, I thought back to an earlier call this week, when I had slipped up mentioning the event off the cuff. I should have known Sarah would dig her claws into such a public occasion.

"Fair point, but it really wasn't that big of a deal. You're blowing this out of proportion now."

"It was to me; these are my best friends." She whined, leaning over the middle seat towards me to emphasise her point.

"Okay, you're being hysterical now. You've clearly drunk too much." I dismissed her, leaning away.

Jesus, she drove me crazy!

"I'm not drunk, I'm allowed to be pissed off." She raised her voice, defiantly.

"Sure you are, but this is embarrassing for you." I laughed. Verity looked like she wanted to scream, her hands forming tight fists against the leather of the seat like she was trying to resist physical violence.

She took a deep breath. "You may be my fake boyfriend but in public your behaviour reflects on me. So, I expect you to respect the people I care about." Fire burned in her eyes.

"That wasn't part of the contract, Doll."

"Fuck you, Axel."

17

AXEL

My rage bubbled in time with the tomato sauce simmering away on the hob. When did this become my Friday night? Cooking for my friends and hosting my 'girlfriend', who was already invading my space on the couch in front of me. Just another one of the many things I could thank Sarah for!

I watched Verity from the kitchen island, buried in one of her books. Unlike her previous visits, when she opted for no makeup and comfortable clothing, tonight she was wearing dark jeans and a black off the shoulder top. She usually wore her hair up but this evening, her messy bun looked more considered. She looked good but I knew it wasn't for me; it was all just to keep up appearances in front of my friends.

"OMG guys, I just got to the part where Erica and James fuck in the woods. Erm, yes please!" She exclaimed, talking into her phone. My ears pricked up at the vulgar words falling from her mouth, as she sent her friends the voice note.

"What the fuck are you reading?" I asked, turning the hob down to let the sauce reduce, circling around the counter to sit beside Verity.

She held her book cover up to me as I read the title. *Punish Me.* My eyes widened and I snatched it out of her hands.

"Hey!"

"Pain seared through me as he slammed deep into my pussy-" I read from the pages, laughing at the explicit content this innocent looking woman was reading.

"Give that back!" Verity shouted, reaching over, basically climbing on top of me. Her knees dug into my thighs as she clambered for the book.

I held it just out of her reach and continued where I'd left off, "ecstasy shot through me as he slid a finger in my arse, I'd never felt so full." Verity's cheeks glowed painfully red as she struggled against me. Her body fell onto mine, her weight pressing against my chest as she stretched to grab it. I closed the book, holding it over my shoulder. "Jesus Verity, what is this?"

"It's a romance novel," she insisted, as she reached around my torso, her petite arms wrapping around me in her determined attempt.

"No, it's porn!"

"It's completely different. I've never read about a pizza delivery guy in any of these." She said defiantly, sitting back and staring me straight in the face, doing her best to be intimidating, but resembling Tinkerbell throwing a tantrum.

"Shall I put it on the TV and prove it to you? Man fucks woman and you're getting horny."

"I am not *getting horny*." She argued, emphasising the end of her sentence. Yet, her body told a different story as I noticed her glazed over eyes and erect nipples. Blood rushed to my dick. *Fuck, dangerous territory.*

At that moment, the buzzer rang. I'd never been more thankful to be cockblocked. In an instant, Verity seemed to realise she was straddling me and hurriedly pushed herself off, adjusting her top as she took a seat back on the chair. I stood up to answer the door and tossed the book onto the island, with a chuckle. Verity shot me an evil glare as I failed to return her property.

I welcomed the three men in as they reached my front door. I introduced Aaron, Brad and George to Verity before heading to the balcony terrace for some drinks.

"Nice to finally meet you, Verity, we have heard a lot about you." Aaron said, clinking his beer bottle to her wine glass. Verity smiled at him.

"All good things I hope." She mirrored the words I'd spoken to her friends and I internally rolled my eyes. I returned to the kitchen to finish off the chicken parmigiana, watching them interact with her outside. Lying to my friends was one thing but it felt like a step too far to have them meet the woman I was pretending to be in a relationship with. It wouldn't be long until Verity would no longer be in my life, and to be honest, I was counting down the days. Verity must have felt my eyes on her as she turned and caught me staring. I nodded towards the steaming plates of food, that I was dishing up in a silent request for help. Without speaking, we took the plates out to the balcony.

"Dinner is served, boys." I announced. My friends taking their seats as we handed out the dishes. After a short moment of quiet, while we all began tucking into our food, Brad spoke.

"Very refined of you to invite us all round for a dinner party." He said, laughing slightly.

"Thank Verity, it was her idea. She wanted to impress you." I cast a glance in her direction, as she looked momentarily surprised at my words.

"Great idea, lucky you getting four strapping men to yourself for the evening." George said, the two performing their usual double act.

"Shut up, George." Aaron interjected. "You must be very special to Axel for him to agree to introduce you to us. We've never met a woman in his life before." I winced at the connotation that she meant a lot to me. There was never a woman in my life long enough to introduce these boys to and that's how I liked it.

"Oh, you're all wonderful company." She pandered, taking a bite of the chicken. "This is delicious, Axel." She complimented with a smile, which didn't reach her eyes.

"I heard on the casting circuit, they're remaking *The Godfather*. I'm gonna go for it!" George gushed.

"Good luck, you're about as Italian as this fucking chicken parm." I goaded, gesturing at the meal in front of us.

"You come to me on the day of my daughter's wedding." George said in a fake accent, mimicking Don Corleone's famous line.

"Point proven." I laughed.

"Oh Verity, darlin', you don't even know what we're talking about! I forgot you're a decade younger!" Brad interjected, looking at Verity opposite him, who was sporting an unimpressed look.

"Yes, silly me, tell me more about this movie." She batted her eyelashes, her voice sickly sweet, sarcastically playing into the perception he had of her.

"Calling it a movie would be doing it a disservice. It's not simply entertainment, it's education. To the simple-minded it might just seem like blood and guns but let me assure you, it's so much more than that."

"Ooo sounds scary!" She lied, cutting into her chicken with more force than necessary. It was becoming apparent that Verity didn't like the assumption that people tended to have of her - that she was young and naive. I watched amused as the scene played out. George and Brad continued to make digs as she tried her best to remain polite, although I'm sure it was killing her!

Once everyone had finished their meals, Verity stacked the plates and took them through to the kitchen. Once she was out of earshot the boy talk began.

"Not bad mate, she's fit." George bleated, seedily. My jaw ticked in irritation.

That's my 'girlfriend' you're talking about, **mate**.

"Good on ya for scoring a young thing like that." Brad agreed. I cringed at his words, I was never a fan of how they spoke about women.

"Man, I don't know how she's gonna handle your lifestyle. She seems even more innocent in person." Aaron deduced.

"Not that innocent." I responded, "you should have seen what she was reading earlier."

"Axel." I heard Verity's warning behind me. I turned surprised as I realised she was now back on the terrace.

"What was she reading? I wanna know!" Brad said excitedly.

"It's in the kitchen if you wanna have a peek." I informed, an unusual uneasy feeling swirled in my stomach as I fed the vultures. Brad scurried back into the apartment, like a man on a mission, past a shocked Verity.

Returning with the goods, he flicked to a random page, standing in front us like a town crier.

"Please daddy, fuck my pussy." Brad read the quote aloud in a mocking high-pitched voice.

George joined him in fits of uncontrollable laughter as they began to take turns reciting paragraphs from the book. Aaron sat quietly, trying not to be sucked into the chaos as Verity stormed back inside.

"Verity, wait!" I called, following her into the kitchen.

She spun around to face me with a stern look on her face.

"Come on, it was just a joke."

"You're right. I am a joke, to you and your stupid little friends." She shouted, gesturing to the balcony where the pair were reenacting a scene from the story. "I've been humiliated, spoken down to and patronised all night and you've not tried to stop it once." Her blue eyes shone with unshed tears as she vibrated with frustration.

"You are an adult, Verity. You are capable of defending yourself, you know." I countered, rounding the island to stand closer to her.

"I know, but these are your friends! I wanted to be cordial and try my best, something you aren't familiar with doing." She shouted, her fury radiating off her in full force. I'd never seen her like this. She had been angry at me before but this wasn't the same.

"You need to stop being such a people pleaser, you're not going to get far in life letting yourself get walked all over."

"You literally don't give a shit, do you? I know this is fake and I mean nothing to you but it's basic common decency." She blurted in aggravation before I clamped my hand over her mouth in an attempt to shut her up. My friends were only just outside the door and were at risk of discovering the truth. Her eyes widened and pupils dilated slightly at my unexpected action.

"You signed up for a boyfriend not someone to fight your fucking battles for you." I hissed, removing my hand from her face and slamming it down on the counter harder than intended, causing more of a scene.

"I hate you." She murmured in defeat, the tears now threatening to spill over.

"At least we finally agree on something, Doll." I released a sigh before rejoining the men outside and taking my seat, with my back to the glass doors.

"Should we call you daddy, Axel?" George said in a mocking tone.

"Fuck off, man." I ran an exasperated hand through my hair.

"Shame she had to leave so soon, I'd convinced these idiots to apologise." Aaron said sympathetically.

"She's not left?" I queried, confused.

"Yeah mate, I just watched her walk out." Aaron confirmed, taking a sip of beer.

I turned back to look at the shut front door. A strange mix of emotions ran through me but anger prevailed. How childish to leave me high and dry in front of my friends, when we were meant to be showing a united front tonight!

I just hoped she had held the tears back long enough to not be papped.

18

VERITY

Axel Ford is the most pig-headed, ignorant, selfish man that I had ever had the displeasure of meeting. He was nearly forty for fuck's sake and still trying to impress his pathetic friends.

I'd never felt so degraded and isolated at a social event in my life. If this behaviour continued much longer, I would be pulling the plug on this whole arrangement. I'd have rather risked legal repercussions, breaching this contract then spend another day pretending to like that arrogant prick.

To add insult to injury, we had to shoot Rosie and Tyler's first sex scene today. *Fuck my life.*

I arrived on set and met with the Intimacy Co-ordinator, Lucy, who Axel and I had met several times leading up to this scene to discuss what our boundaries were and what we were comfortable with etc.

"I know it's nerve wracking being your first ever intimate scene, but just remember, it'll be a closed set and everyone here will be looking after you. If at any point you want to stop, just say so." Lucy said kindly.

"Thank you. I appreciate that." I smiled warmly at her, trying to conceal my nerves.

As I headed to hair and makeup, I pondered how the minimal crew would no doubt be assuming this would be second nature for two love birds a month into their relationship. If only they knew!

The idea of Axel being anywhere near me, let alone touching or groping my body, made my blood boil. I guess I should've been thankful that this would be partially clothed. Rosie and Tyler's first tryst took place in the back room of Cobblestone Cafe. The scene was full of romance, tangled limbs and giddiness to finally be together. So much so, that the pair didn't have time to remove clothes - just a hoicked-up dress and a ripped open shirt.

After getting prepared to shoot, I headed to the soundstage. Lucy was right, it was to be a private affair. Only Lucy, Nora, the sound producer and camera operator were here today, in addition to *him*.

Axel was scrolling on his fucking phone, as per usual, not looking phased at all. He was the complete picture of calm, meanwhile I was shitting myself.

Awkwardly, I played with the hem of my dress whilst I awaited direction. I refused to speak with Axel any more than I already had to and it would appear he felt the same way considering he was seemingly oblivious to me standing all but a few feet away.

"There's my Rosie and Tyler!" Nora clapped, approaching us. "This is the pair crossing the line after weeks of tension and now they're finally giving into the temptation of each other. Remember that heat from the other day, now's the time to channel it. Let's do this!" Axel and I shuffled to our starting places, leaning against opposite sides of the fake doorway.

"Time to live out your book fantasies, Doll." Axel whispered, causing rage to burn inside me, hotter than it was before, I didn't dignify him with a response. Did this man get off on irritating me?

"Action!" Nora called. In an instant, Axel transformed into Tyler in front of my eyes as his whole expression warmed.

"I can't stop myself any longer." He said with a longing look on his face.

"Then don't." I responded as Rosie, triggering him to wrap a hand around the back of my head and kiss me hard.

We began to perform the steps we'd rehearsed, bumping into the sacks of flour, on the right and knocking over the carton of eggs, on the left as we moved through the 'bakery storeroom.' The steps were predetermined but the passion wasn't. As my back hit the shelving unit, Axel lifted my leg to wrap it around his waist. His rough touch on my bare thigh felt electric causing goosebumps to appear on my flesh. Our lips moved in sync and I allowed my mind to give in to the scene, forgetting whose hands were all over me and throwing my head back in half acted pleasure. As I looked into his stormy eyes, his words from the previous night echoed in my brain.

You signed up for a boyfriend, not someone to fight your fucking battles for you.

Unconsciously, I bit down on his lip, harder than I was expecting.

"What the fuck!" Axel cussed, dropping my leg and stepping away from me.

"Cut!" Nora called. "What happened guys?" Axel brought his hand to his lip to check for any damage, glaring at me. I went to open my mouth to apologise.

"I stubbed my toe," Axel spoke before I had the chance. "Let's go again." I narrowed my eyes suspiciously at his cover up, there had to be an ulterior motive. He glowered at me when we resumed our places, I noticed the satisfying red tint to his lower lip and stifled a smirk.

The clapperboard sounded.

"Then don't." Just like the first time, Axel's lips found mine again, firmer this time, his hands more desperate as they explored my body. His fingers wound their way into my hair before he tugged harshly, the pin pricks of pain sent a shock of pleasure down my spine. I knew he was trying to get me back for the affliction I'd caused him but his harsh touch only thrilled me. I let out a breathy moan causing Axel to deepen the kiss as he-

"Cut!" We jumped away from each other, both panting and ruffled. A hot cocktail of frustration and arousal churned in my stomach. "Guys, I know I told you to channel the passion but I'm not feeling the love between the characters." Axel snorted beside me.

Yeah, no kidding.

"Everyone happy to go again?" Nora asked, we nodded in unison and returned, once again, to the doorway.

As the third take started and we spoke our lines, we traced our footsteps through the set. With each step, breathing became heavier, hands roamed further and the throbbing between my legs intensified. From the force that Axel pressed me against the unit, it was apparent he wasn't just acting anymore either. I didn't know what was wrong with me, I hated this man with every fibre of my being. But at that moment, I simultaneously wanted to push him away and pull him closer. Nora's call for cut broke the spell. As her words reached us, we split away again quickly. I stared at Axel, his hair messed from my frantic fingers and lips swollen, I pressed my thighs together subconsciously to dull the ache. *Get it together Verity.*

"Okay let's take five. We need to find the middle ground between a polite kiss and full-on hair-raising heat." Nora instructed, releasing us from the cameras.

I was frustrated that my confused feelings towards Axel were beginning to affect filming. Trust that arsehole to jeopardise my lifelong dream. I needed to clear my head, outside of the sound stage. Hurriedly, I began walking back to my trailer to retreat from the watchful eyes of the crew.

"Where are you going?" I heard him call from behind me.

"Leave me alone, Axel."

"Shouldn't we talk about it?" He caught up easily.

"There's nothing to discuss." I waved him off, not daring to look back.

"I beg to differ." Axel circled around, walking backwards in front of me. God why couldn't he just fuck off?

"Have you followed me to tell me how shit I am at my job? If so, I'm really not in the mood." I said as we passed rows of trailers.

"Not in the slightest."

"Then what do you want?" I asked, passing him quickly, up the stairs to my dressing room, ignoring the electricity between us as I brushed against him.

"I want you to admit it." He prodded, stopping at the bottom as I made my way up.

"I said leave me alone." I opened the door and tried to slam it shut but Axel's strong hand prevented it. He pulled it back open before entering my sanctuary and closed it behind him. I backed up slightly, trying to stand my ground but felt suffocated in the enclosed space.

"Admit it, Verity." He walked over to me, leaning down so close I could feel his breath ghost over my lips.

"Admit what?" I said defensively, instincts screaming to get away from the man in front of me but I wasn't going to give him the satisfaction.

"The reason you struggled with that scene is because you want me." He began to trace a finger along my left collarbone. My heart thudded so hard in my chest I swear he could've heard it.

"Yeah right, Axel. Get your head out of your arse!" I retorted, trying to keep my breathing steady as he began sliding it down my arm.

"I can see the way your pupils dilate from my touch," his finger reached the curve of my hip. "The way your breathing changes around me," I gasped, his light touch heightening all my senses as he ran it over my stomach, beginning to trace upwards on the other side of my body, "and how you fucking loved it when I pulled your hair." He tugged lightly on the end of a blonde curl just above the small mound of my right breast. I felt my face flush.

"You're wrong, I hate you." My voice quivered, my protest sounding weak to my own ears.

"I don't doubt that," a sly smirk pulled at his lips, as his fingers reached my chin, "but I know you're fucking soaking right now, Doll."

"No-"

"Don't lie to me." He cut in, gripping my chin. His hand forcing me to look into his smoky eyes. He was right, my thighs were slick with moistness, I'd never been so turned on in my life. I hadn't admitted it to myself before, but now, standing alone in the confines of my trailer, it was almost impossible to shut out the filthy images in my head.

His dominance made one thing clear, this man could fuck the shit out of me and I hated how much I wanted it.

My eyes flicked down to the large bulge in his trousers before meeting his stare again. He raised an eyebrow in a challenge, I opened my mouth to speak, unsure if I was going to give in or object before he claimed my lips for the fourth time today.

This was unlike any other kiss we'd shared. It was far from delicate, every ounce of frustration, anger and stress was being released as our tongues fought for dominance. In one quick motion, Axel wrapped his hands under my thighs and lifted me around his waist, my legs instinctively caging him in.

"You're fucking desperate for me, aren't you?" He chuckled darkly.

"Fuck you." I hissed, earning another amused grumble from Axel's chest.

"I intend to, Doll." He dragged his teeth across the delicate skin of my neck, causing a shudder to run through me. I'd never burned as hot as I did right now, his touch was molten lava. With ease, he pulled the dress I was wearing over my head with one hand, exposing my red lace balconette bra.

"Well, that's not Rosie's," Axel drawled, pinging the sexy lingerie that was not given to me by wardrobe. He yanked one of the cups down to reveal my peaked nipple before sucking it into his mouth, my hands found the back of his head holding him against me. I let out a low moan as I felt his teeth against my skin.

Axel led us towards the sofa in the corner before placing me on the arm, the cold leather against my bare back was a delicious contrast to the flames rushing through my veins and igniting every nerve ending.

He stood above me, his eyes dark with hunger, a predator and his prey. Staring up at him, I was paralysed with arousal as I anticipated his next move.

"Let's see Verity…" He leant down, running a finger over the matching red underwear covering my most private area. "Just as I suspected. Fucking drenched." I whined at the contact, bucking my hips up for any kind of friction. Not caring how needy I looked in that particular moment. He ripped the panties off me, revealing my slick pussy.

"Who got you this wet, Doll?" He cooed, patronisingly, as he began to tease my centre. I stared at him unamused, unwilling to boost his ego. "Come on, Verity. Don't be stubborn." He dipped a finger inside me. I let out a breathy moan as he began to stroke my walls. "Speak up." I refused to give him the satisfaction, closing my eyes as he pumped faster. "As you wish." He stopped abruptly, I squirmed against him.

"Urgh, is your masculinity that fragile, that you need me to fucking tell you?" I cried, the frustration was almost too much to bear. How was he still this infuriating knuckle deep inside me?

"Just tell me and I'll carry on. You're only sabotaging yourself." He winked with a devilish grin.

"Jason." I said stubbornly knowing it would hit a nerve, Axel's jaw ticked proving me right.

"Oh yeah? Would Jason fuck you like this?" He goaded, slipping his finger out of me and unbuckling his belt. Before I had a chance to react, he swooped my legs over his shoulders and slammed into me. Hard.

Every nerve receptor was alight as I screamed in pain and pleasure. He clamped a firm hand over my mouth to silence me and allowed me a few seconds to adjust to his size before sliding himself almost fully out and back into me with full force. "Would anyone else make you scream like this, huh?" He asked, gruffly.

He fell into a punishing rhythm as I dug my nails into his broad shoulders, my thoughts incoherent with how brutally he pounded me. I bit his hand to free my face from his grip, he smirked. It took everything in me not to cry out his name but I wouldn't give in. I knew that's what he wanted.

With each long stroke, the promise of an orgasm grew stronger. I stared up at the man before me. Sweat slicked his brow, his dark hair falling over his forehead, looking at me like I was the object of his desires rather than an annoyance for once. He buried his face in the side of my leg, stifling a moan of his own, as his movements became more jerky.

"You're taking my cock like such a pathetic slut." He growled, his harsh words fuelling the fire further that was building in my lower abdomen. I closed my eyes, allowing myself to get lost in the feeling as my climax approached.

"I'm gonna co-"

With that, Axel pulled out to the tip and froze his movements.

"What the fuck are you doing?" I panted breathlessly, feeling empty.

"I'll ask you again, Doll. Who made you this wet?" He smirked, awaiting the confirmation.

God, I don't want to say it.

"You're a cocky bastard." I whispered through gritted teeth, his dick taunting my opening.

"That's not an answer." He pulled out completely, and I whimpered. "One word and I'll make all this frustration go away, Verity."

Fuuuuck sake. The way Axel was standing above me, stroking his cock caused my mouth to dry, I *needed* to come.

"You." I mumbled, non-committedly.

"Sorry? I can't hear you?" He mocked, feigning ignorance.

"You!" I declared, louder than I was proud to admit. An arrogant smile tugged at his lips, "Axel, please!" The use of his name and the plea that left my mouth must have triggered something inside him. He spun me on to my stomach and slammed his length into my begging pussy.

"Don't ever forget it, Doll." A sharp spank to my arse shot ecstasy to my clit as he took a hold of my hips. "Fuck, your cunt feels so good." He moaned.

"Axel, I'm going to-" Before I could finish the sentence, euphoria flooded my entire body as a toe curling, mind-numbing, earth-shattering orgasm ripped through me. As the wave continued, Axel swept me up, turning me around again, my legs falling either side of his core as he lifted me. I wrapped my arms around his muscular neck, leaning against his chest weakly from the aftermath of my climax, as he slipped back inside me. Mercilessly, he bounced me on his cock as I clung onto him for dear life.

"That's it baby, come for me again." He whispered in my ear, his harsh thrusts mixing with the sweet pet name caused my brain to malfunction. My vision hazed with each pump as my second orgasm engulfed me. I sunk against his body, spotting the veins protruding from his neck as he tensed, his own climax peaking. A low growl escaped his mouth as he came.

He released my legs and placed me on the sofa, slipping off a condom that I hadn't noticed he'd put on in the midst of the chaos. As the post-orgasmic bliss left my body, the realisation of what had just happened hit me. I was just fucked by Axel Ford! And he made me come, TWICE!

"Do you feel better now?" He asked, re-buckling his belt as I hastily scampered to retrieve my abandoned dress from the corner of the trailer, on shaky legs. I didn't dignify him with an answer. "You're welcome by the way."

"What?" I asked, astonished by his egotism as I slipped the item over my head, recovering my modesty.

"Well, you should be able to film a convincing sex scene now." Suddenly, I was just as frustrated as before we had sex. How is it that less than two minutes ago I was screaming his name and now I wanted to slap the smug look off his face?!

"You're honestly unbelievable." I looked at him dumbfounded.

"I'll take that as a compliment. See you out there, Doll." He chuckled, disappearing out of my trailer and out of sight.

Now alone again, I sank back into the cushions of my seat, dropping my head in my hands as I released a sigh. Just when I thought this situation couldn't get any more complicated, I had to go and sleep with my boyfriend!

19

AXEL

The warm droplets from the shower head helped to work through my thoughts after the unexpected events of yesterday.

I had been fully aware of Verity's interest in me from day one but I didn't know I'd act on it until I could sense her frustration when filming *that* scene. Her whole body was calling for me. When I sensed the number of takes we were going to run through that day, I needed some form of entertainment to get me through the shoot and my favourite pastime currently was pissing her off.

When she stormed back and I followed, my only intentions had been to taunt her further and elicit the anger that I managed to conjure up whenever we were in each other's presence. It wasn't until I had closed the door, confining us like flames in a gas-soaked room, that I knew I was done for.

Her body begged for me, especially those ocean blue, doe eyes and I lost all self-control. Although I was sure she assumed she was just another woman in a long list of co-stars I had fucked to oblivion, that wasn't actually a regular occurrence for me.

I usually made a point not to mix business with pleasure. But it was a damn good stress reliever. One I would bet my life on, that I would be repeating. The way her porcelain skin prickled with goosebumps at my touch, the way my name fell from her rosy lips, the way she dripped with arousal and how her tight pussy clamped around my dick as she fell apart in my arms. It was undeniable that I could get addicted to that feeling.

I shook the image out of my head as I turned off the shower. It was a non-filming day but we were needed on set for a morning of promotional interviews to drum up excitement and interest in the movie. I felt unbothered by the whole thing even though I had crossed the line with Verity less than twenty hours ago - but I expected she had been overthinking ever since.

****

"Ahh, Axel! There you are." Sarah greeted me as I pushed her office door open. "It's so lovely to see you both in the flesh again." She complimented.

My vision zeroed in on the familiar blonde sitting opposite my agent, who was yet to make eye contact with me.

"Fancy seeing you here, Doll." I drawled. Taking the seat next to her. The two of us had been summoned to Sarah's makeshift office, now she was back in the country for a few days, for a pre-interview briefing.

"Axel." Verity greeted, blankly. Without thinking, my gaze dragged over her frame; the white jumper clinging tightly to her chest, her figure-hugging jeans, and her hair pulled back in a loose plait tied with a bow, just begging me to wrap my hand around it.

"I'll keep this short, but I've spoken with the news outlets today and they've all been briefed to ask a specific set of questions only." She handed us two sets of cue cards, "study these and do not, I repeat *do not*, deviate from the pre-written answers. We don't want any unexpected headlines." She warned, waggling a stern finger at us. Verity and I began to scan over our respective sheets.

"What's one thing you love about Axel?" Verity spoke out loud. Reading the answer on the paper - 'his dashing good looks' - I chucked inwardly. "Thank God, you've given me an answer, I would have been speechless." She mumbled under her breath.

"Sure, Doll." *There's definitely something you love about me.* I smirked as Verity shot me a sideways look, deciphering the meaning behind my words. She flicked through the other cards, her expression neutral as she took in the ridiculously curated responses. "Hopefully you can memorise these better than you do your lines, Verity." I nudged her, causing her to stiffen.

"Worry about yourself Axel, I'll be fine." She said, standing up and tapping my shoulder in a clear attempt to seem unaffected by my proximity, as she walked out of the room.

Once the door had closed, Sarah glared at me. "You better make sure her frosty attitude doesn't come across in those interviews, Axel."

I saluted her sarcastically before heading to join my girlfriend at our branded chairs.

"Nice to meet you Axel and Verity, I'm Sam from StarBuzzDaily." A lanky man, who couldn't have long graduated from high school, held out his hand to shake.

"Hey man," I greeted.

"Hi Sam, lovely to meet you!" Verity smiled warmly, her annoyingly adorable dimple appearing on her cheek.

As the camera operator prepped the shot, I grasped Verity's hand in mine and squeezed, to appear the doting boyfriend for the video. Without looking at me, she began to dig her nails into my flesh, her expression remaining stoic. *God, I can get under her skin so easily.* I leant over the arm of the chair to whisper in her ear.

"Are you as turned on as I am, Doll?" She turned immediately to face me, shooting daggers. Her piercing blue eyes, full of rage, captivated me for a second.

"We're rolling." The operator announced, providing Verity with no opportunity to retaliate without it being caught on film. With that, she relaxed her hand to avoid suspicion.

Sam began to rattle through the approved questions, and we dutifully answered as per Sarah's instructions.

"Thank you for your time. We're all so excited to see Rosie and Tyler come to life!" Sam praised before leaving, ready for the next interviewer to jump in his grave. Sarah looked triumphant behind the scenes, satisfied with our performances. The minute the camera stopped rolling; Verity snatched her hand away from mine.

"Careful Verity, the cameras may be off but there's eyes everywhere." I warned. She ignored me, reaching into her back pocket to retrieve her phone. I watched as she scrolled mindlessly through social media. "You seem stressed?" I asked, mockingly.

"What would give you that idea?" Verity responded flatly, refusing to look in my direction.

"You won't look at me, Babygirl. Is it something I said?" I lifted her chin towards me with one finger, instantly noticing how her throat bobbed with a swallow.

"Urgh!" She growled, frustratedly as she jolted her head away from my touch.

"I can think of a way to relieve that tension, Doll." I whispered, smirking as I knew my words would be having a physical effect. As predicted, Verity shuffled in her seat, tensing her legs together. "You're so easy to wind up." I chuckled.

The next interviewer joined us. A short, grey-haired woman who introduced herself as Gemma from The Outlook, a nationwide tabloid.

"Great to meet you both," we smiled in unison, "there is so much anticipation for this adaptation! How does it feel to be involved? Axel, I'll come to you first." She gestured towards me; I turned my charm on.

"It's such an honour to be a part of this project. Knowing the fans had been eager for me to play Tyler from the get-go, I feel grateful that I'm able to give back and hopefully the ladies love it." I winked cheekily, reciting Sarah's words.

"Yes, I'm sure the fandom of *Accidentally in Love* will be lining the streets to see you topless, Axel. What's the workout routine?" She gushed.

"Haha well thank you, Gemma, I'm flattered but I wanted to bring some depth to Tyler, he's not just a six pack, there's so much more to him." I lied through my teeth.

"Of course, of course! And Verity, this is your first role and what a role it is! Not only are you on-screen lovers but we hear life is now imitating art. Tell us what a typical date night with Axel Ford entails?" Gemma's eyes sparkled as she waited for Verity's answer.

"Well Gemma, I'll be keeping some details private but I can say it's endless hours of riveting conversation, he always prepares me the best meals. He's quite the chef, you should try his chicken parm," she listed, I felt my stomach drop as Verity abandoned the script, throwing subtle digs in my direction, "and his friends have been so welcoming. We're like one big happy family." Catching Sarah's panicked expression to the left of the camera, I tried my best to give her a subtle 'what the fuck' look. "It really has been a dream come true."

"That's lovely to hear! So, what's your favourite thing about Axel then?" Gemma seamlessly wormed in the pre-prepared question. If Verity's response wasn't back on script, the only answer I would have accepted would be 'his dick'.

"There's many to choose from, obviously his dashing good looks," I breathed a sigh of relief as it seemed Verity had seen sense, "but do I have an exclusive for you!" Sarah looked as if her eyes were going to pop out of their sockets as she telepathically communicated to shut Verity up. Thinking fast, I slapped my hand on her thigh, squeezing it as a warning, boring my eyes into the side of her head. "Don't worry, Big Shot, it's sweet." She smiled patronisingly at me, as the anxiety twisted in my gut. "He has a whole collection of Sylvanian Families that he's named and tucks into little beds every evening. He can't sleep properly until he's sure they're all safe and sound." *Jesus what is the girl banging on about?!* I furrowed my brow. "Calico Critters babe, that's just what we call them here!" *What the fuck?* "Some people might think it's cringey that a nearly forty-year-old man plays with dolls," she shrugged. I noted the relation to my nickname for her and the implied message, "but I just think it's special." She wrapped an arm around my shoulder before stroking the back of my head, I was frozen still in confusion. Where had this defiant attitude come from all of a sudden? Verity a month ago wouldn't have dared go against Sarah's instruction.

"Okay I think that's enough questions, the cast are tired. Thank you, Gemma." Sarah forcibly stopped the interview, waving frantically at Verity and I to retreat into her office as the reporter left quickly.

We walked across the large room towards Verity's retribution.

"What the fuck was that?" I questioned, catching up to her.

"Checkmate dickhead. You're so easy to wind up." She repeated my earlier words back to me, with a doe-eyed innocent look.

Verity opened the door to the office confidently, letting go before I had a chance to walk in, leaving it to slam in my face. As I was met with the light wood, I didn't know whether to be in awe of this out-of-character Verity who disobeyed us all or to take her back to my trailer and punish her for her insubordination.

20

VERITY

Explosions, Car Chases, and… Tea Parties? Axel Ford's Sylvanian Secret.

> *Axel Ford's Next Movie? Fast & Furriest: The Bunny Chronicles.*

> *Hollywood's Best-Kept Secret: Axel Ford Has More Sylvanian Families Than Oscar Nominations.*

My cheeks hurt from smiling, as I scrolled through the multiple outlets covering the breaking news of Axel's surprising hobby. That would teach him to mess with me so publicly, two could play at that game.

If you'd told me two months ago, I would have been passive-aggressively answering interview questions alongside the biggest star in Hollywood, I would have laughed in your face, and no doubt been incredibly anxious at the prospect, yet this was the predicament I found myself in. Everyday relations between Axel and I only grew more hostile. Even when we'd had sex, it was hateful. It was clear that the act was purely to purge stress for us both. However, it was apparent that it hadn't had the desired effect. I wasn't sure what the future held in store for us but one thing was for certain, I would not be making the mistake of falling into bed with him again!

Just like clockwork, my phone began to ring for my monthly call with Mum. I braced myself to answer, knowing this would be anything but friendly and supportive. I was surprised to see Charlotte's name appear on the screen.

"Hey, who's dead?" I answered curtly.

"Whoa, morbid!" She laughed, "Why would you immediately go to bad news?" My sister asked.

"Haha, sorry. Just been a while since you've called for a friendly chat." I leant back on the sofa, placing my device on the arm next to me and clicking speakerphone on. My sister and I, despite being close in age, had never formed a particularly strong bond. I probably had my mother to thank for that, given we were seen as competition rather than comrades to each other, constantly having grades, achievements and accolades pitted against one another.

"Well, there is more to this call than just a catch up…" She paused, sounding more optimistic than usual. I waited with bated breath for her to continue. "We're pregnant!" She gushed.

"Oh my God! Congratulations!" I jumped to my feet excitedly. I knew Charlotte and her husband, Dominic, had been close to starting a family, but I hadn't expected the news to come so soon. "How far along are you!?"

"Thirteen weeks! I'll text you the scan picture. I've been dying to tell you!" I could hear the lump in her throat, my own tears spilling down my cheeks.

"I'm really happy for you!" I felt like my heart was going to bust with pride.

"They're going to be so lucky to grow up with a famous aunty. We'll have to take them to visit your Hollywood star!" Her words meant more to me than she knew.

"Maybe one day!" I laughed, flopping back onto the sofa. "Thank you for telling me yourself, I normally have to hear everything in Mum's recap of all the amazing things Charlotte and Dominic have done."

"Oh, trust me, I know what it's like." Charlotte agreed, I could hear the exasperation in her voice.

"Has she been boasting to you about the child who forfeited a proper career and is a constant failure to her?" I said sarcastically.

"You're not a failure, Ver and it's not fun on my side either. Constantly having to live up to these crazy expectations. At least you get to have some fun!"

"Sounds like you and Mr Khan have had a bit of fun of your own!" I joked, causing us to erupt into fits of giggles.

"Fair point! Although, I've seen the pics of you and your A-lister! God it'll be so weird if he comes for Christmas dinner, he'll always be Teddy from *Sunset High* to me." Charlotte said, referencing the teenage drama series we binge-watched as pre-teens together and Axel's breakout role. Memories of the two of us rushing home from school to catch the latest episode played in my mind.

My heart sank at the mention of Axel and my sister's enthusiasm. I was so used to a lack of positivity surrounding events in my life from my family, so it was bittersweet to hear this from Charlotte, especially given the true circumstances. I was glad our arrangement would always stay our dirty little secret.

I could already imagine my mother's reaction if she ever found out…

21

AXEL

Another boring Thursday back on set with my lovely co-star. We hadn't filmed much together recently as we had been focussing on Tyler's backstory, so today would be the first time we were back with each other since Verity's little stunt in the interviews last week.

Thanks to her *hilarious* comment regarding my off-set hobby, Sarah had been inundated with offers to promote and advertise the anthropomorphic furry fucks.

What's a cleaner image than enjoying Sylvanian Families!

Sarah's irritatingly excited words rattled around my head. I spotted a large bunch of flowers on the counter. Flicking the attached card open, I read the message:

Wonderful job with the interviews, Verity! S x

Surprisingly, in stark contrast to her initial reaction, Sarah was overjoyed by the response and subsequent press we had received after Verity had gone off script.

"Beautiful aren't they!" I heard a smug voice behind me. "Did you get any, Big Shot?" I turned to see Verity leaning against the door of the makeup trailer.

"I'm more of a Sylvanian Families kinda guy." I shot at her.

"Oh, I hope that didn't ruin your street cred too much." She batted her eyelashes innocently.

She seemed pretty damn proud of herself. Little did she know she was just a pawn in my game.

"It'll take more than a few bunnies to ruin my image, Doll." I dropped the card back onto the tabletop and walked towards the exit, pinching her cheek as I passed. I laughed at the scowl I received from her.

****

"You have got to be kidding me. Why do you have to be so stubborn!" I shouted.

"This is my lifelong dream; I'm not just going to give it up!" Verity retaliated, throwing her hands up in frustration.

"Come on, Rosie. Maybe this is a sign!" I rounded the counter to stand in her eye line, gesturing to the water spraying over the floor.

"Don't be so stupid, it's just a burst pipe, I can pay to get it fixed." Her voice wobbled.

"It's the third one this month! You're just burning money and for what?" I reasoned, grabbing the top of her shoulders, bending down to her height.

"To achieve something, Tyler. All my life people have belittled and underestimated me, I just wanted to prove everyone wrong." Tears began to spill down her face, her crystal blue eyes twinkling.

"I just think it's important to know when to let go." I concluded, wiping a stray tear off Verity's cheek.

"Cut!" Nora called. "That was great guys, the pain was so real. Everyone is going to be sobbing in the cinemas!" Verity and I broke away from each other, sadness still lingering in her eyes.

"Well Blondie, looks like we've finally found one way you're not similar to Rosie." I clicked my fingers as we awaited the next direction.

"What do you mean?" She asked, wiping the remaining tears from her cheeks.

"She's feisty and stands up for herself, you let people walk all over you." I smirked, but she didn't seem to pick up on the humour in my voice.

"I'm sorry Nora, can I just take five please?" Verity asked, her voice sounding thick with emotion still. Nora nodded and she scurried off.

"Point proven." I called as I began to chase after her. Verity ignored me, picking up the pace towards her trailer, "come on, it was just a joke, lighten up."

She continued, swinging the door to her dressing room open as I followed her in.

"You know nothing about me, Axel. You don't know what I've had to deal with or the kind of person I am, so fuck you." She turned to square up to me.

"Whoa, where's all of this coming from, huh?" I asked, condescendingly, a sly smile on my face. She let out an irritated groan at my cocky expression.

"All you ever do is insult me. You are an arrogant, self-obsessed, egotistical, little man." A chuckle rumbled in my chest as I towered over her. "What's so funny?"

"I'm proud of you, Tink." I smirked.

"For what?"

"For standing up to me." She looked shocked, her lips parting slightly as she searched my face for the catch. "And you know I'm not little." I added with a wink, I felt a flicker of heat as I watched her eyes darken at my suggestive words.

"You're unbelievable." She breathed, her voice a mixture of exasperation and arousal. For a moment, she stood there, her gaze darting between my eyes and the quirk of my lips. Then, without warning, she reached out, grabbed the lapel of my jacket and pulled me in. Her lips slammed against mine before I could even react.

My hands roamed her body as our mouths moved together.

"God, I hate you." She whimpered as I bit her bottom lip.

"How much?" I teased, finding the mound of her breast, eliciting a moan from her as I squeezed.

"With every part of me!" She insisted between shallow breaths.

"Every part?" I goaded, raising an eyebrow. "Shall we test that theory, Doll? Get on the couch." I demanded.

"Make me." My cock flinched at her defiance; she knew exactly what she was doing.

"Don't be a brat." I growled pushing her towards the sofa, my mouth never leaving hers. The back of her knees hit the leather before she fell backwards with a gasp. Her ocean blue eyes scanned my form.

I knelt between her legs and pulled down her thong from under the skirt she was wearing. I leant in, my breath ghosting over her porcelain skin, I could smell her arousal.

"Does this part hate me?" I queried, placing my lips to the inner part of her leg. Her breath hitched. "What about this part?" I kissed again, further up this time, nipping her delicate thigh. Her body trembled slightly as her fingers found their way into my hair. "I know this part doesn't." I reached between her thighs, to feel her glistening core. "You're just as wet for me as before." I groaned, beginning to tease her clit lazily with my thumb. She tugged desperately on my curls, willing me to pick up the pace.

"You're so infuriating!" She panted through gritted teeth, I looked up at her under my brow, smirking at her dishevelled appearance: cheeks flushed, hair wild and pussy dripping for me.

"Let me take care of that for you." I drawled.

"Just get on with it." I chuckled at her demand before diving in. Perhaps it was to prove a point, to show her that she wanted me just as badly as the other day, or maybe, though I refused to admit it, it was because there was a small part of me that couldn't stand seeing her upset. Either way, I knew I had to make this girl come - and come hard.

As my mouth made contact, a strangled moan escaped her lips, her fingernails dug deeply into my shoulder blades, the pain spurring me on.

"You taste so sweet, Doll." I purred against her, watching as she threw her head back on the sofa in pleasure. Her thighs wrapped around my head as I circled the bundle of nerves with my tongue.

"Oh God." She cried, as I licked her hungrily, I felt her legs tremble with the wave of her first orgasm taking over her, I worked her through the euphoria, her soft moans lighting a fire within me. I slid a finger inside her, curling to find her g-spot, "Axel-" She panted, hearing my name fall from her lips in such a way caused my dick to throb painfully and I made it my mission to hear it as much as possible.

Her hips rolled and her nails dug deeper as I sucked her clit and thrusted my fingers.

"More." She pleaded.

"You're so needy, Doll." I growled, sliding in a second finger, her breaths became shallow, her hips grinding against my face, it was clear another orgasm was fast approaching.

Knock knock!

We froze, I met Verity's panicked eyes, as I remembered we hadn't locked the door. "Don't come in!" She called as the handle began to turn. I smirked and resumed my movements, slowly licking her folds, teasing her. "I'm getting dressed!"

"Sorry sorry!" A female voice apologised as the handle released. "It's only me, Grace, just wanted to check in as Nora said you weren't feeling great!"

I pumped my fingers faster, as Verity scrambled to form a coherent sentence. "Oh, no, I'm feeling a lot better now thanks!" I smiled against her, *I bet you are,* upping the pace as she tried to keep her voice steady. "I won't be long." Her voice cracked on the final word.

"Okay, I'll leave you both to it." She tapped the door and laughed before leaving.

"Fuck!" Verity moaned, half embarrassed, half on the edge of her orgasm. I shot her a wink and her thighs immediately tensed as her climax rolled through her body. Her moans echoed around the small trailer and I held her hips to prevent her from moving away as I ravaged her cunt.

"Oh God, I hope she didn't hear that!" She started, trying to sit up. I removed my fingers from her before pushing her back against the cushions.

"Where do you think you're going?" I teased, holding her down with a hand on her lower stomach.

"We need to get back to set." She said, flustered, running her fingers through her hair, as she attempted to compose her.

"No, no, you have one more in you, Doll." I assured, my voice low. I lifted her legs over my shoulders and pulled her back towards my mouth. I wrapped my arms around her thighs and licked at her swollen pussy.

Verity whined in protest but tugged at my hair, bringing me harder against her core, her wetness slicking my face.

Such a good girl.

Her hips bucked and I moved my head from side to side, my mouth never leaving her clit.

"Axel, it's too mu- I can't-" She caught on her words as her third orgasm wrecked her body.

There was something so satisfying about a woman who hated me coming on my tongue. After coaxing her through her orgasm I sat back, a triumphant grin forming on my lips as I took in the drained girl in front of me.

"Did you hate that, Doll?" I asked sarcastically.

"Shut up, Axel." She removed her shaky legs from my shoulders and shuffled her skirt back down. "We need to stop doing this."

"Do we? It seemed you were enjoying yourself, Verity. Don't you feel more relaxed now?" I questioned, watching her pupils dilate slightly as I wiped her juices from my mouth, before standing. She nodded irritated in agreement. "I propose a mutually beneficial arrangement."

"Another one? How many contracts am I going to get embroiled in with you Axel?" She rolled her eyes, getting off the sofa and retrieving her underwear from the floor.

"This one would be off the books." I stated. "This is a stressful job and we spend a lot of time together so I suggest a code word."

"A code word?" She asked incredulously.

"Yep, for when either of us need to relieve some tension." She blinked blankly at me, mulling it over.

I could practically see the cogs turning in her head, she could preach all she wanted about how she couldn't stand to be around me but I knew how good I could make her feel. She wouldn't be able to deny herself that pleasure from time to time.

"Ok fine, but I get to choose it." She relented.

"By all means, Tink." I replied, satisfied with the compromise.

"Sylvanian Families." I looked at her unamused. "I'm joking. Erm…" She glanced around the room. "Cookie." She deduced, pointing to an open pack on the side.

"Uninspired but I can agree to that." She held out a hand to shake to seal the deal. "I knew you couldn't resist me, Doll." I winked, pulling her hand towards me and slapping her on the ass, earning a yelp. "Let the fun begin!"

22

VERITY

It had been two weeks since I'd signed *another* deal with the devil. As much as I despised the man, Axel was right about one thing. It seemed the only way I could stand to be around him was when he was seven inches deep inside me.

We'd gotten into a bit of a habit on set when either of us wound the other up of declaring 'cookie' and scurrying back to one of our trailers to work through our frustrations. I wasn't proud of it but it certainly made the days with him slightly more enjoyable.

I had a weekend off but unfortunately; it wasn't going to be Axel-free. We had agreed to accompany each other to an industry party tonight. According to Sarah, it was a great place to network and garner some paparazzi attention.

I slipped on a pair of baby pink strappy heels; to match the backless, silky dress I had picked out from a dozen options. This was a new perk of the job - famous designers sending me clothes to wear!

Checking the time, I had five minutes until Axel would be picking me up. Tonight, he was my chauffeur, affording Clive a night off! Turning back to the full-length mirror in my bedroom, I took my lipstick out of my gold clutch bag and applied the cherry red stain to my lips. My phone rang on my bed, I picked it up to see Axel's name, before I had the chance to answer he'd hung up. Guess that's my cue to leave! I grabbed my Emerald Hart collection necklace that I didn't have time to put on and headed out of my apartment.

I spotted the sleek, black sports car easily in the car park of my building between the Ford Fiestas and Mini Coopers. It stuck out like a sore thumb.

"Evening, Doll." Axel greeted me as I slid into the vehicle.

"Hi." I reciprocated, buckling my seatbelt. Axel looked absolutely devastating. By now, you'd have thought I'd be used to his striking good looks, but every time I went over to his place, even in his casual sweatpants and t-shirts he managed to take my breath away. So tonight, dressed to the nines, it was impossible to deny just how deeply I was drawn to him. He wore a dark navy suit, so deep it was almost black, paired with a crisp white shirt left slightly undone at the collar, he was irresistible. "Thanks for the ride. How long is the drive?" I asked to make small talk.

"About thirty minutes." He replied, changing his gear into reverse. He leant his left hand behind my headrest, looking through the back window, as he effortlessly manoeuvred the vehicle out of the parking space.

Why is it so hot when men do that?

"I hope you don't drive like a dickhead." Axel rolled his eyes at my dig. "I'm surprised you're not drinking tonight?"

"A simple thank you would suffice." He chuckled before turning the radio on to drown me out.

We rode in silence for the remainder of the journey as I put on my jewellery in the car.

"We're here." Axel announced as he turned into a long, dark driveway, lit only by lanterns. The road ended in a large circle with a fountain in the centre, where the valet waited. As we queued behind other flashy vehicles, I took a moment to bask upon the glory of the manor. It was the largest house besides Buckingham Palace, I had ever seen with my own eyes. It looked like something out of *Downton Abbey*!

Axel handed over the keys to a smart-looking man, as we stepped out of the car. My gold necklace dropped from my neck.

"Shit!" I exclaimed, hurriedly picking it up from the gravel before moving out of the way of the other waiting cars. At the bottom of the grand staircase, I attempted to reclasp the accessory around my neck, to no avail.

"Give it here." Axel offered gruffly. I handed it over. The delicate chain looked fragile within his large, rough palm. I turned around to face away from him.

He swept a hand across the top of my shoulders, to move the wispy strands of hair that had escaped my loose updo. His gentle touch caused me to tense, heat searing where he made contact and fire burning in my lower abdomen.

"Who do I have to thank for this little outfit you're wearing tonight, Doll?" He purred. I felt my cheeks flush, thank God he couldn't see my face.

"Ophelia Lancaster sent it to me. I thought it would be perfect for tonight." My voice shook slightly with arousal.

He fastened the necklace and placed it down against my skin, lightly running his knuckle down my spine until he reached the large bow at the base of my back. Shivers tingled through me.

"It looks good on you." He said simply, as if he didn't just set my nerves alight. "Let's do this, Tink." He walked to my side and held his hand out to take as we ascended the flight of stairs and entered the doorway.

I was astonished by the beauty of the building. Long velvet curtains draped at the sky-high windows, ornate painted portraits hung from the wallpapered walls and every room was paved with warm, brown mahogany flooring.

"This is incredible!" I declared, looking open mouthed around the space.

"You'll catch flies if you're not careful." He joked.

"When did you get used to all this grandeur?"

He shrugged, "after you've been to a few of these events, they all start to blend into one unfortunately. The setting just becomes a background to more boring conversation and meaningless networking."

"Cor I should've known you'd be fun at parties." I mocked, rolling my eyes. Axel took two flutes of champagne off a nearby waiter's tray before handing them both to me with a wink.

"Stick with me kid, I'll show you a good time." He said, deadpan.

"Fordy!" I heard a familiar voice call from behind. I turned to see Aaron walking towards us. "Evening, Verity." He greeted, taking my hand in his and placing a kiss to the back of it.

"I thought I'd find you here, plugging away to get some leads." Axel needled.

"It's all about the graft, mate. We aren't all Axel fucking Ford who never needs to audition." He knocked him jokingly in the arm. "Anyway, short and sweet but I think I've just spotted Christopher Nolan in the next room." He scurried off, trying to get a mystery man's attention.

"Could he really be here?" I asked Axel animatedly, "I loved *Inception*."

"I doubt it, Doll. You'll come to learn people can be pretty desperate at these parties so I wouldn't imagine Nolan would bother to show up." He shook his head, clearly over this whole charade. The two of us found a spot in the corner of the room but it wasn't long before the parade of various casting directors, film execs and producers were all vying for the opportunity to pitch to the hotshot.

"So that's the short version of the screenplay." The blonde screenwriter concluded.

"Short version!?" Axel responded bluntly. I squeezed his hand in a silent signal to behave. Although, the poor man had been spoken at for fifteen minutes about a man and his robot dog travelling the world!

"I'll get my assistant to send it to your agent, it would be great to discuss it further."

"Sounds thrilling." Axel replied sarcastically, I nudged him as his tone became harsher. The writer opened his mouth to continue but Axel spoke again. "If you'll please excuse us, we need to find the buffet, I'm craving a cookie."

A sharp intake of air caught in my throat as I processed his words. Axel guided me away from the oblivious man.

"Here?!" I whispered surprised.

"Here." Axel growled.

He pulled me along to the bathroom, locking the door behind us. Bathroom was an understatement; this room was massive! Before I had time to fully assess my surroundings, his strong body slammed me against the wooden door, as his hands roamed my curves.

"What did I do?" I asked bemused, as he began to kiss me relentlessly. Our previous escapades were always a direct result of one of us getting under the other's skin, but tonight, I'd been on my best behaviour!

"Not you, Doll. Everyone here wants a piece of me. I just need something to take my mind off all the noise." I felt a buzz at his declaration, trying not to focus on the fact I was his preferred distraction.

"Okay." I agreed as he trailed open-mouth kisses down my neck, my breathing becoming laboured. Instinctively, I tangled my fingers into his perfectly styled curls, as he sucked a sensitive spot.

"You're messing up my hair, Verity," he whispered in my ear, teasing me. His large hands grabbed my wrists and pinned them above my head causing moisture to pool between my thighs at his dominance.

He reached down, to pull up my dress, sliding my underwear to the side as he began to circle my clit with his thumb, the other hand still firmly restraining my arms.

"Always so ready for me, aren't you?" He purred, feeling my wet pussy. He slid two fingers inside easily and my hips bucked against him. His mouth found mine again and I kissed him eagerly as the heat of my climax built from my core, spreading with ferocity to the rest of my body. I'd never been this quick to orgasm but it was like Axel knew exactly how to get me over the edge.

"I'm so close." I whimpered.

"I know you are, baby. Come for me." He instructed, pressing an uncharacteristically soft kiss to my forehead which caused the building pressure to reach its peak. Blinding pleasure ripped through me as he continued his attack on my clit.

"Good girl." He praised. Axel released my hands for a split second before pulling me away from the door and pushing my torso onto the marble countertop. I heard the familiar rustle of a wrapper, before he recollected my wrists and held them behind my back. I looked up in the mirror and watched as he unbuckled his belt and trousers with one hand. My mouth dried at the vision of him so determined. I caught sight of myself in the mirror, glazed over eyes and red cheeks after the intensity of my orgasm. Usually, I wouldn't like to see myself in this way but something about being in Axel's grasp excited me and made me revel in the image.

I felt him tease my opening with his rock-hard cock and tried to shuffle backwards, needing him to fill me up.

"Patience, Doll." He chuckled before slamming into me. I cried out in ecstasy as he began to fuck me brutally. With each thrust, it was as if his pent-up irritations were melting away. I stared at him as he destroyed me.

"Do you like watching me wreck your sweet little cunt?" He asked, a loud moan of agreement escaped my lips causing him to clamp my mouth shut. "Shh, we're at a work event." He leant down to whisper in my ear. I shuddered against the cold work surface, my second orgasm threatening to crash over me.

"Hold onto the sink." He demanded, letting go of my wrists, I submissively did as I was told. His hand travelled from my mouth down to my throat, the other grabbing my hip as he continued his vigorous movements. "Tap me if it's too much." He instructed, making eye contact with me in the mirror to make sure I understood. I gave him a small nod before he squeezed the sides of my neck, the sensation was exhilarating. He continued to pound me, his hand releasing my hip and snaking under my satin dress to pinch my nipple.

"Come all over my cock for me, baby." My vision blurred as a white-hot light of pleasure shot through every part of me, a scream threatened to escape but luckily there was no sound due to the hold he had on my throat. I struggled for air as my orgasm consumed me. He loosened his grip as I lay limply on the countertop, basking in the sensation of my climax. Axel placed a kiss on my bare back before picking up the pace once again, pumping in and out of me until I felt him release inside the condom. He slumped, pressing a kiss to the side of my neck before removing himself and re-buckling his belt.

"Usually, I would have succumbed to alcohol, but this was a much better solution." He joked, slapping me on the arse.

I lay for a minute, shellshocked, before gaining the strength to sort myself out.

"Glad to be of service but God, do I need a drink now." I said, exhausted from the pounding I had just taken. I straightened my dress as he smoothed my messy hair, with a smile.

"Let's go." He ordered, gesturing for me to take the lead.

I opened the door sheepishly, praying a mile long queue hadn't formed on the other side whilst we had claimed it as our own. To my relief, the party was continuing unaware of the sex-capade that had just occurred metres away.

"Ah Axel, there you are! I just wanted to show you one more thing." The screenwriter from before, spotted us from across the hall and began winding his way over.

"Right, that's it, I'm outta here." Axel declared, taking my hand and guiding me towards the exit.

"But I don't want to go." I argued, yanking my hand away. "I actually *do* want to network, Axel." Unlike him, I wasn't being inundated with offers post *Accidentally,* so I was keen to build some industry relationships.

"Be my guest then, Doll. Are you okay to call a cab?" He asked since he had been my ride there.

"Yeah, works for me." I shrugged. "Bye then."

"See you later." He kissed me on the cheek, to keep up appearances, before disappearing into the throng, leaving me alone.

"Sorry Axel had an emergency and had to shoot off. He'll be in touch." I said to the screenwriter, who looked bewildered as he reached the spot Axel had just occupied. Now alone, and unfamiliar with my surroundings, I decided the best place to begin would be searching for a glass of bubbles. On my way to the bar, I spotted Aaron.

In many ways he was like Axel. They were a similar height, muscular and tattooed but where Axel had a mop of curly dark hair, Aaron had sleek blonde. Ordinarily, he would have been someone who may have caught my eye but compared to the man currently plaguing my thoughts, he paled in comparison. Although we had only met once, at Axel's apartment, Aaron was kind to me that evening and didn't mock me like Axel's other two cronies, so I hoped that would be echoed again tonight!

"Hello, mind if I join you?" I asked, "Axel is boring and left and I need a friend!"

Aaron looked surprised to see me but a soft expression formed on his face, "Hello again, of course Verity!" He passed me a drink, which I immediately began to sink. "How's your night been so far?"

Flashbacks to Axel's face as he fucked me to euphoria flew through my head. "Not too eventful, you?"

"A few promising leads but you never know with these things. Everyone likes to blow smoke up your arse at these events." He said casually. "Have you been here before?"

"Erm, no." I answered, laughing. "First time!"

"Let me take you on a tour then!"

The two of us made friendly conversation as Aaron led me through the quiet grand halls of the manor, concluding at an impressive, secluded balcony. We leant on the stone wall, overlooking the scenic grounds, lit partially by the moonlight. The view was exquisite.

"Thanks, by the way." I said, sincerely.

"Not a problem, I'll charge you for the next one." He nudged my arm with his shoulder. It felt nice to speak to Aaron, whatever this circus with Axel was, I didn't know if you could go as far as to say we were friends. So speaking to someone else in the industry, who seemed normal and kind was a welcome change of pace.

"Not for the tour! I meant how you were at Axel's dinner party. No offence but your other friends are complete dicks." I laughed sadly at the memory.

"None taken!" He chuckled, "and you're welcome. I know a damsel in distress when I see one." He sneered. His previous warm smile became more hostile in the shadows, causing my stomach to twist, unexpectedly. "Axel was a fool for leaving you here tonight, he doesn't know a good thing when it's right in front of him." He leered closer to me, causing the hairs on the back of my neck to stand up.

Suddenly, I became all too aware of how far away the rest of the partygoers were and how I'd blindly followed this almost stranger to a remote location, with no knowledge of my route to safety. Feeling all too alone with this man, who could easily overpower me, I thought carefully over my next move.

"We should probably head back to the party; it wouldn't look good if I was spotted alone in a quiet corner with one of my boyfriend's friends." I faked a laugh, trying to hide my discomfort and appeal to his better nature.

"Oh, it's fine," he smiled seductively, tucking a loose curl behind my ear, "Axel is far from precious when he's in a relationship, sweetheart," I felt a cold sheen of sweat appear on my brow, "we like to share." Something in me sensed that was a lie. His hand snaked around my waist, finding the bare skin on my back, as it travelled lower. My heart pounded fiercely in my chest, as a suffocating dread seeped through every inch of my body.

"If I pull on this bow will all your clothes unravel?" He played with the end of the knot at the bottom of my spine. I moved away from him, panic consuming me.

"Please, get off." My voice shook, tears starting to sting at my eyes. I felt helpless.

"Come on gorgeous, Axel won't mind and hey, he doesn't even need to know if you don't want him to. No one will find us out here to tattle." The second half of his statement sounded more like a threat, he was right, there was no one around to hear me if I screamed.

"I mind." I shouted, trying to turn for the exit. He gripped my shoulder roughly causing pain to shoot through my arm, I yelped.

"Stop making this difficult." He growled, slipping his index finger under the measly strap on my arm. My skin pricked at his touch.

Frozen, I ran through a million scenarios in my head as his finger began sliding towards my breast below the material of my dress. I was paralysed by fear. Just before he reached the peak, chatter in the hallway, outside the room the balcony was off, spiked my attention. My pulse roared in my ears as I seized the moment. I bolted as fast as I could towards freedom, praying if he caught me again, that the passersby would hear my distress call.

The strap snapped at the speed of my exit. I

heard him call my name furiously from behind. I grasped my broken dress and didn't look back. Just focussing on getting back to someone, anyone who could protect me. Weaving through the identical halls, I didn't slow down or check behind until I found the party.

I rushed back into the bathroom Axel and I had occupied earlier that evening, quickly locking the door behind before throwing up bile, when I reached the toilet.

A strangled sob escaped my lips, tears streaming down my face as the adrenaline rushed through my veins. I dug my phone out of my bag and opened the Uber app, typing in my drop off location, with shaky hands. I paused for a moment, debating my options, having already decided that back to the emptiness of my flat was off the cards.

From the safety of the locked room, I had barricaded myself in, I waited for the driver to arrive, hugging my knees to my chest and counting down the minutes until my ride would be outside, imagining the person who would be waiting on the other side of the journey.

When the car arrived, I cautiously exited the bathroom and slipped through the crowd, praying to leave undetected.

Sliding awkwardly into the back seat of the taxi, I scanned the driveway for Aaron, paranoid he would jump me at the last moment. I hastily shut the door and asked the driver to go. As the manor house grew smaller and smaller in the rearview mirror, I felt comfort in knowing

exactly who I was running to.
>I finally released a breath.
>I was safe.

23

AXEL

As the warm whiskey coated my throat, I finally felt my muscles relaxing. I resembled a prize pig at those types of events, everyone always wanted a piece of me, it was exhausting! I was surprised I managed to last even one hour there before I decided to call it a night. I'd completed my obligation to Sarah by going, being papped with my girlfriend and making small talk so I was free from guilt for bailing so quickly. As the alcohol soaked into my veins, the tension released and I kicked off my shoes, sinking back into the sofa cushions. This was the second-best stress reliever to Verity.

It's not ideal that we didn't leave together, Sarah was not going to love the individual photos, but the girl was adamant. She still had such an annoyingly positive and optimistic outlook on this industry full of people that just take and have no regard for the human behind the camera. Maybe I should have stayed to support her but

I'm not a fucking babysitter. If I'm being honest, I suppose it was good to see her arguing for something she wanted for a change!

The buzz from my intercom startled me. It was 11pm, I didn't get many unexpected visitors, let alone at this time of night.

"Hello?" I answered gruffly.

"Please let me in." A shaky female voice asked.

"Verity?" I questioned recognising the speaker, my finger hovered over the button to grant her access.

"Please, Axel." She repeated as I unlocked the downstairs door.

Confusion crossed my mind as I waited for her to reach the top floor. She sounded different to when I had left her at the party and I hadn't expected to see her again tonight. We weren't at sleepover status by any stretch of the imagination! Yet something about her tone made my stomach twist.

A quiet knock signalled her arrival. Pulling the front door open, I was stunned at the image before me. Mascara stained her cheeks, she was holding up the top of her dress which appeared torn and her eyes were red, shining with tears. Verity had never looked at me this way with such helplessness and fear, it was as though she had been broken by some unspeakable horror. Panic swirled in my gut at what could have happened to her.

"Ver-"

"I'm sorry I didn't know where else to go." She whimpered, cutting me off, a sob escaping her lips.

"Come in." I nodded quickly, ushering her inside. "Sit down here." I said, guiding her to the sofa. I immediately wrapped a blanket from the couch over her bare shoulders to protect her modesty. Her entire body was shaking as she stared at the floor. I sat down carefully beside her.

"Who did this to you?" I demanded, unable to control my anger. She winced at my raised voice. "What happened, Verity?" I softened my tone, placing a caring hand on her back, causing her to flinch once again as tears began streaming. "Doll, look at me." I pleaded, removing my touch.

She tilted her face up, her piercing blue eyes boring into mine. "A-Aaron." She stuttered like she was too afraid to say out loud, averting her gaze again.

"What about him?" I asked, concerned.

"It was my fault. I shouldn't have gone there alone with him, I'd had a lot to drink, I-I-" Her breaths quickened as she choked on her words and another cry left her body.

"What did he do?!" I questioned, my fists balling at my sides, trying not to scare her further, as bile rose in my throat at what that cunt must have done.

"I'm sorry, Axel." She whispered, unable to control her emotion.

"You have nothing to be sorry for, Verity. Whatever happened, it is not your fault." I implored, gently reaching for her chin and tilting her face towards me, desperate for her to hear the truth in my words.

"He was going to r-"

"You don't need to finish that sentence." I pulled her into me as she sobbed in my arms, her head buried in my chest.

My mind raced as I thought about Aaron and Verity alone, as he tried to force himself on her. I shouldn't have left her; she should never have been put in that position. I don't know how long we sat there, her bawling, me mentally conjuring up hundreds of ways to destroy the monster who did this to her.

"Did he hurt you?" I asked the burning question, terrified of what her answer could be, letting go of her slightly to assess for any injuries.

"He grabbed my shoulder." She leant away from me sliding off the blanket covering her left arm. A dark scarlet mark emblazoned her skin from the force in which he had grasped her. I saw red.

"I'll fucking kill him." I growled through gritted teeth, adrenaline rushed through my veins as I began to stand.

"No Axel, please don't go, I don't want to be alone right now." She begged, hugging her arms around her body. It took everything in me not to hunt him down and make him pay for what he'd done but looking in Verity's pleading eyes, I knew I had to stay.

"Of course, Doll, I won't go anywhere." I sighed, scrubbing a stressed hand over my stubble.

"Actually, I'm sorry for barging in, I'll get out of your hair." She began unwrapping the blanket, clearly feeling like she'd overstayed her welcome.

"Verity, stay as long as you need." I reassured. "It's late, you can take my bed. I'll pick out some clothes for you to change into." Verity seemed to relax slightly for the first time since she'd arrived at my apartment, nodding in response to my invitation.

"Thank you." She whispered. I stood up and headed to my bedroom to find a t-shirt and joggers - that would definitely drown her - so she could change out of her damaged dress. When I re-entered the living room, she hadn't moved a muscle from where I'd left her, however her sobs had reduced to whimpers.

"I've laid some bits out on the bed for you, feel free to take a shower whilst you're in there too." I offered, assuming she would want to rid her body of Aaron's fingerprints.

"Thank you, yes good idea, I will." She stood, the blanket still tightly wrapped around her frame. As she approached, she offered a watery smile that caused a strange feeling inside of me, almost as if something was cracking in my chest. I heard the door click as she closed it behind her and decided I needed another drink.

Pouring an eyeballed measure into a tumbler, I quickly sank the brown liquor before hastily refilling it again. I gripped the edge of the kitchen island with one hand to steady myself as I downed the second shot. I couldn't stand to see her like this, so broken, so scared. I slammed the glass back on the counter. *Fuck it*, I took a swig straight from the bottle.

All I could picture was Aaron's slimy face and unwanted grip on Verity's body. There was no way he was going to get away with this shit.

Verity's head appeared around my bedroom door frame. Her face now clean and hair wet, slightly waved from the shower.

"I think I'm going to go to sleep if that's okay?" She asked timidly.

"You don't need to ask permission, Doll." I forced myself to smile warmly despite the rage still bubbling under the surface. "Do you need anything?"

"No, I'm fine." She insisted, shutting the door then cracking it open. "Thank you, by the way." Before I could answer she closed it again, leaving me to my inner turmoil.

To distract my thoughts, I decided mindless TV was the answer. I laid on my couch, flicking aimlessly through the channels, drinking shot after shot between the dull options. Eventually I passed out, succumbing to the copious amounts of stress and alcohol coursing through me.

I woke with a start to screaming coming from my room, causing alarm bells to set off in my brain. In a half-sleepy state, I quickly stumbled through to my bedroom, only to find Verity still fast asleep, thrashing violently in my bed.

"Shh, shh." I hushed, walking over to her. "It's okay, it's not real," I sat down gently beside her, brushing a hand through her damp golden hair.

Her eyes flew open at my touch and her body jolted upright before she realised who I was.

"Axel." She breathed, relieved, laying back against the pillows.

"Yes, it's just me. You're safe." Once she had resettled, I resumed stroking the loose strands off her face.

"I was back on the balcony. I could see it all so vividly again." She wept. "I was so scared." The way this woman was looking at me made my heart stutter. I felt as though I was struggling to hold back tears of my own.

"I'll never let anyone hurt you like that again." I vowed, continuing to soothe her until she closed her eyes. I watched as her breathing returned to a normal pace before deciding I should head back to the sofa to try and get some sleep of my own.

I began to stand slowly, so as not to wake her, before tiptoeing towards the door.

"Stay with me." I heard quietly as I reached for the handle.

I turned back to Verity, who was sitting up again, fresh tears threatening to spill down her cheeks. Her beautiful face barely visible in the moonlight. I thought for a moment. I had never considered sharing a bed with her but I couldn't leave her alone, not tonight.

I slid in beside her, tucking in under the covers. I didn't know whether to keep my distance or pull her in to comfort her further. Whilst deliberating Verity snuggled up against me, her small hands fisting my t-shirt to keep me close as she pressed her face against my chest.

Instinctively, I wrapped a protective arm around her small frame before pressing a soft kiss to the top of her head.

"Goodnight, Doll."

24

VERITY

I opened my eyes to an empty room that wasn't my own. Blinking in the sunlight, I remembered where I was and what had happened to me last night. My stomach lurched at the memory.

In the heat of the moment, I had run to Axel for shelter. I knew my friends would have helped, but I also knew on a Friday night, all of them would have been unlikely to be free for a spontaneous visit and didn't need me dampening their nights. Axel knew Aaron and had continuously warned me about what people in this industry were capable of, so I was drawn to his door.

He had been uncharacteristically kind to me to the point where I didn't even recognise him at times. It's a shame he wasn't like that every day, there was a possibility we could have formed a friendship by now. I had woken to find he had already gotten up. I couldn't imagine what I must've been thinking to cuddle up to him, I hoped he wouldn't hold it against me in the cold light of day.

Rolling onto my other side, my shoulder twinged with pain as the memory of Aaron grasping my arm aggressively, came flooding back. *It's over.* I assured myself, taking a deep breath, before sitting upright on the side of Axel's bed. My head pounded from the champagne, adrenaline and all the tears I had shed. Stretching, I stood up and padded across the wooden floor, tentatively opening the door to the living room.

Axel was standing facing away, towards the large windows, with music blasting through his headphones. He was repping bicep curls with a barbell, sweat glistening down his bare rippled muscles. My mouth dried at the sight.

I had been at the receiving end of his power plenty of times but I'd never seen him shirtless - at least not in real life.

Holy shit.

He finished his set, placing the bar on the floor before turning to reach for a bottle of water. "Fuck, Verity." He startled, moving one cup of his headphones away from his ear. "How long have you been standing there?" I shrugged. His tone was harsher than I'd expected after the treatment I received last night.

"Morning." I stated, shifting my weight from one foot to the other, suddenly feeling very unwelcome.

"Kettles just boiled." He nodded towards the kitchen before he readjusted his headphones and turned his attention back to the exercise equipment.

This felt too much like an uncomfortable morning after a one-night stand for my liking. Not wanting to prolong the awkwardness, I took the hint. "I'm going to go, I'll bring these back next time," I called over to him, referring to his clothes that I was still wearing. There was no response from Axel. I was unsure whether I had been drowned out by his music or if he was actively ignoring me. With that, I gathered my belongings and made my way out of his apartment and down to the lobby to call for a cab to take me home to Misto.

A few hours later and I was stepping out of another taxi, stunned by the red brick, Edwardian house before me. It was truly beautiful, with foliage climbing up the walls - a true English gem! I rang the doorbell and waited for Lilah to answer.

"Yay you're here!" Lilah screamed as she opened the dark green door.

"Hello, homeowner!" I squealed, holding up the bottle of prosecco I had brought as a housewarming gift.

"Come on in, the rest of the gang are already here." She beckoned me inside.

I took in my surroundings as Lilah led me towards the front room. We walked through a large neutral hallway with multiple doors leading off to unknown dwellings, until we reached an enormous living area. The room was lined with beautiful sash windows that let in an extraordinary amount of natural light. Complemented by the cream walls clad with panelling. A forest green, U-shaped, velvet sofa sat in the centre, with colourful patterned cushions strewn across it. Soft music played from an unseen speaker creating an inviting ambience. As I observed the room, I spotted many weird and wonderful items that I knew Lilah had collected over the years. This home was truly a perfect mix of the meticulous Zane and my quirky bestie.

"Hey babe!" Jacob greeted, spotting me entering. He jumped to his feet and handed me a glass of bubbles from the collection on the coffee table.

"Hi Jake," I pulled him in for a hug. The moment I arrived I knew the manor house and Aaron would quickly fade into a distant memory.

"Great to see you, Verity!" Amelia said from next to Jake. She wasn't a hugger but offered a wide, toothy grin which conveyed just as much warmth as physical contact.

"And you. It's been a while, you've been so busy!" I responded. It was true, I hadn't seen my friend for weeks now, mainly because she was always with her problematic boyfriend. "But I'm so glad you were free to come tonight."

"Wouldn't have missed it. Sorry I didn't make the launch. I felt awful." Amelia said, with sadness in her eyes as she looked at Lilah.

"No problem at all, I understood. We all have things going on." Lilah responded from the other side of Jake, leaning over to rub Amelia's shoulder kindly.

"Ah I missed you guys, got all my girls back!" Jake wrapped the four of us into a group cuddle. Amelia tensed at my side at the overwhelming physicality but to her credit, she didn't break away.

I allowed myself to melt into the embrace, removing all thoughts of yesterday. As expected, any remaining stress from the previous night vanished the instant I was back with my best friends.

The living room door opening again caused us to separate. A short, blonde man, who I didn't recognise, walked in, wiping his hands on his blue jeans.

"This is Josh, Verity." Amelia introduced. Ah, so this was the *famous* Josh! He held out a weedy hand for me to shake. Damn was this man punching! I generally tried not to be a judgemental person, but from all the awful things I'd heard about this man previously, it was impossible not to feel negatively about him.

"Hi, nice to meet you, Amelia's told us so much about you!" I forced out the nicety, returning the limp handshake.

"Good things, I'm sure." He responded curtly, sounding almost like a threat.

"Of course, there aren't any bad things for her to report, are there?" I smiled innocently. It was only a half lie. Amelia hadn't *directly* told me about any of the shitty ways that Josh had treated her over the course of their relationship. It had always been Jake or Lilah who had updated me with the times Amelia had been left alone crying after Josh had stood her up, cheated on her or had spoken to her awfully.

Looking at this below-average guy in front of me, it really was a riddle as to why a catch like Amelia continued to put up with his BS.

"What's up, party people?" A jovial voice announced, joining the group. I turned to see Lilah's older brother Theo, standing in the doorway.

"I told you, it's not a party. It's dinner with our nearest and dearest." *And Josh.* I knew my best friend well enough to know that she would be sharing my sentiment.

"If there's tequila, it's a party in my opinion. And the Colombian, slaving over the stove in the next room, has plenty of that to offer from the cellar." Theo said, holding up two unopened bottles of the clear liquor in both of his hands.

"Good to see you've given yourself a tour already, T." Zane appeared behind him, a tea towel slung over his shoulder. Zane the homemaker was quite the juxtaposition to the businessman I'd met many times before.

"*Su casa, mi casa.*" Theo winked at his best bud, as Zane rolled his eyes.

"Oh yes, I forgot you were paying the mortgage too, Theo." Lilah laughed.

"Be real, you don't even have a mortgage, sis." He prodded her in the shoulder. "Let's call this payback for all the months you slept in my spare room." Lilah punched him in the arm in response. Theo didn't even flinch, he just ruffled his sister's hair.

"Anyway, dinner is served everyone!" Zane said, ushering us through. I followed my friends to the kitchen. If the living room was impressive, the kitchen was astonishing. I'd never seen so much marble in one place! Laid across a ginormous, rustic table, Zane had prepared countless Colombian small plates for us to feast on.

"This looks delicious, Zane!" I complimented.

"I'm so excited to try it, we hear you're a great chef!" Jacob gushed. "Lilah, you're a lucky gal."

"I know." She said, batting her eyelashes jokingly. "Thanks for doing all of this." Her boyfriend wrapped an arm around her and kissed her on the head.

"Anything for you, *mi Joya*." They truly were the picture-perfect couple.

"Don't make me sick guys. I'm trying to eat here." Theo mocked, making fake gagging noises, causing the rest of us to laugh.

"I thought the idea of your sister and your best friend didn't bother you?" Amelia enquired, as we found our seats.

"It doesn't but I don't need them parading it around." He sat down next to her.

"You're just jealous that she gets to spend unlimited time with him." She joked, nudging him with her elbow. Theo held his chest, feigning heartbreak as Amelia shook her head in a carefree manner. I watched as Josh shot the pair daggers. I was surprised to see he could be jealous of such an innocent interaction, especially considering his lack of monogamy.

Over the next twenty minutes, conversation was minimal whilst we all tucked into the various delicacies before heading back to the living room, to wallow in our food comas. The guys stayed in the kitchen to help Zane tidy up, leaving us to chat.

"So, any juicy gossip now the boys are out of earshot?" Jacob asked, his eyes sparkling with mischief.

"Sorry to disappoint, but I'm afraid my life is blissfully drama free for once." Lilah laughed. "I'm just enjoying basking in the new honeymoon phase after moving in together." I smiled at my best friend, warmth blooming in my chest. It was about time she was truly happy.

"I'm the same." Amelia chimed in, a little too quickly. "Nothing to report." She took a sip of her prosecco. I shared a subtle glance with Jake and Lilah, although we could all hear the denial in Amelia's voice, we silently agreed now was not the time to push her for details about her crappy boyfriend.

"Good to hear it girls." Jake raised his glass before placing it on the coffee table in front of him, looking as though he was about to announce something important. "For once you will be surprised to hear I'm exclusively seeing someone." He gushed.

"Ahh Jake! Who's the lucky fella?" I squealed, sitting forward on the sofa, excitedly, the rest of my friends mirroring my reaction.

"Noah, the guy I met on Valentine's Day!" He said, animatedly, a slight blush tainting his cheeks.

"You kept that one quiet!" Amelia tapped him on the leg, I felt a slight twinge of guilt. I had been so wrapped up in my own tragic love life since Valentine's Day that I hadn't asked Jacob once how his *actual* date had gone.

"Yeah! When are we meeting this mystery man?

You should have brought him today!" Lilah interjected.

"No no, it's still early days." He waved us off. "Besides, V hasn't brought *her* boyfriend." He pointed an accusatory finger in my direction.

"He's a busy man." I defended quickly.

"How are things with Axel, Verity?" Lilah asked. Perhaps I was feeling overly defensive but the way she was looking at me made it feel like an interrogation.

"Things are good." I lied, smiling. "I stayed over last night-"

"Ahh, so, didn't get much sleep I'm guessing," Jacob interrupted, wiggling his eyebrows suggestively.

I rolled my eyes as Amelia nudged him, if only I'd had the night that he insinuated. "So, how's the new area anyways, Lils?" I not-so-subtly changed the subject. "Seen any famous boy band members running around Hampstead Heath?" My friends laughed.

"Unfortunately not! Bit of a piss take to be honest," Lilah joked. "I only bought this house for celebrity spotting." The rest of us dissolved into fits of giggles. We spent the remainder of the afternoon, drinking, eating, chatting and laughing, the kind of cackling that left your cheeks aching. I looked around at my friends, their faces lit with joy and my heart felt like it was going to burst.

Just twenty-four hours ago, my world had felt scary and lonely, now surrounded by these people who I loved so dearly, I was reminded of how lucky I was to have them in my life.

25

AXEL

"Sarah." I greeted, answering the incoming call and switching off the TV.

"Morning, Axel." She replied, her usual tone harsher than normal. "I'm afraid I've got some bad news about your little girlfriend."

"What?" I demanded. My heart jolted slightly at the mention of Verity. I'd been in a constant state of anguish since Friday night and could hardly formulate the words to speak to Verity the next morning. All I could do was work out and try to refocus my thoughts to reduce the fire swirling through my veins and prevent me from beating Aaron to a pulp. So, the last thing I needed was Sarah stressing me out further with these guessing games.

"Well, firstly, she was at the party alone after *you* left early, but I'll come back to that. More importantly, it looks like she hasn't been keeping up her side of the agreement, she was spotted getting cosy with another man later that same evening. The press is going to have a field day with this, Axel!" I gripped the phone, the familiar rage bubbling under the surface. "Axel? Are you listening?" She prodded.

"Yes," I snapped, "so what? Is someone going to publish a story about it?" I quizzed, the anger threatening to boil over as I thought about what this would do to Verity.

"I've been warned that a story is going to break on StarBuzzDaily at 5pm tonight unless we find some way to kill it!" I could hear her tapping her pen on the desk.

"Fuck." I muttered under my breath, running a stressed hand through my hair.

"Yes, well I'm glad you understand the gravity of the situation."

"How do we make this go away?" I asked desperately. The last thing Verity needed was her name splashed all over the tabloids - especially if anyone recognised it was Aaron she was with.

"Well of course I've already discussed this with them and there is one thing you could do."

"I'm listening," I quirked an eyebrow.

"An exclusive interview," *not too awful,* "with a topless photoshoot dressed in Tyler's wardrobe." *You have got to be fucking kidding me.* Despite countless requests to bare all over the years, I had never indulged the press with a half-naked shoot. It was true that I worked hard to keep fit and I was proud of my physique, but I'd rather attend one hundred of those shitty industry events than don a centrefold with my abs oiled up.

"Fine." I grumbled. *If only you knew what I was putting myself through for you, Doll.*

"Great!" Sarah chimed. "I'll get the contract back over to StarBuzz asap so we're out of the woods." Of course she had basically already signed on the dotted line. "Keep Friday afternoon free, I'll send you the details."

"Can't wait, I'll make sure to add a couple hundred more crunches to my morning routine." I rolled my eyes.

"Fab, and while you're at it, go out with Verity again, in public and make it a spectacle!" She demanded.

"Sure." I appeased, "anything else?" I regretted the question before I'd finished asking it.

"No, although I'm surprised at her." She sounded like a disappointed mom, and it pissed me off. "I didn't think she'd be the one breaking this side of the deal, she didn't strike me as the promiscuous type."

"Excuse me?" I spat, bile rising in my throat.

"You know, getting touched up on a balcony, it's vulgar. She needs to think about what sh-"

Seething, I hung up the phone and slammed it onto the counter, before Sarah could finish her sentence and before I said something I'd regret.

A few hours later and Verity was back in my apartment for our regularly scheduled 'date' night. This was the first time we would be seeing each other since she left early on Saturday morning, after the chaos of the night before.

"How was the rest of your weekend?" I asked, trying to hide my concern with a casual question, as we settled onto our usual sides of the sofa.

"It was really lovely. I caught up with some friends and hung out with my cat." An unexpected tension in my chest released with the knowledge that she hadn't spent the whole weekend cowering in her flat.

"Nice, I'm more of a dog person." I joked.

"Never let him hear you say that it'll break his heart." She laughed, scrolling on her phone.

I much preferred this version of Verity. After the devastating way she turned up at my flat three days ago, it was reassuring to see her with colour in cheeks, and a smile so wide that caused her dimple to appear.

"So, to change the topic, I think we need to venture back out in public! Let's double date with your jewellery friends."

"Where's this coming from?" She questioned, raising a perfectly arched eyebrow.

"We were pictured leaving separately the other night. So, let's show the press we're still going strong."

She mulled over my explanation for a minute, "these sound suspiciously like Sarah's words."

"I can neither confirm nor deny, but I'm free Thursday evening, you can pick me up at 8pm." I winked, holding my hands up in a surrender.

"Hmm okay, I'll ask Lilah if they're free and let you know. But Axel, if we're going to do this, at least remember their bloody names!" She laughed. "And don't embarrass me."

I crossed my heart with my finger. "I'll be on my best behaviour, Doll."

26

VERITY

I found myself at The Regal Orchid with Axel, Lilah and Zane on Thursday night. They were not a group of people that I ever imagined I would be splitting the bill with.

As I sat here watching my best friend and her partner laughing endlessly at my fake boyfriend's charm and quick wit, it was difficult to remember that this was all for show. Sitting in the warmth and friendliness of the conversation, it was easy for my mind to let itself go and get lost in the facade.

"That was outstanding." Lilah gushed, sitting back in her chair and placing a folded napkin on the empty plate in front of her.

"Yeah, delicious! Good recommendation Zane." I agreed, sipping on my red wine.

"It's one of my favourite spots." He said, placing his arm on the back of Lilah's chair as the pair exchanged a subtle knowing look.

"I've visited London so many times and never found food this good. Cheers man." Axel raised his glass in the air before taking a large swig.

Zane called over the waiter and ordered a selection of small plates for us to overindulge in for dessert. As I finished my own drink, I watched Axel. Within the dimly lit, wooden clad walls of the restaurant, the shadows danced over the angles of his chiselled jaw. The flash of a camera illuminated his face, startling Lilah.

"Jesus Christ, how do you ever get used to that?" Lilah exclaimed, referencing the paps, eagle-eyed, at the window to our left.

"Comes with the territory." He shrugged, not giving the vultures a second look.

"Okay, next time we'll make sure we reserve a spot at the back or a place with curtains." She laughed.

"We can book a private room." Zane said seriously. I felt my chest tighten with guilt at my friends' concern with Axel's privacy when we were using them for our benefit tonight. My anxiety only increased further at the prospect of a 'next time' and performing this charade again.

"Don't worry, it doesn't bother me, I barely even notice it now." Axel waved off Zane and Lilah.

"Please excuse me, I'm just heading to the bathroom." I pushed my chair back and began to stand.

"I'll come with you." Lilah smiled, following me through the restaurant.

"What is it with girls and not being able to go to the restroom on their own?" Axel joked from behind us.

Lilah and I regrouped at the sinks after washing and drying our hands. I began reapplying my lipstick in the mirror and made eye contact with her through the reflection. She gave me a look which I always dreaded seeing.

"What's going on, Verity?" She scrutinised.

"With what?" A lump formed in my throat, I had known this girl all my life and she could read me like a book.

"I saw the pictures of you crying when you left that party the other night and you left alone too. Where was Axel? What happened?"

I took a deep breath as the actual events of that night replayed in my mind. "I don't want to talk about it."

"Well, I do. You never keep things from me. I'm worried about you. He seems like the perfect gentleman tonight, but I've never seen you look as upset as you did in those photos." She said sternly though her voice was full of concern.

I diverted my eyes, breaking contact with Lilah as I mulled over my response. I knew I had to give her something. There would be no way she would let me leave this room until she'd gotten some information, but all options seemed to have negative consequences.

"It wasn't what it looked like." I dismissed her, putting the lid back on my lipstick.

"I don't understand-"

"Lilah, please drop it." My voice broke slightly which seemed to make her realise now was not the time for this conversation.

"I'm sorry to pry. You're just protecting this insanely famous guy you've known for less than four months. You begin dating him barely a month into meeting and don't think to mention it once to me." She raised her hands in frustration, although I knew it only came from a place of care.

"You can't imagine what it's like for him, he's a private person, so I respected that." I felt my heartbeat rapidly, as I lied through my teeth, hating the fact we were arguing about this.

"Totally understandable, but then why are we sitting having our photos taken over dinner for two hours if he's so *private*." She rebuffed sarcastically. "Something's off." Lilah folded her arms across her chest and leant back on the sink.

I rubbed my hands over my face, deciding I couldn't keep this up any longer.

"You have to promise not to tell a soul." I said releasing an exasperated breath.

"Cross my heart," Lilah responded earnestly, her eyes softening slightly.

"Even Zane." I insisted. Although she'd never confirmed my suspicions, I assumed that anything I told

Lilah would always make its way to her other half, unless specified.

"Oh shit, this is serious then. I promise!" Lilah grabbed for my hand and squeezed it reassuringly.

"I don't really know how to explain it."

"Say it. Out loud." She winked, breaking the tension for a moment.

This was one of the many reasons I loved her. Even in the midst of a heavy conversation, she was always on the lookout for a moment to quote a film to make me laugh.

"For fuck's sake." I laughed, shaking my head.

"Say it." She insisted, giggling as she poked me in the arm.

"Vampire," I rolled my eyes at the *Twilight* reference, "but no, that's not his secret, you idiot."

"Sorry, carry on." Her expression returned to neutral.

"This isn't real." I blurted. Lilah narrowed her eyes waiting for a further explanation. "Axel and I aren't together."

"What do you mean?" She queried, her face twisted in confusion.

"It's all fake. It's all for publicity. Even this dinner tonight, it's all part of the plan." My voice wobbled slightly as I spilled my guts to my best friend.

"Give me a minute to register this." Lilah stared at the floor, dumbfounded for a minute. I could feel my heart beating furiously in my chest as I waited for my friend to answer. I felt awful for dragging her into this.

"That explains the lack of irritation for the cameras then."

"I'm so sorry Lilah. I shouldn't have gotten you both involved without your consent." I apologised, my hand shaking slightly as she continued to hold it.

"You don't have to worry about us, are *you* okay Verity?" Taking my other hand in hers in an attempt to calm my nerves, "how did this happen?"

"It was Axel's agent's idea. It sounded like a good one at the time but I didn't consider how hard it would be lying to everyone I know." I told her, before going through the details of the past few months, choosing to leave out the second arrangement between myself and Axel. I spoke as quickly as I could, aware that anyone could walk into the public bathroom and overhear my confession. Lilah listened carefully, not a hint of judgement on her face, I felt a weight lift off my chest at the relief of telling someone everything.

"Whoa, that sounds messy." She sighed once I'd concluded. "So, how are the two of you really?"

"At first, it was awful, I couldn't stand to be around him but that's a story for another day and a private location." I laughed. "But lately, it's gotten more…" I paused as I searched for the right word. "Complicated."

"You're sleeping with him." She stated, not bothering to ask the question.

"I'm n-"

"Just be careful and protect your heart V." She implored, I nodded.

"I will, we should head back, they'll get suspicious." I mustered a half laugh, the anxiety flooding back as the spotlight was shone on my lies.

"You're right." Lilah released my hands and pulled me into a hug, "but this isn't over. I need *all* the details."

She wrapped her arm around me, giggling as we walked back to the table. Delicious dishes of chocolate cake, macarons, cheese and crackers covered the table. We found the two men laughing, which was an odd sight to see. As friendly as Zane was, he never really let his hair down around me.

"¡*Salud!*" Zane cheered, clinking his glass to Axel's.

"You two seem thick as thieves," Lilah said sitting down on her chair. Immediately Zane took her hand and pressed a kiss to the back of it.

"We had a lot of time to get to know each other. You two were gone for a while!" Zane responded, stroking a circle with his thumb on her skin.

"Sorry about that, lots of girl talk!" Lilah smiled, taking a spoonful of the decadent cake in front of her.

Axel reached across the small distance between us and caressed the side of my neck, I felt myself stiffen more than usual at his touch. As if on cue a camera flashed to capture the intimate gesture. I flinched away from him, catching Lilah's eyeline, she shot me a sympathetic smile. I was suddenly all too aware of the performance we were playing, feeling naked under her gaze.

My attempts to remain normal failed, opting for silence and polite laughs in all the right places, as I guzzled the alcohol for the remainder of the meal.

"We have an early shoot time, so best be off. It was great to meet you properly, Zane, you've got my number." Axel pointed a finger towards the businessman.

"Let's arrange a gym session soon." He smiled, shaking hands. The rest of us said our goodbyes and headed to our separate cars.

Axel shut the door behind me, as he moved around the back of the chauffeur-driven vehicle. The partition was already up. One thing I'd learnt about Axel's driver was he wasn't one for small talk - which at this moment, suited me perfectly.

The car moved away from the front of the building and began its journey back across the city.

"What's up with you?" Axel asked.

"Nothing." I shrugged, hoping he didn't pry further.

"Come on, you've been pissy since dessert." He rolled his eyes but I ignored his remark. "You told her, didn't you?" For a split second I thought about protesting but knew it was fruitless. I dropped my head into my hands. "Well, that explains why you've been so dramatic." He mumbled.

"Fuck off Axel. You might be a pathological liar, but it doesn't come naturally to me." I shouted, the alcohol in my veins heightening my emotions.

"What's the big deal? You've had to tell some white lies to people, it's hardly the secret of the century."

He ran a hand through his hair. "Anyway, I should be pissed off that you broke the agreement and risked this being exposed. You think you feel shitty now, wait until you're plastered as a desperate, wannabe all over the internet." Axel responded, matching my volume.

"I'm already embarrassed to be associated with an egotistical, self-centred prick like you. If anything, it would be a relief that everyone would know I don't really have feelings for you." I spat.

"I could sue you, Doll." He growled as his eyes darkened.

"Go ahead, Big Shot." I returned the intensity. For a moment we were frozen, chests heaving with equal parts fury and desire. I broke the tension, pulling his tie towards me until there was next to no space left between us.

"Cookie?" He smirked, his sweet tobacco scent flooding my senses with the proximity.

"Cookie." I demanded.

In less than a second, his hands found their way to my hips, pulling me onto his lap, my floaty dress bunching up my thighs as I spread my legs over his. How he unclicked my seatbelt without me seeing, I would never know. As I straddled him, his lips claimed mine in an all-encompassing kiss. I didn't know if it was the copious amounts of alcohol or Axel's touch that made me feel so intoxicated but I was feral around him.

"I think you owe me an apology, Tink." Axel drawled.

"I'm sure you'll get over it." I began to grind against him desperately. I felt his engorged erection pressed against the thin material of my underwear, confirming he was as desperate for me as I was for him.

"If you can't keep our secret, I'll have to find another way to shut you up." My pulse pounded between my legs at his filthy words.

"I dare you." I goaded.

"Get on your knees, now." He growled, lifting me off his lap, pushing me onto the floor of the town car when I didn't immediately obey. I watched eagerly as he unbuckled his belt and freed his full length.

"Open your mouth." I shook my head, with a teasing look. He grabbed my jaw, squeezing, to force my lips apart, his free hand drawing long strokes along his erection as pre-cum glistened at the tip. He slipped his cock into my wet mouth, removing his hand from my jaw and wrapping it around my hair in a knot, pulling tight. I moaned around him. My pussy felt drenched as he dominated me. Call me insane, but the thrill that I received from being used for his pleasure was better than any drug.

He allowed me a moment to adjust to his size before mercilessly fucking my mouth. The pleasure was so blinding, I could have sworn I could come just from this. With each thrust, he groaned, pulling my hair tighter and tighter, turning me on even more than I thought possible.

"This is how I like you, Doll. On your knees with my dick buried down your throat so you can't get yourself in any trouble." I moaned enthusiastically at the backhanded compliment. *You seriously have a problem, Verity.* I felt his hand loosen in my hair before he placed it on the seat next to him. "Don't stop. Show me how good you can suck my cock."

Determination coursed through me as I continued to bob my head up and down, each moan I received from Axel spurred me on further.

"That's it, see you can be a good girl for me." He praised, his silky voice sending shivers through my body, he brushed a tender hand across my cheek, looking down at me. "You love this don't you, Doll?" He asked, I hummed around him in unashamed agreement. "I bet you're dripping all down your thighs." I felt my eyes roll back with arousal from the obscene dirty talk.

I swirled my tongue on the top of his head, eliciting a deep groan. I looked up at him through my eyelashes, his head falling back against the seat, one hand clamped on the headrest as he fought against his approaching orgasm. Pressure continued to build between my legs and I gave into the desire.

My breath hitched as my hand pushed my thong to one side and found my pulsating clit. I moved my fingers in time with the long strokes I made along his dick. My eyes fluttered, as I worked myself towards my own climax stimulated further by the sounds spilling from Axel's mouth.

"I knew it." Axel mumbled through gritted teeth, hands clenching the metal of the headrest, "this is driving you crazy." It pained me to admit it but he was right.

Nothing turned me on more than knowing as much as we despised one another, I was the one to reduce him to his most primal self. I increased my rhythm, moving quicker along his cock, circling my most sensitive area more vigorously, moaning against him.

"You wish I could fuck that needy little cunt of yours right here on the backseat and make you come all over the leather, don't you?" He said, his breaths shallow as I bounced my head. He stared so intensely at me I could have tipped over the edge just from his gaze. His dark smoky eyes bored into mine, as I watched him unfold from my actions.

I'd never been so wet in my life. This was pure ecstasy, the need twisting my stomach was almost uncomfortable. "You're so close, aren't you? Do you want to come with your mouth wrapped around my cock?" I whimpered with undeniable want, my fingers rubbing frantically. "Hurry up then, Doll. The journey's nearly over." Axel teased, encouraging my climax.

Desperately, I worked us both in unison, towards euphoria, my free hand grabbed his girth and stroked along in time with my head movements. "Fuuuck, Verity." He moaned as he spilled on my tongue, holding my head down. The salty taste caused my own orgasm to come crashing over me. I convulsed on the floor of the car, still choking on his cock as his head pulsed in my mouth, my limbs tingling with the aftermath. Our groans echoed in the vehicle as waves of pleasure flowed over us.

As the elation subsided, I breathlessly slid back onto the seat beside Axel, as he pulled his underwear back up and buckled his belt.

"Just in time, Doll." He nodded out the window as we pulled up outside my block of flats.

"Right, see you tomorrow." I saluted, getting out of the car. I walked into my building, giggling at the juxtaposition of the calm goodbye after the debaucherous activity that had just occurred.

27

AXEL

Never again. Never again will I subject myself to three hours of being doused in baby oil and positioned in ridiculously suggestive poses whilst a stranger behind a camera, snapped endless shots of me in next to no clothing.

I was used to nudity in the films I'd been in before, but this felt different. Then, I was playing a character but knowing these pictures were purely to ogle me personally made me feel squeamish. Thank God, I was headed for a drink, although I did wish I'd had time for a second shower. I was certain the grease was still slick in some of my crevices.

This was the first time I was meeting my friends since the incident between Verity and Aaron at the manor. Needless to say, he had not been invited this evening. I knew I wouldn't be able to trust myself around him. As much as I would have loved to hunt him down that very night after she turned up devastated on my doorstep, I had made a promise to Verity to not get involved. It pained me to let him walk around like he wasn't a total piece of shit, but I respected the way she wanted to handle it. The last thing she needed was another man overstepping her boundaries.

I opened the door of the Gilded Cage; it was heaving as usual for a Friday. Squeezing past the deep crowd, I found Brad and George occupying a booth towards the back.

"Ahh, here he is, Ken himself!" George chortled as I slid into the seat next to him.

"Ha, good one, mate." Brad affirmed. I rolled my eyes, taking a swig from the bottle of beer that Tweedle-dumb and Tweedle-dipshit had ordered me before I arrived.

"I'll be sure to bring a signed copy when the magazine's out." I jested. "What's going on in your lives outside of your comedic double act anyway?" I half-listened to the duo as they recited various auditions they'd attended, women they'd 'shagged' and what they'd mindlessly spent money on recently: George invested in an obvious MLM scheme, whilst Brad contemplated how he could buy a tiger to be 'just like Tyson' but thank fuck, that idea fizzled out!

I excused myself to the bathroom for five minute's peace and to make a feeble attempt at washing some more of the residual sheen off my arms.

"Alright, geezer!" I stiffened at the familiar voice, my hackles rising instantly. I glanced in the mirror ahead of me to confirm the speaker. "Thought I'd find you here! Thanks for the invite."

"What the fuck are you doing here?" I growled, turning to face him.

"Coming for a drink with the lads, what does it look like?" Aaron replied, in a blasé fashion. My blood boiled in my veins.

"I can see that. But you weren't invited." I snarled through gritted teeth.

"Since when has that been an issue?"

"Since you disrespected my girlfriend."

"Enlighten me?" He responded, waving a hand nonchalantly.

I was taken aback by his ignorance, "the fucking manor house." I exploded.

"Ohhh, I remember now," Aaron tapped the side of his head as if finding the memory, "perhaps if you had paid her better attention, maybe she wouldn't have come running to me for some fun." He smirked, clearly unaware of the seriousness of this conversation.

"This is not about me." I bit back, unconsciously taking a step closer to him, my fists balled at my side.

"You're right, this is about Verity. Maybe you should be having words with her about what happened on the balcony." Rage consumed me, as the image of Verity's distress appeared in my brain. "You were right, she's not as innocent as she seems." He winked.

Fuck it! I'd only promised not to seek him out, I never agreed that I wouldn't retaliate if he approached me.

In a split second, I closed the remaining space between us and yanked the collar of his jacket, driving my fist into his face. Blood appeared immediately from the broken skin on his cheek.

"What the fuck, Axel." Aaron shouted, swinging back at me, instinctively. His punch landed on my jaw, splitting my bottom lip but the adrenaline coursing through my veins prevented any pain from being inflicted. I chuckled at his feeble attempt to hurt me.

"You're pathetic." I grabbed him once again, and slammed his head into the mirror, causing it to shatter and Aaron to cry out in agony. Some of the shards caught my face as they flew off the wall. As the red mist descended, I pressed his head harder against the splintered glass and whispered in his ear, "You're going to wish you'd never even looked in Verity's direction that night, you spineless cunt."

28

VERITY

Although it had only been two days since our double date with Lilah and Zane, I was back at Axel's flat for our obligatory weekend evening appointment. Today I'd brought along the newly released sequel to my favourite romance series, *Discipline Me*. I was looking forward to a few hours of peace and quiet, reading it on Axel's sofa whilst he busied himself and acted as if I didn't exist, as per usual.

"Hello Doll, back so soon?" Axel smirked, opening the door of his apartment. Before I was able to respond to his sarky comment, the sight of him in the doorway stunned me. Axel's usually flawless appearance was tarnished with multiple cuts across the bridge of his nose and cheeks, as well as a bruise on his jaw and a split lip to top it all off.

"What the fuck happened to you?" I asked with genuine concern, reaching a hand towards the purple area.

"It's nothing, don't worry about it." Axel responded casually, as if he didn't look like he'd been in a boxing ring, brushing off my hand and ushering me inside. I tried to bury the feeling of anxiety swirling in my stomach at seeing him so hurt.

"Suit yourself." I shrugged, crossing the room and throwing my bag onto the sofa, in its usual spot. I could tell there was more to the story but we didn't exactly keep each other up to speed with the latest goings on in our lives, so I decided not to press him on it further.

Sprawling out on the cushions, in my corner, I flicked open my new book to page one and began to delve into the saucy story. To my surprise, a glass of wine appeared, on the table, in front of me.

"You're a red girl, right?" Axel asked in reference to the confusion spread across my face. Picking it up, I swirled the glass, bewildered by the kind gesture. "It's not poisoned, Doll. If that's what you're concerned about." He laughed, shaking his head as he sat down on the opposite side, with his own drink.

"Thanks," I slowly took a sip, equal parts touched and befuddled.

Flicking off his shoes, he swung his legs onto the seat and turned the TV on, beginning to scroll as my attention was drawn back to the book.

"Wanna watch something?" Axel's voice interrupted me. I looked behind me, towards the door to check there weren't any unexpected visitors joining us.

"Are you talking to me?" I questioned, pointing to my chest.

"Who else would I be talking to?" He quirked an eyebrow in my direction.

"Did someone punch the attitude out of you? Why are you being so nice?" I put my book down, laughing as I turned to face him.

"Whoa, good to see your sympathy lasted long." He chuckled, taking a swig of his beer, resting his arm on the back of the sofa. I tried not to notice the way his bicep bulged, straining against the material of his thin white t-shirt.

"Sorry, I'm just surprised!" I defended.

"It's fine if you don't want to." A hint of rejection in his eyes, masked with his usual humour.

"No no, I'm not saying that. I was just looking forward to reading this." I held up the pristine copy of my filthy book.

"Ah yeah, 'course you were! Surely once you've read one, you know them all. How different can they be?" He ran a hand through his hair.

"How dare you. I'll have you know I'm reading them for their deep, thought-provoking storylines." I giggled.

"Toss it here then." He held out his hand, I obliged. "Get ready to be seduced by this sexy sequel to James and Erica's love story. Set immediately after the events of *Punish Me*, the pair are faced with more challenges as they navigate their complicated relationship and sexual tastes. With heat, passion and desire firing on all cylinders, will the pair survive their fiery love inferno?" Axel read the blurb aloud in his best Hollywood trailer voice, before chucking it back, a wide grin on his face. "Sounds deep."

"Obviously I just read it for the smut, Axel." I rolled my eyes playfully.

"I know you do, Babydoll." He winked. Butterflies erupted in my stomach at his cocky expression, he knew damn well what kind of things excited me in the bedroom and the reminder sent an electric shock straight between my legs.

"Speaking of softcore porn, how did your topless photoshoot go?" I smirked, referencing the pictures I'd been inundated with on the group chat earlier today, directing us away from dangerous territory. I couldn't stop myself from grinning as I recalled the *'JESUS MARY AND JOSEPH!'* message Jake had sent with the evidence.

"One word. Oily. I will never be doing that again, that's for certain." He scoffed, placing a hand to his face, wincing from pain at the contact.

Now I'm no sadist, but God he looks good roughed up!

"I did think it was an odd venture for you, but I would have thought you'd love people ogling your six pack." A man like Axel Ford, who looked like he had been sculpted by the Gods surely enjoyed the attention it garnered?

"Contrary to popular belief, I'm not one to whip my clothes off on cam when I'm not playing a character! They'd been bugging me for ages to do it and I finally had a good reason to." Axel's voice sobered; the jokey tone removed as he looked wistfully towards me. It felt like he was conveying a message, that I was somehow related to his decision to participate in the uncomfortable shoot but there was no sense in that.

"Well, you looked great and I'm sure you've made a lot of people's day. What a selfless man you are!" I mocked, breaking the tension.

A gruff chuckle escaped Axel. "*Da Vinci Code*?" He asked, pointing the remote at the screen.

"Oh God no, way too boring for me! I'm more of a *Clueless* kinda girl." I placed the book on the coffee table, replacing it with the glass of red before taking a sip.

"Ugh, I can't stand schlocky romance films. They're far too happy for me." He stifled a shudder.

"Sorry hard," I held my hand up in surrender, laughing at his sour expression. "Question, why did you take this job then? I can't imagine this would have been your cup of tea either."

Axel paused for a moment, seemingly collecting his thoughts. "I don't want directors to think I'm a one trick pony, gotta keep the portfolio broad."

"Yeah, I guess you've got to do a few Twilights to get The Batmans." I nodded proudly whilst Axel shot me a puzzled look. "You know, Robert Pattinson."

"Yes, I know Verity, it was just a weird thing to say." He shook his head, stifling another laugh.

"Fuck off." I jested, picking up a scatter cushion and launching it in his direction. He caught it easily, a cheesy grin spreading across his face. "Well, you must be relieved we're almost done then!" I said with a playful laugh. "I can't believe we shot our last scene together yesterday. Feels like just the other week I found out what a prick you can be." I nudged him with my foot.

"Aw, listen to you, sounds like you're going to miss shooting with me, Doll." He teased with a flirty smirk.

"Keep telling yourself that, Big Shot." I aimed for humour though I wasn't sure it hid the slight edge to my voice. The thought of not filming together for the foreseeable future hadn't fully sunk in until now. A month ago, I'd have been over the moon at this revelation but now I was left grappling with an odd, uncomfortable twist in my gut that I couldn't quite wrap my head around.

"Whilst we're spilling secrets, why'd *you* take the role?" He tucked the cushion I'd chucked at him behind his back.

"It was a huge opportunity and hopefully help towards going to the Oscars!"

"Going to? Don't you mean, winning one?" He quirked an eyebrow.

"I mean I'd be honoured but I'd settle for just walking through the door." Axel laughed slightly at my unexpected dream. "Plus taking *Accidentally* proved I wasn't wasting my life with my career choice. Although it's unlikely to make a shred of difference, I'll always disappoint my family." I circled the rim of my wine glass with my finger whilst discussing the awkward subject.

"You're the star of what will likely be one of the biggest releases this year, surely they're already proud of you?" He questioned. "Just booking the job is a huge achievement in itself."

"Ha, you don't know my family." I muttered, half under my breath.

"Let me guess, nothing is ever good enough, constant comparisons and unattainable expectations." Axel reeled off effortlessly.

"You hit the nail on the head."

"Thought so. I have some experience with difficult family members. Trust me Doll, it doesn't get easier once you've 'made it'." He said in quotation marks. "That's when people's true colours really show." I'd never seen this side of Axel, he was looking at me with legitimate care, it made me feel secure enough to open up to him for the first time.

"Mum." I stated simply, raising my hand momentarily.

"Dad." He mirrored my movement and offered me a sympathetic smile. "I've got it!" He exclaimed, typing *True Romance* into the search onscreen. "It's a cult classic and the perfect mix of action and romance. Plus, it just so happens to be one of my favourite films!"

We settled into comfortable silence as we watched the story unfold. Every time there was an onscreen death or major plot point, I noticed Axel turn to gauge my reaction, he was like an overexcited school kid, checking in to make sure I was paying attention and hoping to find I was enjoying it as much as he was. There was no denying, tonight was different to our usual forced evenings.

During the final shootout, my phone lit up in my lap. I half lifted it to see the notification, trying not to miss any of the action but the familiar name caught my eye and made my stomach drop.

Aaron Baxter spotted Friday night battered on the streets of London - who bruised this brute?

My blood ran cold as I glanced over at the bloodied man, deep in concentration. With shaking hands, I unlocked my phone and clicked through the photos attached to the article. My chest felt tight as I looked at the predator who had cornered me. Blood stained his clothes; his nose was swollen and purple. Compared to Axel's minor ailments, he looked as though he'd gone ten rounds with Mike Tyson.

"Axel..." I started, my voice cracking slightly as I broached the topic, the pieces of the puzzle beginning to click together. He whipped his head towards me instantly, sitting bolt upright.

"What's wrong?" He asked, pausing the film and moving beside me when words died on my tongue. His jaw tensed as he took in the images from my phone, that I had turned towards him.

"You agreed to leave it." I whispered, looking up at him with pleading eyes.

"He approached *me*." He said sternly.

"What did you do?"

"He got what he deserved." His eyes darkened and a growl rumbled in his chest. "No one touches what's mine."

Before I registered my actions, I tugged his shirt, bringing him closer. At the invitation, Axel closed the small distance and collided his lips to mine. My hands roamed his hair, whilst he wrapped a strong arm around my waist, lifting me easily onto his lap. This kiss, whilst just as desperate as the others felt different, it wasn't caused by anger and frustration, it was something deeper, stronger somehow. My heart raced wildly in my chest as flashes of Axel defending me flooded my mind. He had put himself in harm's way for me, driven by a need to protect me.

It struck me then; he must truly care.

Immediately, I pulled his top over his head, frantically, exposing his rippling abs, taking a moment to drink in the Adonis-like image of him. My eyes flicked back to his smug face as he raised an eyebrow.

For the first time, I was no longer denying my attraction for Axel Ford, and it was liberating. I ran my fingers along the dark lines of the tattoos covering his chest, revelling in the knowledge that we could take our time enjoying each other tonight. No runners waiting to usher us back to set; no car journeys which were always over too soon and most importantly; no prying eyes. Tonight was ours and I intended to soak in every single second of it.

"You're so beautiful." He breathed, the compliment knocking the wind out of my lungs. I pressed my lips against his again, feeling his cock harden as I began to grind on him. His hands travelled up to the curves of my breasts, a moan spilling from my mouth.

I deepened the kiss, causing a wince of pain from Axel. "I'm sorry, does that hurt?" I whispered, pulling back slightly and stroking a finger across his cut lip.

"No, it's all good, Doll." He smiled, his grey eyes looking at me with something softer than just burning desire. His rough hands found the hem of my top and pulled it over my head exposing my bare chest. He sucked on my erect nipple. I groaned at the feeling of his teeth grazing the sensitive area, causing him to bite harder. He slipped a hand under the elastic of my joggers, finding the wetness between my thighs.

"I bet you've touched this pretty pussy thinking about me before, haven't you?" He purred, moving my underwear to one side, beginning to circle his fingers around my swollen clit. I whined at his filthy language, humming in agreement. His movements stilled. "Show me."

My breath caught at the demand. His authoritative tone confirming he wasn't playing around. I shimmied off his lap quickly and slid down my trousers, sinking into the cushions in the corner of the sofa, draping my legs over his right thigh. Axel watched me hungrily, his own breathing laboured with barely restrained arousal. I slipped my hand into my bag beside me and retrieved the small velvet pouch. Axel's eyes widened as I removed the silver bullet, tossing the bag onto the floor.

"Verity Sloan carries a vibrator in her handbag."
He chuckled, running a finger up my inner leg, causing
goosebumps to appear. "You are full of surprises."

I giggled, suddenly feeling slightly shy at what I
was about to do, I'd never done this in front of anybody
before. Axel must've sensed my insecurity. "Let me see
how you make yourself come when I'm not around,
Doll." He whispered in encouragement. My mouth dried
from the request and I flicked the vibrator on.

I slowly began to draw the bullet up between my
legs, Axel leant over my torso, kissing the side of my
neck, causing bolts of electricity to jolt through me. The
toy reached my most sensitive area and my breath
hitched. I moaned as the vibrations pulsed on my clit.

"That's it, baby." Axel murmured, his Brooklyn
voice like gravel. His right hand still tracing circles on my
upper leg, sending shivers down my spine. "You look so
fucking hot with your hand between your thighs,
whimpering and thinking about me." I let out a pathetic
cry as I watched Axel stroke himself through the material
of his jogging bottoms whilst surveying me, causing the
pressure to build in my lower stomach. "You're going to
come soon aren't you, Doll." He purred, I nodded
weakly, my eyelids fluttering closed, the pin pricks of
pleasure almost too much to bear.

His touch travelled towards my dripping core. My
eyes snapped open at the feeling of two fingers slipping
inside, which he curled to tease my most sensitive spot.

"Axel," I breathed, my head falling back in
pleasure, the combination of his thick fingers thrusting

inside me and the vibrations of the bullet against my wet pussy caused my legs to tremor as my orgasm approached.

"Good girl, make a mess all over my hand." Blinding pleasure ripped through me at his permission, I bucked my hips against the toy and the punishing rhythm of his movements. Axel whispered words of encouragement as he coaxed me through my climax. I struggled to turn the bullet off, the sensation overwhelming and dropped it onto the sofa beside us before pushing his hand away from me.

"Ax, it's too much." I whined, he stilled, a smug chuckle rumbled through his chest. He leant over and pressed a kiss to my forehead. Despite the earth-shattering orgasm I had just had, I craved *more*. "I need you inside me." I begged, looking at his hard cock hidden by the grey fabric of his trousers. He smirked, lifting his body from the sofa slightly to pull down his joggers and boxers.

"Come here," he growled, grabbing my hips and lifting me back onto his lap, placing me against his throbbing cock. In that moment, I realised this was the first time I was seeing Axel fully naked and what a sight it was. He really was the picture of a Hollywood leading man with muscles upon muscles and a smile that threatened to tip me over the edge alone. I could feel the head of his dick press on my stomach disrupting my daydream of appreciation, a bead of pre-cum glistened at the tip.

"Oh fuck, I need to get a condom." He cursed, his voice shaking as he was clearly holding himself back.

"I'm on the pill," I said, hurriedly, I met his eyes, a look of confusion and surprise flashed there. "Please Axel, I want to feel *you*." I implored. A groan escaped his lips as he lifted me and impaled me on his cock without a second of hesitation.

We moaned in unison, the feeling of him stretching my pussy was overwhelming.

"God, Verity. Your cunt feels so fucking good." He buried his head in the crook of my neck, biting lightly on the skin. His hands caressed my hips, guiding me up and down his thick shaft. The friction of skin on skin was mind blowing, Axel bucked against my hips, he felt impossibly deep inside me as I continued to bounce on his cock.

I slid a hand into his unruly hair, tangling the strands around my fingers as I gripped tight, my other arm wrapped around his neck, keeping me close to him as I rode his dick desperately.

Pressing my chest against his face, Axel nipped and sucked on my left peak as he moaned into my breast. The sensation was otherworldly.

"Ax-Ax-fuck-" my breath quickened as my thoughts jumbled incoherently.

"Spit it out, Doll." He growled through gritted teeth, I looked at him with half opened eyes, despite the cuts to his face, his beauty was undeniable, his hair messed from my frantic fingers running through it, lips swollen from our kisses and looking at me so intensely I forgot how to function.

"I'm gonna com-" Before I could finish the sentence my second orgasm rushed through me. My toes curled. All corners of my body tingled with euphoria. Before the wave had fully flooded over, Axel swept me up in his arms and carried me across the room. I clung around his strong neck, pressing kisses to his face and shoulder.

The feeling of cold glass against my bare back, shocked me. It heightened every sensation as Axel restarted his movements, pumping into me as I held on desperately to his broad frame. I dug my nails into the tops of his shoulders, threatening to draw blood from the intensity.

"Your cock is so big!" I cried out, as it hit a spot so deep inside I didn't know it was possible. He smirked confidently, sliding out and releasing my legs to the ground, which resembled jelly from the two mind altering orgasms I had already had the pleasure of.

"Face the window." Axel ordered, spinning me around, he bent me over slightly, before sliding the tip of his erect dick inside my begging pussy once again. "Enjoy the view." He drawled before slamming into me with full force. My hands pressed flat against the glass steadying myself, as he continued thrusting punishingly, so hard I was certain the window would break!

The lights from streetlamps and cars, multiple floors below, twinkled as the world moved normally, whilst my brain was being fucked to oblivion. I should have been concerned that someone might have seen me like this, but all I felt was a sense of pride from being ravished by a man like *him*.

The cool against my nipples in contrast from the heat radiating from Axel was intoxicating. I felt the familiar buzz of my climax begin to build in my stomach all over again. He reached between my thighs, rubbing my clit with his fingers and whispered sweet nothings in my ear until I came a third time. I fell limply against the glass, his muscular arms wrapping around my waist to prevent me from crumbling to the floor.

"That's it, Angel, you've done so well for me tonight." He praised, I whimpered an incoherent response. I was putty in his arms as he manoeuvred me, laying me down on the rug in the centre of the room. I watched as he positioned himself above me, re-inserting his cock.

"Axel," I moaned, unsure if I was going to survive another orgasm but not wanting it to stop. He drove into me brutally, the hard floor beneath us ensuring I felt every inch of him.

"I can't get enough of you, Verity." His smoky eyes bored into my soul as he gritted his teeth. The declaration caused my heart to stutter, I tried not to think too deeply about the meaning behind his words.

"Axel, please come inside me." I begged, unable to hold back the feeling of another climax approaching. My words must have triggered something in him as he quickened his pace before releasing. My pussy constricted around his cock, my legs shaking and eyes tearing up at the intensity.

"Fuuuck!" Axel exclaimed, collapsing into a heap on top of me, being as careful as he could to not crush me from his position. I sighed contentedly as pleasure hummed around my body. My limbs felt impossibly heavy and light at the same time as exhaustion washed throughout.

Axel rolled off me, his arms wrapping around my frame, pulling me to his chest and tucking my head under his chin. I smiled against him, my eyelids remaining shut as I laid there in blissful contentment listening to his heart rate and breathing return to normal.

29

VERITY

Buzzzzzz!

I awoke with a start to the sound of my phone aggressively vibrating on the wooden floor. Axel's arm constricted around my waist and he let out a low groan as I reached away for the device.

"Axel," I complained, he loosened his grip allowing me to lean forward and grab my phone. Surprise jolted through me when I saw 'Mum' emblazoned on the screen. I flicked my eyes to the time, *7.38am*. She never called this early in the day. Quickly I answered, hoping everyone in my family was okay, feeling particularly concerned for Charlotte's unborn baby.

"Mum? Hello?" I answered.

"Finally awake then! I've been trying you for the past five minutes." My mother's shrill voice insulted. *It's not even eight.* "Anyway, what's your exact address, Verity?

Your father and I want to pay you a visit. We're in the car on the way to London."

"You're what?!" I exclaimed, sitting bolt upright. Axel moaned beside me as I released myself from his grasp, pulling the blanket from the sofa over and wrapping it around my body.

"Clean your ears out, girl. We've just got onto the A2, text me the address quickly and pull yourself together." She hung up abruptly, leaving me frozen.

"What's happened, Doll?" Axel croaked sleepily, touching the back of my arm. It was not the time to think about it, but God his morning voice was sexy!

"My parents are on the way to visit me." I sighed, rubbing my eyes to get rid of the sleep.

"That's fine, isn't it?" I turned towards him, a puzzled look on his face.

"They don't know where I live. I can't take them to that shithole, Axel, my mum will never let me hear the end of it." I placed my head in my hands as I imagined the look on my mother's face when she was met with the damp-stained ceilings, peeling wallpaper and whatever kind of rodents that Misto hadn't been able to catch yet. This was going to be a disaster.

"I know you mentioned she's tough on you, but surely it wouldn't be that bad for them to see your flat?" He questioned, reassuringly.

"Trust me, this would end my life." I knew I was being dramatic but knowing Eleanor Sloan, the minute she realised I hadn't been living in a swanky five-star apartment, I would never be able to change her mind about my life choices.

"Bring them here then." Axel said casually, the offer rolling effortlessly off his tongue.

"You can't be serious?" I shot him an inquisitive look.

"Why not? It's not like I have a six-foot portrait of myself on the wall and you said yourself the view was impressive." He winked.

I slapped him on the bare chest, taken back slightly by the firmness of his pecks. "Don't you think it's a bit soon to meet the parents?"

"Easy Doll, I'll head out for the afternoon and leave you to weave your web of lies on your own." He stretched and I watched as his muscles rippled. I would have done anything to stay wrapped up with him. Considering the several hours I'd spent lying on the floor I was feeling surprisingly well-rested which I could only imagine was due to being cocooned against this magnificent-looking man all night.

"At this point, it's basically second nature." I shook my head, laughing. "Whilst you're offering out favours you can go feed Misto." Standing up, I kept the blanket around my body and reached into my bag on the sofa to retrieve the key before chucking it at Axel.

"Yes ma'am." He saluted. I felt my pulse quicken as I looked down at him, he was completely naked, my gaze dragged lazily across his perfect form. I heard him chuckle and my eyes flicked to his, he smirked, cockily. "Give me your phone, I'll type in the address for your parents." He held out his arm offering to take my device as he entered the information. I ignored the need pounding between my thighs, now was not the time to be horny. My phone beeped immediately in Axel's hand. "They're forty minutes away."

"I need to get dressed." I said to myself, out loud. Stalking round the living room, I collected up my scattered items of clothing from our sex-capade the night before. "You need to as well!" I ordered and to my surprise, Axel leapt into action without protest.

I worked for the next thirty minutes, putting the place back together, giving the apartment a quick hoover and clean whilst Axel headed to the local bakery to pick up some pastries. I kept checking the time, anxious about my parents' impending arrival and Axel's whereabouts. The last thing I needed today was a meet and greet between him and my devil mother! The door clicked signalling his return.

"Where the hell have you been? It's only a few mins walk." I exclaimed, perhaps a little more aggressively than necessary.

"I'm Axel Ford, I can't just pop to the shop and get back quickly. It's a bit of a surprise to the public seeing me queuing for freshly baked bread, Doll." He tossed the Danish pastries onto the kitchen island.

"Careful or your big head won't fit out of the door!" I began decanting the baked goods onto a plate I had taken out ready.

"Right, I'll get going-" Axel started, interrupted by the intercom.

"Fuck! They're here already." I flapped my hands, panicked. Axel laughed at my display, pressing the buzzer to let them in. "What the fuck did you do that for?" I asked, feeling sick with anxiety.

"Well, what was your plan? Leave them out there in the rain?" He gestured towards the window.

"You're still here!" I accused, pointing a finger at him.

"What do you want me to do? Abseil down the side of this building?" Axel was still laughing, clearly unfazed.

"Ah! Hide or something!" I smoothed my hair down in the mirror in the kitchen, anticipating the judgement from my mother regarding my appearance.

"No, I'll just leave. It's all cool, Verity. They might not even recognise me." He smirked, knowing that was far from the truth.

"Just go you pain in my arse. I'll call you the minute they leave." I shoved him towards the door.

"Good luck, Doll." He smiled kindly. The unexpected warmth calmed my nerves a fraction. He opened the door, only to be faced with my guests.

It felt like time stood still, their eyes widening as they took in the man before them. Not only was this the first time they were meeting my insanely hot, famous, older, boyfriend completely unexpectedly, but his face was covered in cuts and bruises. Not the first impression I would have liked my family to have of him.

"Ah, good morning, Mr and Mrs Sloan." Axel held out his hand informally. "It's lovely to meet you."

He schmoozed as my parents returned the shake. "I'm Axel, please come in."

"Oh, we know who you are." A goofy smile spread across my dad's face and I tried not to recoil into the corner from the awkwardness of the situation. "Please call us Richard and Eleanor." He responded, as they walked into my fake flat.

"We recognise you from our daughter's bedroom walls as a teenager." My mother interjected. *Fuck my life, thanks, Mum. I'd managed to keep that one a secret up until now.* I saw her eyes flick to the gash on Axel's lip but she didn't mention it, it seemed she *could* be tactful when she wanted to be. "Verity and her sister were huge *Sunset High* fans.' I didn't know for certain but part of me felt like she had disclosed that information purely to embarrass me.

"Is that right?" Axel shot me an amused smirk and I tried to hide my scowl in return.

"Hi Mum, Dad." I greeted my parents, hugging them gingerly. My mother gave me a wooden embrace and a guarded smile, though I didn't expect anything less.

"Hi Bug." My father said, with his usual pet name, ruffling my hair. I felt a slight twinge of guilt at not reaching out to him since moving to London a few months ago, for all the grief Eleanor gave me, he was always supportive.

"Oh wow, the sights from up here are out of this world! You can see Tower Bridge in all its glory." My mum proclaimed, making her way across the room to the floor-to-ceiling windows.

"It's pretty spectacular isn't it." Axel agreed, crossing the space to join her. "Verity told me it was the main reason she picked this place. Did you know some nights she presses her face up against the glass and has her mind blown just from taking it all in." I felt my cheeks flush from his comment. I knew exactly what he was referencing to get under my skin. *Arsehole.* "Anyway, I won't intrude any further, have a lovely day. It was great to meet you both."

"You're not joining us, Axel?" My mum questioned with a disappointed edge to her voice.

"Unfortunately not, Eleanor, I'm needed on set today." Axel lied, "but I'm sure I'll see you again soon." He took my mother's hand and placed a kiss on the back of it before leaving. I could have sworn her cheeks glowed with a similar redness to mine for a moment. *That slick bastard!*

"Pastry?" I offered, breaking the silence once the door shut behind Axel.

"They look delicious, thanks Bug." My dad declared, taking a maple and pecan twist.

"Oh, I couldn't possibly." My mum tapped her completely flat stomach softly, "I'll take a coffee instead. Is that a La Marzocco?" She pointed towards the counter.

I turned to see the coffee machine I'd never paid much attention to. Beats me but trust my mum to know the swankiest appliances. "Yeah." I exclaimed, trying to fake enthusiasm.

"An espresso will do just fine." She stated, taking a seat on the sofa.

"And you, Dad?" I rounded the corner towards the spaceship-looking appliance, God knows how that thing worked.

"Just a water please, I'll grab it, where are the glasses?" He said through a mouthful of pastry. Shit, I didn't know that either. I surveyed the front of the cupboards, praying one would jump out at me. To my disappointment, they all remained uniform.

Hmm, if I were to store glasses anywhere, where would I put them? Eenie, meenie, minie, mo. I tentatively opened the door above the coffee machine and breathed a sigh of relief when I was faced with several tumblers. *Lucky guess!*

I passed it to my dad, who filled it up from the tap before joining my mum on the couch. *Right back to this confusing contraption!*

I should not have been this intimidated by a hunk of metal.

Come on Verity, time to channel your inner Rosie, this should be second nature by now. After staring at the apparatus for a few more seconds I decided to employ my old friend Google, searching the model I found a semi-comprehensible manual on how to make the 'perfect espresso.' I followed the steps until I was satisfied with the shot of caffeine I had produced.

I carried the plate of the remaining goodies and the coffee over to my parents. Placing myself down on the side furthest from my mother.

Anxiously, I picked at my apple Danish, nervous to strike up conversation. I watched as my mum tasted the coffee, feeling a millimetre of relief, when a satisfied 'hmm' left her mouth.

"So, why are you here? Not that I'm not happy for the impromptu visit…" but my mum was anything but spontaneous. This trip was most definitely predetermined and I was the last to know.

"We had a day free this weekend and thought how nice it would be to drop in and visit our youngest daughter to find out more about her new high-flying life!" My mum rattled off. Translation: she was convinced I was barely getting by, didn't want to give me notice to prepare and turned up unannounced to confirm her suspicions and lord it over me. Well, more fool you, Mum. I was one step ahead for once! I had a fake flat provided by my fake boyfriend to show off.

"This is truly a beautiful flat, Bug." My dad gushed, Eleanor looked around the room, desperately trying to find something to insult.

"Yes, it looks like you have finally made a good decision." She relented, "I have to admit, I wasn't expecting the place to be this nice." She continued, although it looked like it pained her to give me a compliment. I forced a smile, it didn't feel good that the only time I'd ever impressed my mother was a complete lie.

"Crikey Verity, is that a replica of Sting from Lord of the Rings?" My dad pointed to the mounted sword on the wall by the kitchen. So that's what it was then, I did think it was an odd interior design choice to mount a random weapon.

"Yeah…" I agreed.

"Does it glow blue when orcs are near?" My dad said, giggling like a schoolboy. "Do you have any mithril knocking about whilst we're at it?" He wiped away tears from laughing so hard at his own joke. My mother rolled her eyes, bitterly.

"No dad, there are no orcs in London!" I jested, enjoying seeing him so himself. *What the fuck is an orc? Or mithril for that matter!*

Now that we were all settled, I eased myself with the thought that maybe this visit wouldn't be so hard after all. My mother had been placated and my father thought we had a shared love of something nerdy, I was certain I could survive the next couple of hours.

30

AXEL

I followed the directions on the map until I reached the small brick building in the heart of Shoreditch, that I had picked Verity up from once before. From the outside it looked quite quaint but nestled between a fried chicken shop and an off licence, I could imagine it wasn't the place you'd want to take judgy parents!

I let myself into her top-floor apartment and the stark contrast to my own hit me. Verity's personality shone through in every corner, despite how run down the place was, it was cosy and welcoming. I perused the walls which were covered in frames of Verity and her friends, some of which I recognised from the launch event. An involuntary smile formed on my face as I looked at her happy expression, a dangerous feeling I'd never felt before, stirred in my chest. A soft tickle jolted me from my thoughts.

"What the fuc-" I started, looking down to be met with the piercing green eyes of who I assumed was the famous Mr Mistoffelees. "You scared the shit out of me, little one." I reached down, scratching the back of his head, he purred appreciatively. "Right, where's your food then, Mr?" I began to search the small kitchen area, opening various cupboards before I found the bag of biscuits. I poured a pile of food into one of the bowls and filled the other with fresh water. "There you go, man." *Jesus, I'm talking to an animal.*

With the cat satisfied, I settled down on Verity's sofa, placing my hands behind my head. Thoughts of the previous night played in my brain. I didn't know what this girl had done to me. Last night felt different, the conversation at the start was deeper, more genuine. I could feel her care in a way I hadn't before. And most notably, it was the first time we had fucked without declaring 'cookie' since establishing our barely-friends-with-benefits codeword.

It was *also* the first time after one of our 'dates' that she had stayed over, that had usually been an unspoken boundary but last night we hadn't talked about it, we'd just passed out after sex, tangled in each other. Strangely, I hadn't wanted her to leave. Waking up to her this morning felt comforting in a way I hadn't expected. I couldn't remember the last time I'd shared a 'bed' with anyone else.

That being said, I didn't get the best quality of sleep on the rug. I felt my eyelids getting heavy whilst I awaited Verity's call for the all clear.

"Axel?" Verity's voice awoke me from my nap. I felt a warm weight on my chest, glancing down to see a pile of black and white fluff, curled up. "I called you; they've gone."

"Didn't hear it, I dozed off." I grumbled, reaching up and instinctively stroking the cat on top of me.

"Clearly! What were you hanging around for anyway? I'm not really in the mood for round two?" I looked up at Verity, her hands on her hips, as she stared at me angrily. You wouldn't have thought I'd just done this woman a favour.

"Don't flatter yourself," I winked, enjoying winding her up as usual. "I needed to give you your key back." I pointed at the metal object on the coffee table. "And needed to get mine from you."

"Ah yeah." She replied, looking awkward, before digging out my key from her pocket and placing it next to hers. "Well, it seems the two of you have gotten well acquainted in the meantime, you traitor Misto! Do you know he prefers dogs!?" She stage-whispered towards the purring animal, still sleeping blissfully. I stretched, causing him to wake and spring off me before I sat up on the couch. Verity joined me, sighing heavily.

"How did it go then? Worth the lie?" I asked.

"Actually, not too bad thank God." She responded before laying her head back on the sofa and closing her eyes. I took a moment to drink her in, the delicate slope of her nose, her perfectly sculpted cheekbones, her usually immaculately styled hair slightly damp from the rain. I'd spent countless hours in her presence, but I was still taken aback by her beauty. "What's mithril by the way?" Her ocean eyes shot open, catching me staring.

"What?" I laughed, her random question taking me by surprise. "It's the strongest metal known in Middle Earth; in Lord of the Rings they use it for armour. Why? Do you need it to protect you from your mother?" I nudged her playfully, ignoring the shock of electricity from the physical contact. *Oh no, these kinds of feelings cannot be good.*

"You dork." She giggled. "My dad spotted your fucking sword and now thinks I'm a huge nerd so thanks for that." She rubbed her hand on her face. "Can't wait for all the shit I'll get for Christmas now."

"Sounds great to me, if you don't want it, I'll happily take them off your hands." I grinned, beginning to stand.

"I can't believe you finish your scenes tomorrow. That's come around so quickly!" Verity shook her head.

"I know, one more day and then I'll be on US ground again for a few weeks. Back in mid-May for reshoots though, so not too long." I found myself reassuring both Verity and I that I would see her again soon, although I wasn't sure why.

"Yeah." Her voice sounded distant.

"Right, I'll make myself scarce." I said, breaking the tension between us, I stood from the seat and faced the front door.

"Axel," I turned back to look at her, "thank you for today, I really appreciate it." She smiled sweetly, her adorable dimple making an appearance.

"Don't mention it, now I've been here, I can understand why you wouldn't want them to see it." I looked around in mock horror.

"Good to see you're back to being an arsehole." Verity rolled her eyes.

Walking the short distance, I opened the door and began to pull it shut behind me until I heard Sarah's voice in my head. Reopening the door, Verity looked at me with surprise.

"Forget something?"

"May 20th. Keep it free, I have a family wedding and you're my plus one." I explained, deadpan. Starting to feel a little strange inviting her under false pretences.

"Another genius idea from Sarah?" She guessed correctly.

"Perhaps, but it could be fun." I shrugged awkwardly in the doorway.

"Sure, I'll put it in my diary." She agreed, matching my tone.

I smiled warmly, "see you in a month, Doll."

31

AXEL

After nearly five months, I was back on American soil. Usually, I would enjoy being back in the familiarity of New York, eating good pizza, catching a Knicks game and seeing my oldest friends but over these past two weeks, something had felt different to usual.

Even when I was doing the things that I loved most, I found my mind wandering to thoughts of the girl back in England.

Fuck, I know what this means.

I rounded the corner of the block and approached the entrance to one of my favourite sushi restaurants, SoHo Sashimi, largely avoiding the paparazzi thanks to the baseball cap I was wearing. One of the great things about being in New York was that everyone kept themselves to themselves and there were so many celebrities in the state, it wasn't a phenomenon to spot one. I could usually walk down the street and not be bothered by anyone and feel somewhat normal for once.

Opening the door of the building, I spotted my mom sitting in a booth along the back wall. She flashed me a wide, toothy grin when she saw caught my eye, filling me with warmth. I hadn't seen her since I moved to London for the shoot and being an only child, we had always been particularly close.

"Hello, sweetheart!" She cooed, standing up and wrapping her arms around me.

"Hi Mom." I smiled, returning the embrace. "Missed you."

"I've missed you too." She squeezed me tighter before releasing me. We took our seats and perused the menu making light conversation as we waited for our sushi to arrive.

"You're looking well." My mom complimented, picking up an edamame that we'd ordered to share.

"Thanks, I've had a lot of free time to work out in London." I took a swig of Soju. I was glad the bruises, from my run in with Aaron, had finally faded. She would have only worried.

"I saw the photoshoot; you've certainly been eating your greens." She laughed and I internally cringed.

"Jesus Mom, I can honestly say first and last." I rubbed a hand over my face, trying to wipe the embarrassment off.

"Well, the ladies at my book club were overjoyed and were begging to get signed copies!" She winked. This was not the conversation I wanted to be having with my mother.

"I know you're joking but just in case, that's definitely not happening." I assured her, desperately thinking of a way to change the subject. "Anyway, the wedding in a few weeks should be nice, and it will be good to see everyone."

"Yes, they're all excited to see you too." Mom said, as she picked up a maki roll with her chopsticks. "Have you spoken to your dad recently?" She asked cautiously, dampening the mood.

My relationship with my father was tenuous at best. Throughout the early years of my acting career, when I was mainly shooting commercials and minor roles in sitcoms, my dad made it no secret that he was less than impressed with the path I had chosen to pursue. I was making fairly decent money and booking jobs pretty consistently but every day he would cut me down with how *this will never go anywhere* and that I needed to get my head out of my ass and step up to provide for the family. When I booked *Sunset High*, it felt like I had hit the jackpot! A regular on a confirmed show with over twenty episodes and the strong possibility of future seasons. It was like finding the golden ticket for a young actor.

When I told my parents, my mom was overjoyed and I'd never seen her filled with so much pride that I was achieving the goals I had set out for myself. My dad on the other hand, only had negative opinions and told me he was embarrassed that his son was going to be involved in a 'sissy teen romance for prepubescent girls to drool over' and no pay check would be worth the ridicule that I would supposedly bring on him.

That was the day my mum left my dad.

"Not since the end of April." I shrugged.

After *Sunset High*, I decided I would never accept a role like that again. I focussed only on projects that I thought might have impressed him, although even when I had been nominated for prestigious awards and revered in the press for my performances, I had never heard him say he was proud of me or even happy birthday for that matter. Yet he never forgot to call me at the end of every month to request his usual payout to fund whatever he was short on at the time.

I knew in my head that I should have cut him off years ago, but I was lucky enough to be in a financial situation where I had more money than necessary and he was still my dad. I didn't have it in me to let him suffer.

"Hmm, I'm sorry he still puts you in that position, honey." My mom comforted, "you know I never agreed with the weight of expectation he put on you, but I always hoped he would grow up one day and you would be able to rebuild your relationship." She leant across the table and placed her hand on mine.

"Unless my bank account ever runs out, I don't think we'll ever be in a place to have a normal conversation. For years that made me feel shit but now I just don't care, I guess." It wasn't so much that I didn't care, but more that I had grown numb to his indifference.

"It's his loss, Axel. He's missing out on knowing a wonderful son." She gave me a loving smile which I returned. The two of us ate in silence for a beat. "I can't wait to meet your lady, Verity, isn't it?" Her eyes gleamed with eagerness and I felt a pang in my chest. I hadn't felt the slightest bit of guilt lying to anyone I saw day to day in London but sitting opposite my mother, beaming with pride it felt like a hot knife to the stomach. Coupled with the unusual emotions I was currently trying to decipher in regard to my stunning, blonde-haired co-star, the sushi was starting to lose its appeal.

"She's looking forward to it too. Plus, it's her first time in New York so lots for her to explore whilst she's over here." *At least I think so.* I hadn't spoken to Verity since I shared the invitation in her apartment two weeks ago but something about her screamed NY virgin.

"Oh great, make sure you plan lots of activities for the two of you."

"Yes, I'll make sure the agenda is jam-packed." I laughed.

We continued to chat about the upcoming movie, the latest scandals in my mom's Pilates class and how I was planning on spending the remainder of my time in America before bidding goodbye to each other. Although the night was full of engaging conversation, I couldn't stop my mind drifting back to Verity.

Entering my apartment, I kicked off my shoes and wandered through to the kitchen deciding to pour myself a glass of whisky. I settled onto the suede coach, clicking the TV on to find something mindless to turn my brain off.

My phone dinged with a text message.

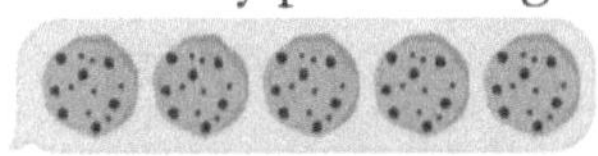

A shock shot to my groin.

Fucking hell, Verity. Three thousand miles away and you're causing this kind of physical reaction from me. I chuckled as I rang her number before I could stop myself.

"Evening, Miss Sloan." I purred.

"Axeeeellllll," she slurred jubilantly through the phone, "why are you calling?" She hiccupped down the line.

"You text me damn cookie emojis!" I tried to hold in my amusement at her blatant intoxication.

"Oh yeah! Are you coming then?" I could practically hear her eyebrows waggling suggestively.

"You know I'm in New York, Doll. What time is it?" I pulled the phone back. *8pm.* "It's gotta be like 1am right? Where are you?" An unexpected feeling of concern surged through me as I imagined an inebriated Verity, alone on the streets of London in the early hours.

"At home." Relief washed over me. "I was flicking through TikTok and fell down a rabbit hole of Axel Ford edits. Damn you're hot."

"Oh my fucking God Verity," I howled, unable to hold it together any longer. Only she could admit something so daft and it could somehow still stroke my ego.

"I'll send them to you." She shouted, excitedly. The volume of her shriek caused me to hold the device away from my ear momentarily.

"Please don't! I'll be fine." I laughed, shaking my head and taking a sip of my drink. "What have you been up to then, Tink?"

"Simmys with the girlsssss!" She elongated the last syllable; I'd never heard her so animated and I knew I should send her to bed but selfishly I wanted to think of reasons to keep her on the phone.

"I have no idea what that is, but it sounds like you've had a great time!"

"I would be having a *greater* time if you were here…and you would too." She whispered, causing a shiver to run down my spine. I ran a hand through my hair as I imagined what she could be wearing and how fucking good she would look in it.

"Verity Sloan, you are relentless!" I snickered, trying to douse the fire in her before she got out of control.

"There is something we could do while we're a million miles apart." A beep began to ring in my ear. I checked the screen to see Verity requesting a video call. I considered my response for a second before I answered, deeming my curiosity too high to ignore.

After a moment, Verity's face appeared on the grainy screen. She was a vision. Even with her face flushed, hair dishevelled, and make-up smudged from the night, I had never seen anyone so beautiful.

"Hey you." I drawled, unable to hide my smile.

"Why are you so fit?" She giggled, "and so far awaaaaay!" She pouted and I wanted to wipe the look off her stunning face.

"You're gorgeous." I complimented simply, Verity gave me the biggest, goofiest, sweetest smile causing her dimple to pop out. My heart felt as though it could burst from the way she was looking at me. "I'll be back soon." I reassured her, although there was nothing I wanted more than for her to be in my arms in this instant.

"Not soon enough. I want you now! I miss you!" She exclaimed, "...and your dick." Her cheeks turned the prettiest shade of pink and she tried to hide her smirk.

I rolled my eyes playfully. "Patience, Doll."

"I'm horny nowwww." She whined. Usually, the whole begging thing didn't work on me but the bulge in my pants said otherwise. I found her playful demeanour adorably endearing.

"Well, you know how to take care of that. Still got that vibrator?"

"Yes, shall I show you?" She asked, my cock hardened slightly at the thought but I knew she wasn't in the right state of mind.

"Not tonight. I think it's time you went to bed, Verity." I encouraged kindly, sensing the tiredness creeping up on her at the late hour.

"Okay, I guess you're right." She yawned, proving my point. "But…don't be a stranger. It's been too long since I've heard your voice." A shy tone coated her words as she blinked her ocean blue eyes at the camera.

"I won't, Doll." I smiled, reassuringly.

"Goodnight, Ax, I'll be thinking about ya." She hung up, leaving me faced with my own reflection.

As much as I hated to admit it, I would be ending my day thinking about her too.

32

VERITY

Today was the day I was going to see Axel after a month apart and to say I was inexplicably anxious was an underestimate. Usually, I wasn't nervous in his presence but from the start of our contract, a lot had changed. Not only had we entered into our complicated enemies-with-benefits situation but now we were treading dangerous territory with our most recent escapade being unprovoked by our codeword, not to mention the drunk phone call I had made two weeks ago. I was mortified when I woke up the next day and remembered how I had been so vocal about missing him. But an unexpected *'morning, Doll'* text from Axel, reassured me that I didn't need to relocate and change my identity.

Since then, the past fortnight had been filled with semi-regular exchanges, checking in on each other. The time difference prevented any real conversation flowing but the consistent messages had my head scrambled. I felt my heart rate increase every time my phone beeped with a notification, like a damn teenager waiting for her crush to text.

"ETA ten minutes, Ms. Sloan," Clive announced from the driver's seat.

"Great, thank you!" I said, my stomach was doing flips as signs for Heathrow Airport became more frequent, although I wouldn't be rocking up to general departures today. Clive was escorting me to Axel's private jet which was waiting on the concourse for a departure at 11.05am sharp.

I spent the remainder of the journey trying (and failing) to think of all the inflight entertainment that I could consume on the plane. Clive drove us through a private entryway to the tarmac and a large white jet came into view, which I was almost certain belonged to the American movie star. We parked alongside a town car, which Axel was lounging against, scrolling through his phone. He didn't look up from his device as we stopped mere inches from him.

"Safe trip and enjoy your time in New York." Clive said, removing the key from the ignition.

"Thank you, I will." I grabbed my handbag from the seat beside me as I heard the door open. I turned to shuffle out of the car only to be met with a pair of striking, smoky grey eyes. I felt my cheeks burn.

Fuck, has he got hotter?!

"Hey, Doll." He drawled, offering me a hand as I sat stock still. He was just wearing a simple black t-shirt and matching jeans but he looked goddamn edible.

"Hey." I replied, quietly, my previous nerves still choking me out. I took his hand in mine and climbed out of the vehicle. I stood awkwardly beside him, seemingly forgetting how to function as a normal human being as I considered how to greet my fake boyfriend, turned fuck buddy, turned situationship.

"Here are your bags, Ms Sloan." Clive broke me out of my daydream and handed me my two large suitcases.

"I'll take it, cheers." Axel smiled, grabbing the holdall and wheelie case, as I thanked Clive before he returned to his car. "Right, you, let's go." He nodded towards the plane. I wasn't afraid of flying, however the thought of being trapped in a metal cylinder with Axel Ford for eight hours, terrified me!

"Make yourself at home, there's a drinks fridge in the corner." He gestured, as we walked into the aircraft. "Let me give you the grand tour." He led me down the centre aisle. I looked around at the expensive interior. I had never seen a plane like this!

"This is insane." I breathed, unable to fake nonchalance.

Every wall was mirrored, every surface was made of dark wood and the floor was fully carpeted. The jet was bigger than my apartment for sure, with several sections along its length.

"This is my favourite area, here." Axel gestured to the 'room' containing two cream recliners with a small table in between on the right side of the plane and a large forest green sofa lining the left side. Axel sat down in the chair facing the cockpit and clicked a seatbelt on.

"Tour's over then?" I queried, taking a seat in the chair opposite and securing my own belt.

"Yep." He responded simply, looking out of the window as the plane began to taxi to the runway.

"Well, what's through there then? The cleaning cupboard?" I joked, curiosity getting the better of me.

"Ahh well that's my private bedroom, Doll, maybe you'll see it someday." He shot me a look that made my thighs tense together and my heart flip, I rolled my eyes, trying my best to pretend his words didn't affect me.

After we reached altitude, the seatbelt light turned off and with the sound of the ding, Axel unbuckled and moved to lounge on the sofa to the side of me.

I delved into my bag and pulled out a new book to get stuck into. I was no further than page two before Axel piped up.

"New series?" He asked with a smirk, pointing to my book, *Soho Seduction.*

"Why? Do you wanna borrow the other one?" I joked.

"I'll bear that in mind if I ever have a lonely night." He laughed. "I suppose you can use the bed back there if you need some alone time." He winked. I bit my lip, the last thing I wanted was *alone time*, but I wasn't about to yell cookie and join the mile-high club.

"Just let me read, please." I turned my attention back to the pages and tried to block out the superstar beside me. Although I was forty thousand feet in the sky, it didn't feel too dissimilar from curling up in Axel's living room. The cosy vibes surrounded me as I fully immersed myself in the story.

My eyelids fluttered open to find the book closed on the table and a fluffy blanket wrapped around me. I stretched and tried to come to, glancing across to see Axel in the same position as before on the sofa, reading.

"How long have I been asleep?" I croaked, my throat dry. Axel startled at my question, taking off the glasses he must have put on whilst I was dozing.

"Erm," he rolled up the paper and looked at his silver watch, "around four and half hours I reckon."

"Jesus, didn't realise I was so tired!" I yawned, straightening in my seat, the blanket falling off me slightly. I couldn't stop the smile that pulled at my lips at the thought of Axel tucking me in. "What are you reading?" I asked, nodding towards the scroll in his hand.

"Just some script, I get sent them all the time, figured I'd have a skim through." He shrugged, dropping the manuscript.

"All right, Big Shot. Not all of us are dripping in offers, you know?" I jested.

"Shit yeah, sorry, that sounded a bit dickish." Axel laughed. I was bemused, he had never apologised for anything before. Maybe it was the altitude messing with his head!

"Tell me about the wedding then, whose is it again?" I asked, trying to get my bearings before the hours of socialising.

"Jackson and Addison, he's my cousin, my mom's nephew." He informed me.

"Are you two close?" I asked, sipping on the glass of water on the table in front of me.

"As close as you can be when you spend most of the year travelling around the world." He replied, a solemn look crossing his features. "But I've always got on well with my mom's side." He smiled.

"That's understandable." I remembered back to the conversation we had back in Axel's apartment when he insinuated a strained relationship with his dad. "Will your dad be there?"

"Hmm," he chuckled with no humour, "definitely not."

I shuffled awkwardly in my chair, realising I'd touched on a sensitive subject. "If you ever want to talk about it, Ax, you can." He met my reassuring gaze. "You helped when my crappy mum was in town…seems only fair I'm here for you too." I shrugged.

"Thanks, Doll." He said in a hushed tone, there was a charged energy surrounding us, not the usual type, one I couldn't quite put my finger on. He slapped his hands on his thighs and stood up. "Right, I'm going to see what food there is in the kitchen." He spoke, cutting the tension and disappearing off down the aisle.

I rested my head back against the chair and let out a deep sigh as we flew the last few hundred miles. *How do things between us get more complicated by the minute?*

The New York buildings flew past in a blur as we transferred from the airport to Axel's apartment building and back into Axel's personal classic red Chevy in his underground parking lot, taking all our luggage with us.

"It's weird to see you in the driver's seat." I prodded, glancing over at him. It was only the second time he'd driven us anywhere, and there was something so attractive about it…to be honest, everything he did was attractive to me.

"Ha, yeah, I love driving but not much opportunity to just drive aimlessly for hours, especially when you are usually accompanied by paparazzi." He nodded to a blacked out 4x4 alongside us, a camera flash sparked in the window.

"Fucking hell, do they ever give it a rest?" I complained, pulling the sunglasses on my head, over my eyes. As much as I didn't like them hanging around, the reality that I was here purely to be seen publicly with Axel was at the forefront of my mind.

"They'll give up eventually, it'll calm down the closer we get to the venue. Once they've got the money shot, they'll go," he mirrored my movements, donning his aviators. Axel looked more like a movie star than ever. One hand on the steering wheel, the other arm leaning on the edge of the open window, his hair tousled from the wind. I found myself staring at him more than I'd like to admit.

True to his word, as we crossed into Rye, I realised we were now alone on the road. The town was quaint and looked like it was straight out of a postcard. After around an hour, we reached the white waterfront mansion where the wedding would be taking place in a few hours. The sun beat down on the crystal blue water and refracted light into my eyes.

"What a beautiful location!" I gushed.

"It is, I think it belongs to Addison's family."

"Jesus Christ, I do not think I will fit in here." I laughed.

"You'll be great." He smiled warmly, triggering a flutter in my stomach. Axel carried our bags into the house and led me up the grand staircase and along a never-ending corridor, until we reached a corner room.

"This is us." He said as we stopped outside one of the many doors.

"Us?" I startled.

"Is that okay?" He laughed slightly at my shocked expression before pushing it open.

"Yeah, yeah, of course, no worries at all." I word-vomited, half out of thrill and half from terror. Of course I would be sharing a room with him, the family might've found it a little weird if we had requested separate beds.

"Come on, Doll, we better start getting ready."

We walked in and Axel moved our cases to one of the corners. Along the left wall was an emperor size bed, which looked insanely comfortable, images of being fucked on the plush mattress flashed in my mind before I could stop them. A large free-standing bath sat in the middle of the room which only spurred on my filthy mind as excitement swirled through me at the thought of bathing in front of or better yet *with* Axel. He walked over and pulled back the voile curtains, opening the double glass doors behind them to reveal a balcony, which overlooked the picturesque lake. He stepped out and into the rays of light. I wished that I could take a photo of this God, illuminated by the sunshine, with the blue water behind, so I could save it in my mind forever - or better yet, make it my phone background!

He turned back to me as I was unpacking my belongings, trying desperately to rid my wicked mind of all the vulgar thoughts floating around in there. "I didn't know what colour tie you were wearing, but hope this is okay?" I held up a floaty, floral dress that I had worn to my aunt's wedding a couple of years back and prayed he wouldn't turn his nose up. I knew I should have texted him to ask!

"It's lovely Doll, but…" My heart was in my throat as I braced myself for the insult, "I got you something." He declared, fetching a box from a room I hadn't yet explored. "It was delivered here this morning."

"Oh, wow Axel, really you shouldn't have." I thanked, as he handed me the gift.

"I didn't want you embarrassing me." He joked, it was noticeable that there was no malice in his voice.

"God, you never stop the digs, do you?" I laughed, placing the item on the bed.

I lifted the lid to reveal white tissue paper. Cautiously I unwrapped the garment to find a stunning light blue silk dress.

"You'll look beautiful in it." His compliment dizzied me. I couldn't wrap my head around the fact that I was in America, with Axel and we were…friends? I daren't consider there was anything more at play here. I was merely an actor, who had signed a contract and was now fulfilling the agreement. But the way Axel looked at me and the way he made me feel, there was no mistaking I wasn't just playing a part anymore.

33

AXEL

My eyes snapped to the bathroom as Verity opened the door and stepped out. I felt my jaw drop. She was a vision. The blue material clung to every line and contour perfectly, my gaze followed the long slit up the side of one of her legs which stopped just above her knee. The halter neck, with a deep V, looked as though it was made for her, the sky-blue material draped over her effortlessly, complimenting her stunning ocean eyes. There was a thin ribbon of silk which she had wrapped around her neck, the end hanging over the curve of breast.

She looked completely different to usual but just as beautiful.

"Wow." I whispered, making eye contact with her. Her cheeks flushed red and she tucked a stray strand of hair that had escaped her up-do, behind her ear.

"What do you think?" She asked coyly

"You look phenomenal, Doll." I complimented, walking towards her. My hands buzzed with the need to touch her skin but I held back, unsure if that was crossing a line.

"You too, Ax." She smiled, picking up the matching blue tie off the bed and placing it around my neck. I watched as her hands looped the fabric into a knot and she chewed her lip in concentration. She was so close, the sweet scent of her perfume flooded my senses, I was sure she could hear my heart pounding in my chest.

Once finished, she looked up at me through her long dark lashes, still holding the end of the tie with only a few inches separating us. Her breathing shallowed, her pupils dilated and I knew she felt the same as I did. This was dangerous, we'd been here before but for some reason, tonight felt brand new. Her eyes darted to my lips and I leant my head down ever so slightly-

Knock knock!

"Come on man, gotta go!" A male voice, who I recognised as Jackson's best man, called through our door, breaking the tension. I checked my watch.

"He's right, we should go." I sighed gruffly, taking a step backwards, away from Verity. She blinked and turned away before I had the chance to fully gauge her expression.

"Let's do this." She agreed, picking up her clutch bag and walking past me to the door.

I couldn't make sense of the cocktail of emotions twisting in my stomach as I followed behind her.

The wedding took place at sunset, outside on the green, overlooking the water. The happy couple were silhouetted against the pinky, orange sky as they spoke their vows in front of friends and family. I didn't usually care for romance, but I had to admit that the ceremony moved me. Maybe it was the fact I'd been away from home for a while or maybe it was the girl on my arm, but I felt the weight of their vows heavier than any time before.

After the formalities had been completed, it was time for everyone to let their hair down. The champagne was popped and the mingling began. Verity had told me she was anxious to be introduced to so many of my family members at once, but watching her converse so easily with them all, she had no reason to be. She was pure sunshine as she charmed, chatted and giggled with the guests. I kept my hand on the small of her back whilst we did the rounds.

We sat with my mom and the rest of the bridal party for the duration of the four-course Michelin meal, seated around a large table, draped in a white cloth. The drinks continued to flow as my family members attempted to embarrass me with stories from my youth. Verity laughed along and demanded to see photographic evidence of some of the tales, which thankfully, did not exist.

"Cor, I'm stuffed!" Scarlett, my youngest cousin, sighed, patting her stomach appreciatively.

"Me too. That was incredible." Verity agreed. The two had been gossiping non-stop since they found their name cards next to each other for the meal. For moments of the chatter, I sat back and watched Verity in awe as she spoke, spellbound by her charisma. "I'm off to the ladies room." She said, placing her napkin on the table and standing up before excusing herself.

A minute after Verity had left, I noticed Scarlett and my mom sharing a mischievous look.

"What is it?" I asked disconcertedly, leaning back in my chair.

"I like her!" My mom stage whispered, excitedly.

"Me too, Aunt Jeanie!" Scarlett agreed, clasping her hands together. "Although that's not surprising, considering we must be about the same age." She moved into Verity's vacant seat, next to me, nudging me with her elbow.

"God, you make me sound ancient." I chuckled, ignoring their seal of approval. It was complicated enough acknowledging my own feelings towards Verity, let alone my families too!

"Poor girl looks like she's been cornered by boring Uncle Bob," Scarlett nodded towards her. "She'll be stuck there for hours!" She laughed, I followed her gaze to see Verity, looking glorious, deep in conversation.

"Looks like she's handling it well though, bless her." Mom responded. We all knew too well how mind numbing it was to be collared by Bob whilst he recited events from his week on the ranch.

"I better go and save her." I said, standing up from my chair, leaving the two of them to gossip behind my back, as I crossed the room to her.

"Ladies and gentlemen, if you can all please come to the dancefloor. The new Mr and Mrs Porter will be starting their first dance." The emcee declared to the room. I reached Verity and instinctively, took her hand, leading her to the front of the crowd.

As the music started and the newlyweds began to sway to the string quartet, Verity and I never released our grip of each other. I tried to focus on my cousin and his new wife, but I couldn't divert my attention away from the fire burning between us.

"All couples, please join."

Verity looked at me nervously, waiting for me to take the lead. "Come on then, you." I nodded towards the floor, now filled with pairs, arms around each other, moving in time with Jackson and Addison.

I wrapped my arms around Verity's waist and pulled her in close, as she put hers around my neck. We moved in silence as the music played.

"Having a nice evening, Doll?" I asked, getting lost in her sea-blue eyes.

She looked up at me smiling so sweetly I felt like my heart was going to burst. "Of course." She implored.

My gaze traced every feature of her beautiful face, her cheeks slightly pink, lips her usual shade of rouge and that adorable dimple. "Your family are lovely."

"They love you, Verity." I chuckled slightly. "I can see why." The words slipped out before I could stop them. The same spark of electricity that we had in the hotel room ignited again, her eyes flicked between mine and my lips. I pulled her closer towards me before ducking my head and whispering in her ear. "Let's get out of here."

I led Verity, hand in hand, away from the dance floor towards the grand doors. We stepped outside and the cool, coastal air hit us. Verity leant against the railing of the veranda, shivering slightly from the breeze. I took off my suit jacket and wrapped it around her shoulders, before standing beside her to take in the view.

"Wow, this place feels like a dream." She gushed, staring out at the moonlit water.

"Thank you for coming with me tonight." I leant on the wood beside her, my arm brushing hers slightly, goosebumps raising at the minimal contact.

"Well, free flight, free food and free accommodation. What girl would say no?" She laughed almost awkwardly, as if she was feeling the same shift in our relationship that I was.

Silence surrounded us for a few minutes, the only sound was the sea lapping against the shore and the whirlwind of thoughts speeding through my head.

Verity turned to look at me, the wind displacing the loose tendrils of hair framing her face. I stroked a curl behind her ear, causing her breath to hitch, my hand traced along her jawline until it reached her chin, pinching it between my thumb and finger and finally pulling her face towards me.

My lips brushed against hers, as we teetered on the brink before giving into the need. I kissed her hard, pouring every ounce of pent-up desire from the past twenty-four hours, hell the past month, into it. Her fingers found the hem of my collar keeping me close as our lips moved together.

"There you are, they're cutting the cake." Scarlett's voice called, "come on lovebirds, chop chop." Verity giggled as we broke the kiss, I held her for a few more seconds, as she beamed up at me before she followed my cousin back inside. I took a moment to resettle myself, running a hand through my hair as I released a deep breath.

I'd crossed the line and one thing was for certain, the situation had never been more complicated.

34

VERITY

It had gone twelve, when we decided to call it a night, leaving the bride and groom and their remaining guests, partying away on the dancefloor.

As I followed Axel back to our room, I tried to hide the spring in my step, I was unsure whether it was fuelled by the copious amounts of fizz I had drunk or the intoxicating kiss that I shared with Axel on the veranda, but I felt so light that I could have floated up the stairs.

We entered the room and I shut the door behind us, as Axel opened a bottle he had brought from the reception. "Want one?" He asked casually, as if he didn't reduce me to a giggling teenager this evening.

"Sure! Don't threaten me with a good time," I winked, confidence surging through me.

"You're a funny one, Verity." He laughed, shaking his head, pouring two glasses of expensive alcohol.

I skipped over to the dressing table, placing my clutch on the desk and slipping my heels off before facing the mirror. Removing the final hair clip, I opened my bag and took out my phone to check my notifications for the first time this evening. I spotted a message from Jacob from three hours prior.

> Don't listen to them babe. They're just jealous. We all know it's real! x

Confusion washed over me. What could he be referring to and what was so important about it that he would message at 2am UK time?

Curiosity got the better of me and I did something that I promised I would never do. I Googled myself.

News article after news article appeared, flashing headlines questioning the validity of Axel and I's relationship. Tears welled in my eyes as I clicked onto each link and couldn't help but scroll through the opinions of strangers.

They're never seen on normal days out, everything always looks so set up!

*Of course it's a stunt, why would Axel be with **her** out of choice?*

He must be getting a HUGE pay check to put up with Verity! She was so annoying in that interview!

"What's happened?" Axel asked, concern coating his words as he put a flute of champagne on the table in front of me.

I couldn't find my voice, instead I turned my phone screen towards him. "Oh, Verity. Why are you looking at those?" He asked, furrowing his brow.

"There's so many." I choked out a sob, scrolling through the hundreds of search results.

"Don't listen to them, they're just writing it for clicks." He waved a hand dismissively, "it's silly to pay any attention to them!" His blasé attitude along with the correct assumptions from complete strangers made me feel stupid. I stood up from the stool, anger burning through my veins.

"That's easy for you to say, you're not being torn apart." I cried out.

"They're vultures! Just ignore them." He grabbed me by the shoulders to steady me as I shook with anger and upset. I couldn't believe I'd let myself get so wrapped up in this made-up relationship, this facade that clearly everyone apart from me was able to see through.

"I don't even know why I'm crying, they're right aren't they, this isn't fucking real!"

His mouth met mine with intense urgency, erasing all thoughts of the salacious media, and the demons haunting my thoughts. I deepened the kiss instantly, needily pulling him closer.

"Does this feel fucking fake to you?!" He growled against my lips, I tangled my fingers in his hair, his tongue swept against my bottom lip and I granted him access. His hands explored every inch of my body, reaching towards the scarf of my dress and untying it, letting the fabric fall away from my breasts, before it slid down my body to reveal the lacy thong I was wearing. He stood back, admiring me with dark eyes. "Fuck, Doll, you drive me crazy." He whispered, his eyes following the contours of my body. He swept me into his arms, my mouth found his again as I wrapped my legs around his waist and he carried me over to the bed. He threw me onto the plush, feather duvet, breaking our kiss once again.

I watched with bated breath as he undid his tie and removed his cufflinks at an agonisingly slow speed. I whined desperately, the heat between my legs almost too much to bear. "You're soaking, Doll." It wasn't a question; his eyes were fixed on my dripping core. "I've been thinking about the taste of your sweet cunt all month." He licked his lips, unbuttoning his shirt before tossing it to a random corner of the room. I groaned at the filthy images in my head, I'd be lying if I said I hadn't spent many a night with my vibrator between my thighs dreaming about his tongue.

"Please, I need you so bad." I almost sobbed, he was now completely naked and the sight of him made my toes curl. He chuckled devilishly before crawling over me, kissing his way up my bare body, leaving a trail of goosebumps in his wake. He hovered over me, his dick agonisingly close to my centre.

"Axel, I need you inside of me." I begged, the head of his cock teasing my opening.

Before he responded, he laid down beside me and pulled me over and up, so that my pussy was above his mouth. "I told you; I've been dreaming of this." He purred against me, his breath ghosting over my folds. "Hold onto the headboard." He demanded, I submissively did as I was told as he dug in. A loud moan ripped through me as he licked and sucked with fervour.

"Fuck, Axel." I cried, my thighs trembling around his head as I tried not to lean my full weight on him. He made a frustrated sound at me before folding his arms over my legs, pulling me hard against his face. The familiar sensation of an approaching orgasm began to build in my lower abdomen, I looked down at the man below me. His eyes closed in pure ecstasy as he ate my pussy like a man starved. "Fuck, fuck, Ax-" He opened his eyes, watching as I came undone above him, as our gaze locked the wave of my climax cascaded over me in full force. My whole body trembled with pleasure; each swipe of his tongue was like a bolt of electricity. I doubled over, losing my grip on the headboard.

"Just as delicious as I remember." He complimented.

Before I had the chance to make sense of my surroundings Axel had lifted me back down his body. I locked eyes with him as he lowered me onto his hard cock. We moaned together at the sensation as I began to rock my hips against him, instinctively. "That's my good girl." He praised, spurring me on. He bucked up beneath me, hitting my g-spot with each stroke. My forehead was pressed against his, nose to nose, lips brushing with each thrust. This was more intense than anything I'd ever experienced, there was no doubt that this was real. "I missed this so bad." Axel breathed against me, I nodded in agreement, feeling too overcome with emotion to verbalise my thoughts. Just as I felt my second orgasm approaching, he sat up and I wrapped my legs around his waist, his cock sliding deeper inside of me. We began to move in time, Axel pumping into me slow and deep, as I clung onto his shoulders. He held my waist, guiding me along his dick, as waves of euphoria spread to every corner of my body. "I missed *you*, Doll." He groaned against my skin, his face buried into my neck as I hit the peak and felt his cock twitch.

"I missed you too, Axel." I cried out, throwing my head back in pleasure as I came. My vision blurred and I saw stars as he released inside me with a guttural groan.

After a moment, I slid off him and laid down on the covers to his side. Axel snaked an arm around me and pulled me close.

"What have you done to me, Verity?" His free hand ran through his hair as he exhaled, sweat beading on his forehead.

Laying on his chest, he traced circles along my back as we both came back down to Earth. I tried desperately to ignore the niggling feeling in the pit of my stomach that threatened to cloud my happiness tonight.

As my eyes shut from exhaustion, the events of the evening played on a loop in my mind and I fell asleep with a smile on my face.

35

AXEL

The morning sunlight streamed through the balcony doors, shining golden rays on Verity's porcelain skin. She looked like an angel, asleep on the pillows next to me.

I'd been awake for the past thirty minutes and was yet to force myself to start the day as I had no desire to leave Verity alone in this bed. I watched her sleeping soundly, a content smile on her face, as her chest rose and fell with each breath. I thought back to where we were four months ago compared to today and the tumultuous journey we had been on together. The confusion I had been feeling recently melted away completely last night. Stroking a hand along the contour of her face, a warm sensation spread across my chest.

A sleepy sound escaped Verity's lips as she stretched her body and her eyes flickered open.

"Morning Doll," I said softly, playing with one of her curls. She smiled sweetly, knocking me off guard with her beauty.

"Morning," she replied, her voice cracking slightly.

"How're you feeling?" I asked, thinking back to her watery eyes as she read countless callous news articles about us, last night.

"Pretty damn great, to be honest." She smirked, chuckling to herself.

I couldn't help but join in her laughter, "good to hear it, but I meant the stories."

She sobered slightly. "Ahh yeah, it sucks but like you said, it's all clickbait so trying to let it wash over me."

"Yeah, they're just jealous anyway, who wouldn't be?" I winked, flexing my bicep sarcastically. Verity rolled her eyes, slapping my arm and giggling. I pulled her to me and hugged her close.

Verity's hand fell on to my chest and began tracing along the lines of my tattoos.

"These are so intricate," She spoke, moving her finger along my inked abs. "Do they mean anything?" She asked, referring to the large black vines along my torso. Nestled in the plethora of mixed leaves were unique pieces that had been added over the years.

"They're my different projects. Although I do love collecting memorabilia from my favourite films, I'm not one to take from my own sets." I advised, "instead, I've been adding to this over the years, each addition is a reminder or a memento of that time."

"They're beautiful," she complimented, her blue eyes scanning me appreciatively, "what's this one for?" Verity asked, pointing to the mountain peak on my left pec.

"It's for *The Quiet Reverie*. That's what I was working on when *Accidentally* started and why I had to do everything virtually to begin with."

"Ah yeah, it was set in the Appalachians, wasn't it?" She exclaimed, her excitement over my previous movies made me metaphorically puff my chest with pride.

"Correct, but an insider secret, it was actually filmed in Canada!" I confessed, giving her a peek behind the curtain.

"That's so interesting." She gushed. It was a joy to discuss the trivia with her. I was so used to people only caring about being seen with me or leeching off my status, rather than having genuine appreciation and interest for my work.

Her hand travelled up towards my shoulder, stopping on my collarbone. "Let me see, this is from *Confession*." She correctly guessed, pointing at the detailed flip lighter used in the scene when my character set another alight.

"Wow, you're quite the Axel Ford connoisseur." I chuckled.

She blushed slightly before defending herself. "Don't have to be a mega fan to have seen a few of your movies, Ax." I wasn't usually a nickname guy, but I'd grown fond of the way it fell from her lips. "There was one point I couldn't go to the cinema without you popping up on screen." She rolled her eyes, giggling slightly.

"Fair point." I smirked, watching as she followed the lines once again before pointing to the holly on my bicep.

"And what's this? Big Christmas fan?"

"No, Verity." I laughed. "It's my mom's birth flower."

She smiled sweetly at me. "The connection you two have is lovely."

"Yeah, she's dealt with a lot and always put me first." I shrugged, "I wouldn't be where I am now without her sacrifices." I looked down at my favourite tattoo feeling thankful for the woman who raised me.

A moment of silence passed between us. Verity, shuffled up the bed into a sitting position, pulling the duvet around her torso to cover her bare breasts. I joined her, leaning against the headboard.

"So, what now?" Verity spoke, breaking the tension. It was obvious she was talking about our relationship going forward and not just what we should have for breakfast.

"Now," I turned to face her head on, to assess her reaction, "we drive back to Manhattan and I take you out on a real date." Her ocean-blue eyes widened for a split second, "why do you look so surprised?" I laughed, bewildered by her expression.

"I was not expecting that! I thought I'd be lucky to get any small talk out of you let alone a whole day together," she joked.

"Point taken. I guess I haven't been the most chivalrous." I held my hands up in mock surrender.

"You can say that again, Big Shot." She threw me a look and without thinking I clasped her face and brought her lips to mine. It felt so natural to be with her like this.

She hummed against me before breaking the kiss. "Mm, I like *this* Axel." She whispered.

"Come on, you, we should get on the road." I chuckled.

"Alright." She yawned, stretching before she stood up. The sheet fell off her body and I couldn't stop my eyes trailing down her perfect frame, fuck I wanted her. "Oi, stop looking at me like that if you want us to get going!" She scolded, I noticed the way she clenched her thighs together slightly as I stared at her hungrily.

"Sorry, Doll." I winked. She turned away and I leant forward spanking her ass, causing her to squeal.

****

I unlocked the door to the penthouse and let Verity into my home. The drive back from the wedding had been surreal, as she read and I drove, much like any other time we travelled together, but this time it all felt completely different.

I watched as Verity explored my place, trying to gauge her reaction. Much like my London apartment, the furniture was neutral and the decor was minimal with the odd piece of film merch dotted around for the film fanatic in me.

"What is it with you and amazing views?!" Verity exclaimed, gesturing to the cityscape beyond the wall of floor-to-ceiling windows. "You can literally see every tourist spot in NYC from here!" She leant against the glass looking adorable as she gawked at my hometown.

"There's the Empire State! And the One World Trade Center!" She pointed at the buildings I'd seen hundreds of times.

"Quite the little tourist aren't you!" I laughed.

"You have got to be shitting me, look at your view of the park!" She gestured wildly, moving to the other side of the room, looking out towards the never-ending view of Central Park ahead of us. Walking up behind her and wrapping my arms around her waist, I rested my head on her shoulder and followed her eye line.

"Point to where you want to go then, Doll." I whispered. "We'll grab lunch on the way." She circled her finger on the window highlighting an area near Bethesda Terrace. "Sure." I kissed her neck before releasing my grip.

On the walk to the famous fountain, I took Verity into my favourite bakery, ordering us two salt beef bagels and sodas. We meandered through the park, stopping occasionally for Verity to take pictures of the various locations that she remembered from movies or the odd fan photo when I was recognised.

"Well, if the acting falls through, I could always find a backup career in photography after the number of pictures I've taken of you and different girls today!" She laughed, with no hint of jealousy as we continued our journey.

"You should think yourself lucky, Verity," I slung an arm over her shoulder. "Getting to hang out with your celeb crush all day."

She glared at me, knowing exactly what I was referring to. "I hoped you wouldn't bring that up." She groaned, her cheeks tinting red with embarrassment.

"Ahh, it's cute!" I ruffled her hair; I couldn't deny the pride I'd felt when her mother let her obsession with *Sunset High* slip. "I've been waiting to bring it up if I'm honest." I chuckled as her blush deepened.

"I was more of a Chase girl." She bluffed, shrugging me off. Chase being the other heartthrob of the show.

"Ouch." I clutched my heart in feigned heartbreak causing her to giggle. "It's just down here." I pointed to the set of stairs, cascading from the pavement.

The terrace was surprisingly quiet for a Sunday, but I was thankful for the minimal tourists as we began to walk down to the fountain.

"Stop there and pose!" Verity called, taking out her phone and snapping a picture of me. "You look fit."

"Are you *sure* you're a Chase girl?" I teased, taking her hand and leading her to a patch of grass to the side of the staircase, in the shade which overlooked the fountain and lake.

We sat down and unwrapped the food before chowing down on the delicious meat filled sandwiches.

"Who would have thought back in January, we would be here now, enjoying a bagel together, not trying to kill each other!" Verity mused, nudging me slightly.

"Who said I didn't bring you out here to murder you?" I raised an eyebrow.

"In Central Park in the middle of the day? You're not a very bright murderer." She laughed.

"Maybe that's all a part of my plan. Lure you into a false sense of security."

"I've never been afraid of you Axel, irritated by you for sure but never scared." She shrugged her shoulders slightly. Her statement, although said in jest, rang true. One of the pitfalls of being in my position was how people always saw the star power and not the man. Verity had never been intimidated by my status, I used to think she was timid and a pushover and despite the grief I gave her, she never put up with my bullshit, always questioned when I did something she didn't agree with, when I had been rude on purpose or dismissive towards her. She didn't let me walk all over her like others may have, but until recently, I'd failed to see how strong she was. "It's so beautiful here, I can see why you call New York home." Verity said, breaking me out of my thoughts.

"Well, I don't know if it will always be my home." I shrugged.

"Are you thinking of staying in London after the film's done?" She asked, her voice apprehensive yet hopeful.

"If there's a reason to." I locked eyes with her, trying to convey how I was feeling without scaring her off. I took her hand in mine.

She leant forward and pressed her mouth to mine in a gentle kiss which was unlike any we had previously shared. The way her lips felt told me everything I needed to know.

The noise of a camera shutter triggering broke us apart. I spotted the paparazzi hiding in the bush a few metres away. *For fuck's sake.* I felt the urge to fiercely protect this new part of my life, which was ironic given the fact this all began with the hope of ending up on a front page.

I no longer wanted to parade Verity to the masses, instead I wanted to keep her all to myself and prevent anything from going wrong.

36

VERITY

After the most mesmerising forty-eight hours in New York, Axel and I had touched back down on UK soil last night, to carry out some post-production commitments that we had, now that the editing of the film was well underway.

I felt just like a popstar when I stood in the recording booth, staring out at the sound producers as I recited lines over and over, changing the intonation and expression on each go. It took everything in me not to break out into song and do a poor Ariana Grande impression, but I thought better of it - I was tone deaf and didn't want to give the engineers migraines from my awful attempts at whistle tones!

"Thanks Verity, can we just try that one, one more time please? It's the closing voiceover of the whole film so wanna make sure we've cracked it!" Tom, the Head Producer, spoke through my headphones.

"Sure thing, Tom." I gave him a thumbs up through the glass and cleared my throat ready to speak the monologue once again, in my best rom-com voice. "So, there we were. Two strangers who had become something more. Who met in a tiny hole in the wall, where coffee smelt like hopeful mornings and the air was thick with the aroma of sugary cakes. A man on a mission to find the best Americano and a woman who just needed someone to notice her. It was unexpected yet undeniable. Despite the odds, we found ourselves here, in the place where we first collided, accidentally in love."

"Woo that's it! Thanks Verity, I think we've got all the extra soundbites we need from you - you're free!" Tom clapped his hands together, whilst the other Engineer, Jim, entered the room and began setting up for Axel's turn in the booth.

I spotted Axel through the window, taking a bite of a pastry that the studio had provided. I couldn't stop the butterflies from fluttering furiously in my stomach as I watched his movements. He looked up, catching me staring doe-eyed, before flashing a signature movie star smile which nearly knocked me over.

Shuffling quickly out of the sound-proofed room, I made my way back over to the hunk.

"Good job, Doll!" He complimented, wrapping his arm around my shoulders.

"A compliment from Axel Ford? Never thought I'd live to see the day." I winked, stealing a bite of the croissant.

"Hey, I think you're great at lots of things, some on camera and many more in the privacy of my apartment." He leant in and whispered the end of the sentence in my ear, those damn butterflies journeyed downwards, and I wished we were alone.

"Hey Axel man, you're up!" Tom called over to us in the corner, before putting his headphones back on.

"Gotta go, don't miss me too much." He smirked, brushing his lips over mine as he passed by, leaving my dumbfounded and insanely horny.

I sat down on the black leather sofa behind Tom and his assistant and watched like a love-sick puppy, as Axel delivered his lines with ultimate perfection. During one of the breaks, whilst Axel had a drink and read over some new sections of the script, Tom and Jim turned their focus to music.

"Much luck hunting down any up-and-comers Jimmy?" Tom asked with hopeful eyes.

"Unfortunately not, every demo I've heard just isn't quite cutting the mustard." Jimmy sighed, exhausted. "Who'd have thought it would have been so difficult to find an edgy, undiscovered band for our title song?"

A lightbulb went off in my brain!

"Tom, Jim, sorry to butt in and for the eavesdropping but I may be able to help you!" I sat up on the couch, eagerly.

The two men looked at me with confusion and raised eyebrows.

"My friend runs this amazing music blog, Under the Radar, where she promotes and reviews loads of bands that have gigs in London. I'm sure you will have probably ticked a lot of them off your list already but may be worth a deep dive! I can put you in contact with her if that would help?"

Jim and Tom looked at each other, as if communicating telepathically before Tom turned back to me.

"Do you know what, what the hell, it can't put us in a worse position! What are her details?"

"Really?! That's awesome, she'll be so pleased. Her name's Amelia Sani, she uploads to www.undertheradar.com and @undertheradar on Insta. Pass me your phone and I'll put in her number." I replied animatedly, taking the device as it was handed to me, this could be such a huge opportunity for her to get her foot in the door within the music industry! I quickly typed in the digits and gave it back to Tom, whilst Jim appeared to already be scrolling through her Instagram page.

"Anyone you'd recommend?" Jim asked as he flicked through the pictures.

"Oh God, I'm no music buff but I am biassed. My best friend's brothers in a band." I leant over and clicked on the photo of Theo and his bandmates rocking out on a stage, at one of the gig's Amelia attended. "That's them!"

"The Velvet Echoes, cool name." Jim complimented, "Captivating and raw, The Velvet Echoes are a dreamy concoction of alternative rock and indie vibes, the atmosphere created by their music is both exciting and emotive." He read the quote aloud.

"That sounds like exactly what we're looking for. Thanks so much Verity, we'll be in touch with Amelia and see what she has to say." Tom held out his hand to shake, before opening the blog on his computer and having a read. "I'll be right back, mate." He said to Jim and disappeared into the hallway, phone to his ear.

"Guys, we doing this?" Axel called through the speakers, confusion in his eyes at what was taking so long.

"Sorry about the delay Axel, but your girlfriend may have just answered our prayers out here."

"Okaaaay then, I hope that isn't as weird as it sounds…" I shot him a dirty look. Of course he would take that to mean something filthy. He winked from inside the booth.

"Just music stuff!" I called through the mic.

"Jesus, don't trust her, she has awful taste." He said with a smile. I flashed him my middle finger through the glass in response. "Ready to go?"

"For sure, let's crack this." Jim agreed, turning the record light to red as Tom re-entered the room. He smiled warmly at me as he retook his seat and turned his attention back to Axel and the dials in front of him.

My phone buzzed in my pocket.

My heart swelled at Amelia's message. We'd really grown close over the near-on year of knowing each other through Lilah and I was overjoyed to be helping her in any way that I could. She was a boss bitch at anything she turned her hand to but I knew marketing was just a means to an end for her. Her true passion was music and sharing her opinions on undiscovered talent, in the hope that she would be able to support bands being signed or to grow their fanbase. This opportunity could really set her on the way to achieving that at a higher level.

After an hour or so, Axel completed his obligations, signalling the end of our *Accidentally in Love* chapter. We thanked the crew and walked out of the studio building. When we reached the street, he turned to me.

"Well, that's it then. It's all up to the director and editors now!" Axel announced, rubbing the tops of my arms with his hands.

"I can't believe it's done. I'll miss being on set." I admitted sadly, thinking back over the past few months and how quickly working on my first lead film had gone.

"I won't miss Tyler's clothes that's for sure!" Axel grumbled. When I didn't laugh at his joke, he pulled me in for an all-encompassing hug. "I will miss working with you though." He kissed my hair.

"You know this isn't goodbye right?" I responded. Half to him and half to convince myself.

"Of course, but we'll both be busy on new projects soon and I won't get to annoy you every day on set." He rested his chin on the top of my head and I melted into his chest, inhaling his woody scent.

"Well, you'll be booked and busy, Axel, it's yet to be determined for me." I responded, fully aware of my rookie status in comparison to his mega stardom!

"Nonsense, that's what the agreement was drawn up for."

The mention of the contract made me feel sick. Our relationship was only committed to last until after the first week of film release. With the editing underway and the premiere in November, I couldn't ignore the ticking clock ringing in my head, which had six months left. Axel said himself that whatever was going on between us was no longer fake and that these feelings were real. But with how complicated our relationship had been - and continued to be - it was scary to let myself believe the contract was now redundant.

"What's the matter?" Axel asked with genuine concern, unwrapping himself from me when I had failed to respond to his words.

"I guess I know that you won't be obliged to miss me at some point in the near future." I said, sounding more pathetic than I had intended, looking down and picking at my nails.

"Hey, look at me." Axel implored. When I didn't immediately obey, he lifted my chin with two fingers forcing me to stare into his ash-coloured eyes. "Fuck November, Verity. I'm not going anywhere." He kissed me with such passion it conveyed a thousand words. "Let's go get lunch to celebrate, Doll." He took my hand and led me down the street to a destination unknown.

At that moment, I decided to trust Axel fully and rip up the contract in my brain. If he was all in, then so was I and a silly bit of paper wasn't going to ruin that.

37

AXEL

The next few months flew by in a whirlwind, since saying goodbye to Tyler and Rosie, Verity and I had grown closer than ever. With all this new free time it was the perfect opportunity to give Verity a much-needed education in good cinema.

Though Verity protested we came to an agreement that we would alternate choices each date night. At first it was picking off a carefully curated list I'd written up but eventually she'd negotiated her way into adding her own frivolous options. More often than not, to my dismay, these were musicals.

If you'd have asked me at the beginning of filming how many I'd been subjected to, the answer would have been two, the obligatory *Grease* and *Mamma Mia*, forced upon me by my mom. And if you asked me now…it would be fifteen (and counting) which was far too many in my opinion.

"So, what is today?" I sighed, flopping onto the couch, unfortunately for me the rota said it was Verity's turn.

"*Hamilton*!" She sing-songed, doing jazz hands in the direction of the TV. I wanted to roll my eyes but she was so adorable I wrapped my arm around her shoulder instead, pulling her to my side.

"I can't say no to this can I?" I laughed as she clicked play.

"Are you sure you haven't seen this?" She asked, raising an eyebrow.

"Huh?"

"Stay tuned for act two!" She winked. I let the joke fly over my head.

So began the next three hours of solely music and choreographed dances, I noticed I was watching Verity just as much as the screen as she laughed at the jokes, gasped at the twists and cried at the tragedy as if it was her first time watching, but the way she mouthed every single line told me she'd seen this far too many times already.

"What did you think?" She asked, looking at me expectantly.

"Hmm," I thought over my answer. I'd never admit it out loud in fear that she'd surprise me with tickets to the West End, but I quite enjoyed it. "That one was slightly more bearable, I suppose." Verity clapped her hands together, her face lighting up like a kid on Christmas.

"I knew you'd be a Hamil-fan!" She gushed.

"A what?!"

She ruffled my hair, "don't worry, your secret's safe with me." She shot me a wink.

"Well, you'll be a Ringer before you know it."

"Excuse me?!" She exploded.

"A Lord of the Rings fan, duh."

"Oh, that sounded really filthy." She giggled, blushing slightly.

"Honestly, Doll, you and your dirty mind." I shook my head, laughing at her.

Despite the poor entertainment choices, nights like these with Verity were my favourite. No prying eyes, no paparazzi, just us in the privacy of my own home, getting to know each other.

"Can I ask you a serious question?" Verity blinked up at me, from across the table at our newly found favourite London restaurant. Another pastime we had acquired was touring little known food spots to find the hidden gems, but from the back of the restaurants these days to avoid the press.

"Anything." I answered immediately. She chewed on her lip slightly, seeming uncharacteristically shy, I reached for her hand across the table, stroking reassuring circles on the back.

"Am I your first?" She asked, coyly.

"Are you asking if I was a virgin before you, Verity?" I laughed, half amused, half concerned.

"Don't be stupid, obviously not." She giggled, "I meant your first stunt relationship."

"Of course you are." I said simply, taken aback slightly.

"Hmm." She mused, sounding pleasantly surprised by my answer.

"You seem shocked by that?"

"Well, it just seemed to come so naturally to you." She shrugged, taking a sip of her red wine before continuing, "and I've seen stories of you with previous co-stars before."

It seemed my fuckboy persona hadn't been lost on her, I'd never been ashamed of my public appearance until now and the realisation that I was potentially muddying Verity's image caused a sinking feeling in my stomach.

"Verity, do you not think I'm capable of getting a *real* girlfriend?" I teased, I hoped she couldn't see through my blasé facade, an unusual, uncomfortable pain in my chest twisted like a knife.

She rolled her eyes, a smile pulling at her perfect lips. "Of course not but I'm extremely jealous of any woman that's got to be with you." She half joked, a sadness in her voice.

"Don't worry, Doll, none of them come close to you." I raised our clasped hands and pressed a kiss to hers, her 'jealous' words reassuring me but the concern still waivered below the surface.

A further side effect of having plenty of spare time was that I had developed an unhealthy obsession with checking my emails for any update on the Gus

Kensington blockbuster. As of my fifth time of refreshing today there was still radio silence.

As the weeks passed with no answer, I started to accept the possibility that the role had passed me by. I wasn't a newbie in this industry, I knew every job wasn't guaranteed but this was the first time I'd sacrificed job satisfaction and my integrity as an actor in the hope of being cast. If I'd have known *Accidentally in Love* would have been nothing more than a blemish on my filmography, rather than a step towards my end goal, I'd have never accepted it in the first place.

But as I lay here now with Verity snuggled up against me, I found it difficult to regret the decision I'd made last year. I turned off the bedside lamp, pulled her closer and breathed in her sweet scent, silencing the negative voices.

38

VERITY

"I got it, I got it, I got it!" I ran into Axel's apartment hurriedly, throwing my bag and keys on the kitchen island where he was cooking dinner.

"The Christmas one?" He asked excitedly, wiping his hands on a tea towel. I nodded enthusiastically, vibrating with happiness. "That's incredible, come here you!" He praised, picking me up and spinning me around before pressing a kiss to my lips.

"Couldn't have done it without you helping me run lines!" I gushed, he lifted me onto the kitchen counter, positioning himself between my thighs.

"Of course you could, Doll. I always had faith in you." He began kissing my jaw, his lips trailing down my neck to my collar bone. A breathy giggle escaped me as I melted into his touch.

"I'm just going to jump in the shower and then I'll tell you all about it," I said, trying to keep my breathing under control. "Or maybe we can resume this afterwards." I laughed as he nipped my earlobe before pulling away. I forced myself to hop off the counter and away from him although my body was screaming at me to jump his bones.

I basically skipped to the bathroom, overjoyed with the news that I had received on my way home. I had been getting nervous after wrapping *Accidentally in Love*, as the phone didn't appear to ring quite as often as my agent and I had hoped it would. However, a few weeks ago, an independent British-made Christmas film, being marketed as a *Love Actually* inspired movie, came knocking and as of today, I was their new leading lady! My agent assured me I had achieved this on talent alone but I couldn't deny the feeling that my connection to the movie star currently cooking me Bolognese, may have had something to do with it.

I undressed in the bedroom, throwing my clothes onto the chair in the corner. A cat's cry startled me as the items fell on Misto curled up on the seat. Mistoffelees had joined me in the apartment around a month ago, after a lot of cajoling on Axel's part. The time that I spent in my own apartment had dwindled since filming ended as we regularly chose to fill our free time with each other's company. Eventually, he wore me down and convinced me that it made more sense for Misto to move here, then for me to keep commuting across the city to see and feed my furry friend every day. However, I was still getting used to his new fave spots to have a snooze in.

"Sorry buddy!" I apologised, stroking his head before I walked into the bathroom and turned the shower on.

After five long months, the night before the premiere for *Accidentally in Love* had arrived. I was so nervous I could be sick but as I approached the location from Axel's instructions, for our surprise date night, the anxiety melted away.

I was led into screen three by a staff member at the cinema, where Axel met me in an empty room. He was dressed impeccably in a black suit and had styled his usually unruly curls. He looked insane!

This was one of those cinemas where the seats were plush, velvet sofas rather than the flip down chairs. On the table to the left side, Axel had set up a bottle of champagne with two glasses and on the right-side table, sat two large boxes of popcorn.

"God, what film are we watching? It's not done well on ticket sales!" I nudged him in the ribs playfully.

A killer grin spread across his face at my joke, sweeping me off my feet. He took my hand and pulled me towards him, before dipping me and capturing me in a passionate kiss. "Evening, Verity." He greeted, as he stood me back up right. I giggled, feeling like I had walked straight into a romance novel.

"Hello Axel, this is incredible, thank you." I smiled, as we took our seat on the couch. "But what are we watching?" I took a handful of the popcorn.

"Being the night before your first major film premiere, I thought you deserved a treat." Axel signalled to an unseen staff member. The lights went off and the film began to play. The title card of *'Cats: The Musical*, certificate PG, 1998' flashed onto the screen.

"Oh my God, it's my favourite! How did you know?" I gasped, grabbing his arm tightly.

"Mistoffelees." He snorted, "hardly a riddle to work out."

"Aw, that's why I-" *Fuck!* That was close. I caught myself before three little words rolled off my tongue. "-I think you're the best!"

He didn't respond, but wrapped an arm around me, pulling me in closer and placing a kiss on my head as the music began to play.

Two hours later and the musical concluded. I had used all my will power to avoid bursting out into song on various occasions. The film would have been hard enough for Axel to enjoy as it was, the last thing he needed was me wailing like a strangled cat in his ear.

"Well, what's the verdict?" I turned to face him.

"It was…a film." He grimaced slightly.

"I can't believe you actually sat through it and didn't fall asleep or go on your phone!" I laughed, "I loved it in case you wondered."

"I figured that might have been the case." He chuckled, "I wouldn't have subjected myself to that for just anyone, you know?" His smoky eyes bored into my own.

"Thanks." I whispered, butterflies fluttered in my stomach with anticipation of his next words.

"It's because I love you." He said simply. I felt my heart swell with the confession, my breath hitching.

"I love you too." I implored, tears threatening to spill from my eyes. I leant forward, pressing my lips against his in a sweet kiss that quickly dissolved into fiery passion. His hands found my hips, pulling on top of him, I buried my fingers in his hair, as I deepened the kiss.

"I love you so much." He breathed, kissing my neck. I felt like I could burst from his words alone, it was obvious we'd been falling for one another but for some reason I didn't expect Axel to say it so freely. He nibbled on a sensitive spot below my jaw, causing heat to pool between my legs. I ground against his hardening cock, the sensation driving me wild.

"Let me show you how much I love you." I purred in his ear, sliding off his lap and into the space in front of him.

"God, what did I ever do to deserve you, Doll?" Axel asked, watching me tie my hair up with a hairband from my wrist. I shuffled his suit trousers down his legs to free his raging erection, the head of his cock already glistening with pre-cum. I licked my lips hungrily before taking him into my mouth. Axel groaned loudly as I swirled my tongue and began bobbing my head.

"Fuuuuck." He moaned, I hummed around him, getting just as much pleasure out of this as he was. I looked up at him, fluttering my eyelashes innocently. "Jesus, Verity, you can't look at me like that and expect me not to bend you over this seat and fuck you until you can't take it anymore." He growled, wrapping his hand around my ponytail and pulling my mouth off him, a string of drool still connecting my lips to his erection. "Get up here." He demanded. I was too dick-drunk to protest, clambering to my feet before I had the chance to make another movement, Axel had somehow bent me over the back of the chair in front of us and ripped my tights, pulling my thong to one side as he slipped his cock into my wet pussy with ease. I moaned loudly at the feeling of being stretched open and imagining the filthy image we must be, fucking so openly in the cinema. The thought of someone walking in on us, only got me hotter!

He thrust into me brutally and I dug my nails into the velvet of the seat. I felt him tug my hair, pulling my body up against his own so his mouth was in line with my ear. "You're a fucking incredible woman, Verity." The sweetness of his words and roughness of his touch was a dizzying combination, my orgasm approached quickly, my thighs shaking as I struggled to stay upright. "That's it Babydoll, let me feel you come around my cock." My climax crashed over me, my legs buckled, my back arched and Axel had to hold me to prevent me from crumbling to the floor as I let out a guttural moan.

He pulled out of me before lowering me onto the soft material of our sofa and positioning himself in between my hips. He placed my legs on his shoulders. God, he looked insane towering over me like this, the dim cinema lights casting shadows across his chiselled face and his frame so broad I felt merciless to his power. He teased my pussy with the head of his cock and I whimpered pathetically.

"Please Ax." I begged.

"Please what?" He smirked, I whined, moving my hips in an attempt to gain any kind of friction. Seems even though he was in love with me he still loved to wind me up.

"Please, fuck me." I mewled, frustratedly. He chuckled at my desperation before plunging into me hard.

The angle of my legs meant his dick hit the deepest spots inside of me, each drive of his hips caused stars to multiply in my eyes. "God, you feel so good." I cried out, breathlessly. He turned to kiss my calf before reaching down towards my pulsating clit. I groaned at the sensation of him circling the bundle of nerves with his thumb and hitting my g-spot.

"You gonna be a good girl and come for me baby?" He asked. I nodded weakly letting my arousal hit its peak, I felt him quicken and my eyes fluttered closed as the ecstasy began to flow through me. "Look at me, Doll." He commanded.

I opened my eyes as instructed and watched the man in front of me come apart in time with my own orgasm. As the waves washed over us, we slumped onto the sofa, wrapped in each other's arms.

"That was a much better phrase to instigate sex than 'cookie'." I giggled, tracing the tattoo on his arm with my index finger.

I felt his chest rumble with a laugh as he stroked my hair and kissed the top of my head.

"I couldn't agree more, Doll."

39

VERITY/AXEL

VERITY

My hands shook with nerves as Axel and I settled into the black limo that was taking us to the premiere in the centre of London. I couldn't believe it when I saw my old driver Clive at the wheel. It felt full circle.

Axel looked like the quintessential movie star, in a full black tuxedo and shirt, the lapels were satin which matched his tie. He looked incredibly handsome, I still felt as though I was living in a fairytale, sitting beside him.

I slid across the seat to be closer to him and smoothed down my maroon dress. I was lucky enough for a top designer to have sent me the gorgeous outfit I was wearing. It was a full-length gown, with various layers along the skirt and thin straps at the top. I'd never felt so beautiful.

"No one's going to look at me tonight, Doll, everyone's going to be fixated on the gorgeous woman on my arm!" Axel complimented, lacing his fingers with my own and bringing my hand up to his mouth, placing a kiss there.

"Great, thanks, that's made me even more nervous now!" I half joked.

"I'll be with you all evening, you'll be fine." Axel reassured before leaning closer, "failing that, I'll relieve any tension when we get home." He purred in my ear, causing heat to rush between my legs and goosebumps to appear on the side of my neck. His hand travelled to my thigh, squeezing slightly and I tried to hide my physical reaction to such a simple touch.

The butterflies fluttered with arousal at the idea of us returning later, I didn't know how I was going to concentrate on the film with thoughts of Axel fucking me, clouding my mind. "Don't distract me!" I giggled, intertwining my fingers with his once again, removing his touch from the sensitive spot on my upper leg.

"Who did you invite in the end then?" He asked, rubbing a circle on my palm with his thumb.

"Just the usual lot; Lilah, Jake and Amelia. Oh and Theo and his band will be there too obviously." I replied. After putting Amelia and the sound producers in contact, they amazingly decided to employ The Velvet Echoes to record the title song of the movie's soundtrack!

"No family then?" He asked tentatively.

"I thought about it, but they can come to the next one…" I answered, becoming deep in thought. Charlotte had a three-week-old to look after, I wanted to ask my dad, but I couldn't without also inviting Mum and the last thing I wanted was her negativity ruining my big night.

My phone pinged. It was a message from Charlotte, Dominic and my baby niece, Zoe. The happy couple were beaming, whilst Zoe slept soundly.

Best of luck tonight, Aunty Verity and Uncle Axel, wish we could be there <3 xx

All unpleasant feelings melted away from the warmth of my sister and her new little family, not to mention the familial nickname she'd called my boyfriend.

The roar of the crowd lining the fences in Leicester Square, flooded my ears as Clive pulled up at the red carpet.

"It's showtime, Doll." Axel said, pressing a kiss to my cheek. Adrenaline surged through my body as the car door opened to the swathes of people and flashing cameras.

Axel and I stepped out of the vehicle, taking hands immediately as he began to lead me down the carpet. I heard various voices shouting our names trying to catch our attention to get the best shot. Axel slipped his arm around my waist and held me tightly.

"I'm right here, Doll." He whispered into my ear, clearly sensing my anxiety as the faceless humans clicked away.

After a few more minutes of smiling until my cheeks hurt, we were free from the glare of the lens' and onto meeting the fans of the book and upcoming film. I got to meet so many friendly people who were so excited to see our adaptation which helped to calm my nerves as we entered the cinema to see the final cut.

"Ah Verity Sloan! We love you!" I heard a group of familiar voices chant from the left side of the building. I turned to see the animated faces of my best friends.

"I'll be right back, Sarah's signalling me for a chat, I'll find you before we go in." Axel said, squeezing my arm before walking towards his agent.

"Can I get an autograph?" Jake joked, giving me the biggest hug as I reached the gang.

"You look amazing!" Lilah screamed, holding me at arm's length as she examined my outfit. "You have to let me borrow that dress!"

"I would but it's unfortunately just on loan for tonight!" I laughed.

"Ah heartbreaking!" She sighed, dropping her arms to her side.

"Oh come on Lils, as if Zane couldn't buy that for you anyway!" Jake ribbed, only to be met with a deadpan expression from Lilah, "love you!" He said, buttering her up.

I turned to Amelia and Theo who were accompanied by the remainder of the band, standing next to the lively duo.

"Congrats Verity!" Theo fist-bumped me.

"Congrats to you guys too, I can't wait to hear the song!" I returned the sentiment, clapping my hands together excitedly.

"Well, we wouldn't have had the chance if it wasn't for you and this scamp right here." Theo thanked, patting Amelia on her shoulder as she rolled her eyes jokingly. I was surprised that she hadn't flinched away from him, given her dislike of physical contact.

"Yeah congratulations, Verity, don't let this one steal your limelight tonight!" Amelia laughed.

"Soak up all the spotlight you want Theo, I'm not precious! I think it's nearly time to find our seats, you guys head in and I'll go find Axel, I want us to walk in together." I hugged and kissed my friends goodbye and walked in the direction that Axel had gone moments prior.

AXEL

"What's up Sarah? Can't this wait?" I asked my agent, with slight irritation, as we stopped in a quiet corner of the cinema lobby. I felt guilty for leaving Verity alone, though thankfully she had just found her friendship group.

"Well, I thought you'd want to hear the news as soon as possible?" She asked, dangling the carrot. My heart rate increased as I anticipated her next words.

"YOU GOT *REQUIEM*!" She announced, throwing her hands in the air in celebration. "I heard from Kensington's team last night but wanted to pass it on in person. Told ya I could get it!" She winked.

This was the most amazing news. I couldn't wait for the film to end and update Verity. As much as I wanted to run straight to her and tell her everything now, this was her first ever film premiere and I didn't want to take any of the enjoyment away from her with my news.

"Oh wow, that's great. Where is it filming? I'll have to let Verity know if I'll be away." I said thinking out loud.

"Verity?" Sarah turned her nose up. "Why would she still be in the picture? The contract ends next week."

"As far as I'm concerned the contract ended months ago." I confessed, revealing my true feelings. As much as Sarah thought she controlled every aspect of my life, I didn't owe her an explanation regarding how things had progressed with Verity.

"Axel, you can't be serious. I thought *she* was the newbie but here you are actually falling in love with your stunt girlfriend, it's laughable!" She responded snorting with amusement. I felt my blood boil at the lack of respect for the woman I loved.

"You don't know anything about our relationship," I growled, my fists tensed at my sides.

"Actually, I do. I curated the whole thing!" She chuckled, before taking a step closer to me and placing a hand on my chest, looking deep into my eyes, all traces of humour gone. I wanted to recoil at her touch but I stood my ground. "You've just gotten the role you've worked so hard to achieve, with the director who's been at the top of your list and you're going to let a silly little stunt distract you from that. Let's be real Axel, you'll break her heart, just like all the others. Why even bother stringing her along?"

I took a deep breath, I hated to admit it but she was right, I'd always been selfish and put my job before others. Why would being with Verity change that now? I could see how this would all end in tears. It might not be tomorrow, next week or even this year, but I would inevitably fail her.

"You can cut her loose now, she's dead weight, you got what you wanted." Sarah implored.

"Axel?" Verity's quiet voice sounded from behind me. "What's she talking about?" I turned to look at her, confusion twisting her perfect features, before I had the chance to answer, Sarah spoke for me.

"Axel booked a very prestigious role thanks to you and your fake little relationship." She sneered, "he needed his reputation sweetened up to land it and your annoyingly innocent persona fit the bill to achieve that, but he's done with you now and right on time for the contract expiry too - I honestly couldn't have planned it better if I'd tried!" Sarah concluded, looking awfully pleased with her scheming.

Every part of my body was screaming at me to step in, to tell Verity that she meant everything to me but the look on her face, the heartbreak that I had caused, left me silenced.

"So, you *were* getting something out of this arrangement then." Verity turned to look at me, tears falling from her ocean eyes. "You were using me from day one and played me for a fool." Her voice shook, each word cracking my heart.

"Ver-" I began before getting cut off again.

"Of course he was, you didn't actually think he would ever love a girl like you. You're a nobody." It was as if I could see physical stab wounds from Sarah's bitter words, I knew Verity never deserved any of this pain, our entire relationship was based on my egocentric decisions. I'd done exactly what everyone had assumed I would have, corrupted her innocence and shattered her happiness. I had to do the one selfless thing I could think of. I had to let her go.

Verity turned her attention back to me, ignoring Sarah. "You should win an Oscar for your performance." She choked on her tears, disbelief and anguish swirling in her eyes.

It killed me but it was over and there was no going back.

I braced myself before destroying her heart completely, "there's a reason I'm the most sought-after actor in Hollywood, Doll."

40

VERITY

It was like watching Dr Jekyll turn into Mr Hyde. The man I had fallen for and thought that I had known, was now a complete stranger in front of me.

I backed away from Axel dumbfounded and heartbroken, leaving him with his cackling sidekick and ran for the nearest exit. To my left, the cinema screen was packed full of celebrities, journalists and my best friends eagerly awaiting the showing of the film. I couldn't go in there, I couldn't lie and play happy families as I had once done, months before. To my right, the red carpet was still lined with fans and paparazzi who would ambush me with cameras and questions if I headed that way. I felt trapped and needed to get out.

I spotted the fire exit and prayed it led somewhere private, whilst I texted Clive to meet me. Thankfully, the door led to a private back alley, where the limo was ready and waiting.

"All ok, Miss Sloan? I wasn't expecting you for a couple of hours yet!" Clive asked, concerned, as I sat in the back and buckled my belt. "No Mr Ford?"

"I'm fine." I sniffled, still registering the events from the lobby. "No, just me."

"Very well, where are we going?" He asked tentatively, usually Clive knew to drop me at Axel's apartment but in his absence, he must have realised the reason for my tears.

"My apartment in Shoreditch, please." I asked. My heart broke further when I remembered Misto would not be waiting on the sofa for me, but I couldn't risk going back to Axel's and running into him. I would have to ask one of my friends to get him tomorrow for me.

I stared out of the window, watching the buildings pass by, Axel's words swirling in my head as I second guessed every interaction I had ever had with him. Every touch, every compliment, every expression of love, they were all nothing but lies. I was crippled with the pain of my broken heart, sobbing in the back of a car when I should have been revelling in the joy of watching my first film on the big screen.

I bid Clive goodbye and forced myself up the stairs and into my cold and lonely flat. I dragged my body into my bedroom and fell onto the covers, curling up into a ball as I let the sobs wrack my body. I stayed there until I succumbed to sleep.

An unknown length of time later, I was awoken by the sound of Lilah, Jake and Amelia tumbling into my room, startling me initially as I'd forgotten momentarily that Lilah had a key, in case I ever needed her to pop in for me.

"We were so worried!" Lilah breathed, hugging me tightly.

"What happened?" Amelia asked, sitting beside us on the bed.

"When Axel came in alone, we just knew something was wrong and had to find you." Jake concluded, joining them on my other side. The mention of Axel's name was like a branding iron to my heart and more tears fell.

"I don't really want to talk about it." I tried to smile weakly but I'm sure it looked more like a grimace.

"Of course, whenever you're ready, Verity." Amelia reassured.

"Come on, you can't sleep like this." Lilah gestured to my dress, "I'll get the shower going and help you take your makeup off." My friends coaxed me off my bed and into the running water. I got myself into my pyjamas, feeling hollow as I went through the motions.

"We'll stay here tonight, pet." Jacob assured me. "If there's anything you need just shout, we'll just be in the other room." I snuggled into my covers, barely able to thank them despite their genuine care. I didn't know what I did to deserve these people.

As the morning broke, I didn't want to open my eyes and realise that last night's events were real and not a nightmare but the reminder that my friends were bundled up in the living room gave me the boost I needed to get out of bed.

Walking out of my room, I found Jake curled up in a blanket on the sofa watching *The US Office* and Amelia in the kitchen, making coffee.

"Morning, did you manage to get much sleep?" Amelia said, pulling me in for a quick-yet-affectionate hug.

"I think I managed to get a bit, but I couldn't turn my brain off." I responded, rubbing my puffy eyes, sore from crying, "where's Lilah?" I looked around for my friend.

"She went to get Misto, she should be back any minute, she got up hours ago." Amelia informed me. I felt comforted in the fact she knew me well enough to know I would feel better with my furry friend back, but it also marked the end of this chapter with Axel. I would not be going back to the apartment that until yesterday, I had called our home and where I had imagined we would have celebrated the release of our movie and decorated for Christmas next month.

As if on cue, I heard the faint meow of my black and white cat, as he padded into the kitchen, unaware of my inner turmoil. I scooped him up and squeezed as the tears began to fall once again. "Thank you." I blubbed as Lilah appeared in the doorway.

"Axel's lucky I was unarmed when he opened the door or I would have stuck to my word and killed him." She said, venom coating her words. Lilah wasn't an aggressive person but she loved her friends fiercely and would do anything to protect and support them. I hadn't even needed to express the reason behind my upset for her to know exactly what was wrong and what I needed.

"Did you speak to him?" I asked weakly, digging to discover information about how he was doing this morning.

"If you call a grunt and a point, conversation, then yes and it was riveting. Fucking arsehole." Hearing how unbothered he was caused my heart to break all over again. *Of course he doesn't care, Verity, he never did.*

I took the mug of coffee that Amelia was holding out and nodded towards the sofa. "Come on then, I'll fill you all in."

Three of us squashed up on the couch, kicking Jacob off as he took one of the throw cushions and sat cross legged on the floor in front of us. They listened intensely as I recited last night's debacle and filled in Jake and Amelia on the conception of our relationship.

"So, he was using you from the start? And you thought it was real?" Jake questioned, trying to get his head around my mind-fuck of a situationship.

I sighed, "no, I was aware it was a stunt at first. I agreed to it…" I looked up sheepishly at my friends' confused expressions. "I know it was stupid; I'm an idiot for putting myself in this situation."

"No you're not! Don't say that!" Lilah reassured me. "It's not your fault he's clearly a sociopath." She muttered under her breath.

"So yeah, we started officially dating about six months ago, or that's what I thought. But I guess he just thought my acting wasn't good enough to make the world believe our love story. He needed me to *really* fall for him to seal this deal he and his agent were working on secretly." I barely got the last sentence out as fresh sobs clogged my throat.

"I'm so sorry, V." Jake apologised, pity in his eyes. It was clear my friends didn't know what to say but just having them here was more comfort than they could have imagined.

"Anyway, chuck me the remote, I just need a distraction." Jacob handed me the controller and I flicked to the first channel. As if God was laughing at me, a fucking *Accidentally in Love* trailer blessed my screen.

"You have got to be kidding me…" I groaned as the overly happy music of Theo's band, began blaring through the speakers, accompanied by compilations of my 'ex-boyfriend' and I. "At least the song sounds good."

"Let's turn this off." Lilah said, reaching for the device.

"No, leave it on." My morbid curiosity got the better of me. "I didn't get to see any of the film, so may as well watch this." I laughed sadly. Every clip sparked a new memory, I recognised every set and remembered the feelings between myself and Axel at each stage. Tears fell silently down my cheeks.

"*Accidentally in Love* with Axel Ford and introducing Verity Sloan, now in cinemas." The voiceover announced, my friends cheered at the mention of my name.

"Axel Fraud more like." Jake sneered. A surprise giggle escaped my lips.

"You can say that again." My voice cracked and

my friends bundled me into an unconditional hug. Although I couldn't see the light at the end of the tunnel right now, I knew if I was surrounded by people like these, eventually, I would be alright.

Twenty-four hours later, I finally managed to convince my friends that I was okay to be left on my own for a bit. As much as I wasn't over the breakup and what had happened at the premiere, I knew I needed some alone time to fully process everything.

I sauntered around my flat, noticing how bare a lot of the shelves and cabinets were, as I'd moved so many of my personal belongings into Axel's apartment over the past few months. My heart sank at the thought of having to face him to get it all back one day soon.

Making myself a drink, I leant on the kitchen island and released a deep sigh. "How did we get here, hey Misto?" I said to the cat, intertwining himself through my legs. I felt sad that it was over, I felt stupid that I had allowed myself to be fooled and I felt angry that he had the audacity to even do it in the first place.

My phone began to vibrate furiously in my pocket. I took it out to see who was calling. Mum. Bar Axel, she was next on the I-don't-want-to-hear-from list today. I hesitated before sliding the circle on screen to answer.

"Hello, Mum." I greeted flatly. "How can I help you?" I doubted she was checking in to see how the premiere went so her reason for calling was a mystery to me.

"Good morning, Verity. We are in the car, about

five minutes from your apartment. Just checking you're home? We saw some pictures of you online and your father insisted we travel across to check you were okay." Firstly, of course it was my dad who cared the most and secondly, they'd be about to arrive at Axel's!

"Stop!" I shouted.

"Verity Eleanor Sloan, that is no way to speak to your mother." She began scolding.

"I'm not there, come to this address." I butted in and recited my real location. I hung up knowing I only had fifteen minutes before their arrival, if I was lucky!

My mum's words rattled in my head. Pictures. Shit! Someone must have spotted me last night and uploaded the photos online. Whilst anticipating my uninvited guests' arrival, I searched my name on Google, only to be met with a flurry of images of me, fleeing the cinema, tears cascading down my face. Headlines with shitty puns such as, *'Verity gets the Axe: Is it all over for Hollywood's co-star couple?'* and *'Sloan Ranger: Verity spotted ditching her debut premiere in tears!'* littered the screen, all accompanied by delightful pictures that clearly showed my heartbreak evident by the tears and snot running down my face. At least my dress looked nice, I guess.

In no time at all, my parents were standing at the door of my shoddy flat, confusion on their faces as they took in the limited decor and damp patches.

"So glad to see you, Bug. I saw the photos and had to pop in to check on my youngest." My father pulled me in for a hug that I really needed.

"Thanks Dad, I'm fine really." I desperately tried

to hold in the tears, not wanting to show my true emotions, as he let me go.

"Where on Earth are we, Verity?" My mother questioned, silently judging the place as she walked around in a circle. Her voice was like nails on a chalkboard with how fragile I felt.

I knew I couldn't lie to them forever and that they would eventually find out that I didn't live in a multi-million-pound penthouse, overlooking Tower Bridge but fresh from a breakup - or perhaps a better term would be dismissal? - was the last moment I imagined coming clean.

"You might want to sit down for this." My dad obliged, taking a seat on my scruffy sofa. My mother gave it a quick glance, before remaining bolt upright as if she thought it was littered with fleas or worse, was second hand! "I've not been totally honest with you. Where you visited me before was Axel's apartment, not mine. I was too ashamed to bring you here, so he let me use his to avoid you having to find out about this place." A dagger stabbed in my gut as I recalled the kind act, he had done that day and considered it was probably just another step to manipulate me. "This is my real home. A slightly decaying, freezing cold, matchbox. Welcome." I held my hand out, gesturing to the lacklustre space around us.

The pair of them didn't say a word. I looked at the floorboards, anxiously, whilst I waited for one of them to say something. Anything!

A few moments later, my mum walked past me and reached the front door. "Verity, you never fail to disappoint me." She spat out before leaving. The slamming of the door made me flinch and it took everything in my power not to crumble into a heap of tears. I knew this would be her reaction but it didn't mean it hurt any less. I continued to stare at the floor, waiting for Dad to dutifully run after his wife.

A beat later, he rose from the seat. I daren't look up at him as he followed my mum's footsteps. However, to my surprise, instead of moving past, he stopped in front of me. Slowly, I raised my head to meet his eyeline.

"I'm sorry about your mum, you know what she's like. It's no excuse and I will talk to her I promise. But Verity, listen to me, you have nothing to feel ashamed of. You're a go-getter, look at you, your own London flat and a fancy movie under your belt!" The warmth of his words and the kind look in his eyes caused the floodgates to fly open and I broke down, inches from him. He held me tight as I shook silently in his arms, the emotions of the past two days coming to a head. "I just want to make sure you know that I love you, I'm so proud of you and the only thing I care about is that you're safe, well and happy and I can see that you're not quite feeling your best right now."

"Thanks," I choked out through guttural sobs. "We broke up, Dad."

"I know, Bug, I know." He said, stroking my hair in an attempt to soothe me. "The right man is out there and he will treat you like the princess you are. Until then, your old man will always be here to pick up the pieces and try to help put them back together again."

We stood there for what felt like a lifetime, until my howling had reduced to shaky breaths. "You should go, Dad. Mum will be waiting." I declared, breaking away from him. He half smiled as he headed for the exit, "and thanks for what you said."

"Anytime kiddo." He replied, shutting the door.

41

AXEL

It didn't truly register that it was over between me and
Verity, until I opened my apartment door to her friend,
Jake, carrying an empty cardboard box and wheeling
along a suitcase.

I looked around him, expecting to see Verity, but
the hallway was barren.

"If you're looking for my tiny blonde friend, she's
not here and she won't be coming. I'm on clear-out
duty." He said. My heart sank at the thought of never
seeing her again.

"You better come in then, I'll show you round." I
welcomed him unenthusiastically. It had been one week
since the premiere and although the breakup had been
my decision (and fault), I hadn't been able to bring
myself to separate Verity's belongings from my own.
Seeing her shampoo in the shower and her extra clothes

in the wardrobe allowed me to almost kid myself that she
would eventually be coming home.

We meandered in silence from room to room,
with me passing Jacob various objects that belonged to
Verity. Every item he placed in the box felt like he was
ripping out a piece of my soul.

We completed the rounds back in the living room
as I showed Jacob out of the door.

"Jacob?" I said, following him into the hallway.
He paused, turning back to face me. "Please just tell her
I'm sorry." My voice broke slightly on the last word,
echoing the crack in my chest.

Jacob's expression was unreadable as he balanced
the overflowing box on top of the suitcase. "How dare
you." He began, "you manipulated her, led her on, made
her fall in love with you and then broke her heart when
she wasn't worth anything to you anymore." He spat,
vitriol burning in his eyes, I felt my blood run cold.

"She's never been worthless. I ended things for
her own good. I would have eventually let her down
regardless." I said, telling Jacob what I'd told myself since
that night.

"Everything you do is selfish. *Your* feelings, *your*
gain, *your* perception. This isn't about you! Did you ever
stop to ask Verity what *she* wanted?" I was stunned to
silence, "all she's ever worked for is to be successful in
this industry and you threatened that with your stupid
proposition. Thank God it hasn't come out it was fake
otherwise she'd likely be ruined. But lucky for her, she'll
just be seen as another notch on Axel Ford's bedpost."

My stomach lurched uncomfortably at what the media would now surely say about Verity, they'd paint that I never cared about her at all and she'd have no reason not to believe it.

"Please Jacob, just pass on the message, I don't want her to think she mean anything to me." I begged, unable to defend what I had done.

"No, I won't. Just stop." He said simply, turning to pick up the box of Verity's things and grabbing the handle of the suitcase. "You'll be fine, you've reignited your player rep and got what you wanted at the end of it, I hope it was worth it." I watched as he walked down the hallway carrying the remaining tatters of my heart.

I shut the door behind me, looking around at my apartment, everything looked colder, greyer. There was no colour without Verity. Taking a seat on the sofa, avoiding Verity's usual corner, I stared at the black screen of the TV, unable to muster any energy to move. What the fuck had I done? I'd lied to the best person I'd ever known. I'd let her believe that every moment between us had been fake when that was far from the truth. She made me feel things I didn't think were possible, she made me better, whole. And I'd pushed her away at the end when I should have explained everything and begged for her forgiveness. My chest was hollow as I thought about how Verity must have felt the night of her first premiere, leaving alone whilst I sat and relived our relationship on screen.

Each scene that played felt like a gut punch, I was barely watching, instead replaying the image of Verity's eyes welling up when I stamped all over her happiness.

I dropped my head into my hands, not realising I was crying until my palms became wet with tears. I let the agony of my heartbreak consume me, my sobs becoming violent.

Jacob was right, this had been a selfish decision when I thought it was the opposite. I had been protecting *myself*, scared of how *I* would feel if *she* had ever decided to leave *me*. I was a coward, the least I could do now was let her move on with a better man.

A couple of weeks later and the hole left from Verity's absence was still apparent. I had stopped going out with my friends, preferring to stay in and continue through the list of films that she had recommended, in an attempt to fill the crater in my chest.

However, today, I had no choice but to leave. I was meeting Gus Kensington in a local coffee shop to discuss *Requiem*, which was due to begin filming in Scotland, after Christmas. The irony of drinking an Americano and eating a cinnamon swirl was not lost on me, as I recalled the scene that Verity struggled to get through.

"Thank you for making time in your busy schedule to meet with me, Mr Kensington." I acknowledged, taking a sip of the caffeine.

"No problem always got time for my actors, especially my lead. What did you want to discuss?" Gus responded, I'd heard rumours of how friendly of a director he was and he was certainly living up to the notion.

"Firstly, I wanted to thank you for waiting for me to get my act together and ultimately, offering me the role. It's been a dream of mine to work with you, I've always been inspired by your art." I gushed, trying to conceal my admiration for my hero sitting across the table.

"Aw thanks chief, you're a brilliant actor, I'm glad we've found the perfect project to work on together." He returned the compliment, his words of encouragement making what I was about to say more difficult.

"That's the thing I can no longer accept." I confessed.

"I'm confused?" Gus raised an eyebrow, leaning back on his chair.

"I hurt someone incredibly important to me to get this and I can't, in good conscience, continue with it. I'm incredibly sorry to let you down last minute, this decision has not come easily." I analysed Gus' reaction to the news but he was difficult to read. "I'll cover any financial damages caused by this. My Agent, Holly, will be in touch to arrange the compensation."

"Holly? I thought it was Sarah who'd been badgering me for months?"

"I wasn't expecting to see you today, Axel?" Sarah said as I walked into the London office of the agency unannounced.

"I won't be staying long." I assured, taking a seat in front of her desk. The small room was panelled with various posters of films that I had worked on, thanks to her efforts.

"To what do I owe this pleasure then?" She smiled. I took a deep breath preparing myself for the inevitable argument this was going to cause.

"I'm afraid I think it's time we part ways; I appreciate everything you have done for my career over the years and I think you're great at what you do but I don't think we are compatible anymore." Sarah's face puckered at my words.

"Axel, you can't be serious. I've just scored you the biggest job of your career." I could tell she was trying not to raise her voice.

"I know, but I'm not happy." I stated, simply.

"We aren't in this for happiness Axel, you're in this for success." She spat, condescension coating her words.

*"But I **was** happy." I sighed, half to myself.*

"Oh, here we go, this is about that stupid kid, isn't it!" She laughed bitterly. I tensed my jaw, sitting back and letting her rip me apart. "You really are too easy to manipulate Axel, I dangle the girl in front of you and you ruin your career over it. In all the years I've worked with you I never knew you to be so pathetic." She crossed her arms over her chest.

"This is precisely why this has to end." I sighed. "I used to be like you, only in this for the money and the fame but it was miserable, Sarah. I want more than that out of life."

"I'm no longer represented by Sarah Mackie." I confirmed, matter of factly.

"I have to say, this is devastating news, it's going to be difficult to find someone as good as you," he paused, taking a sip of his drink, "but you gotta do what you gotta do for love. She must be very special," he smiled warmly, shooting me a wink. "You shouldn't let that go."

42

VERITY

I wish I could say the month after my first film release had been a positive one. Although the reviews had come back well from the critics and the book fans seemed to be satisfied with our portrayal of their beloved characters, I couldn't bring myself to feel proud of any of it without feeling the whiplash of reciting Axel's parting words in my head.

I hated him for what he did, how he used me without concern and ruined every memory. Yet, at the same time, I couldn't hate him completely. I missed our nights critiquing films, feeling his body against mine in bed and the way he made my heart skip a beat whenever he smiled in my direction.

But that was gone and it was never real. At least not to him.

From the photos I'd seen online of Axel wandering the streets with some pretty blonde woman, he had already moved on. As much as seeing the images felt like a knife to my already shattered heart I just hoped for her sake, she was aware of every clause in the contract.

The only thing getting me out of bed right now, was my new role in my upcoming film, *The Twelve Dates of Christmas Eve*. I found myself in yet another romantic comedy but this time, with a much larger cast. The story followed twelve different festive dates on the 24th of December that spanned singles, long term couples and friendships all celebrating the holiday.

We meet my character, April, as she's heading to an evening at the pub with her childhood sweetheart, Nathan and their friendship group. However, as the evening unfolds, she discovers her boyfriend is cheating on her with one of their close friends and it all comes to a head. I was hoping my fresh heartbreak would help me get into the emotion of the character.

When we all met at the table read a couple of weeks ago, I was anxious given the initial hostility I had received from my co-star on *Accidentally in Love* but meeting Niall, who played Nathan, he was the complete opposite and now a week into filming, I knew that if I fluffed a line or forgot a direction, he would not make me feel stupid for it.

He was warm, friendly and encouraging, an all-round delight to work with in comparison to the rude, arrogant and condescending Axel. But for some reason, I found myself missing the fire. I cursed my brain for feeling this way, this was what had gotten me into this mess with Axel in the first place.

Everything about being on set reminded me of him, even things as insignificant as the sound of the clapperboard or the greasy food at craft services. His ghost was everywhere.

Now, as I was arriving to set at the start of the second week, I was hoping it would be a happy Monday. I stepped out of the car and rounded the corner, only to be met with what I first mistook as a mirage leaning against the iron gate.

Axel looked at me with a half-smile and I stopped still in my tracks. He walked towards me, meeting me where I was frozen.

"Axel-" I started.

"Sorry for the ambush, but I needed to speak to you." He said sheepishly, sliding his hands into his pockets.

"You have my number." I shrugged, trying to fake nonchalance though my heart was ripping at the seams.

"I assumed you'd blocked me." He stated.

"And yet you didn't try." I began walking past him, knowing I needed to escape this conversation if I wanted to keep my emotions at bay. Before I made it to the gate, I felt Axel's hand grasp my wrist, trapping me in place. Fire burnt at his touch. I yanked my arm away, glaring up at him as his smoky eyes bored into mine. "Don't touch me."

"Sorry," he held his hands up in surrender, looking at me as if I were an animal he was trying not to frighten off. "Please, don't walk away. Let me explain."

"You've had five weeks to explain and all I've had is radio silence."

"I thought it was for your own good that I left you alone." His voice sounded different, almost sincere but I'd learnt not to believe a word this man said.

"You've been assuming a lot lately." I snapped back, checking my watch. "If you'll excuse me, I need to go to set. Goodbye, Axel."

"Verity, please." He begged as I began walking away, refusing to look behind me in fear I'd crumble.

Trust Axel to come here and make it all about him.

43

AXEL

Like the crazy stalker I was, I checked the email on my phone to re-read the call sheet information for *The Twelve Dates of Christmas Eve*. One of the benefits of being me was being able to blag my way into receiving information that probably should have stayed classified for security reasons. Mainly to stop obsessive fans of the stellar cast, lining the gates to get a glimpse. The irony wasn't lost on me that I had now become one of those people.

Checking the time on my phone, Verity was due to arrive within the next five or ten minutes.

As if on cue, I glanced up from my screen just as she approached, the golden December light streaming behind her, casting a radiant glow through her blonde hair, like a halo.

In her usual fashion, she walked towards the gate without acknowledging my existence or the coffee cup in my hand. Since the first time I had met her here, hadn't quite gone to plan, I decided going forward I would bring her favourite coffee order as a way to hopefully break the ice and allow me to explain my side of things. This was the third time I had waited since then and I was certain it would be the third time I would be completely ignored - but I had a different plan this morning.

"Morning again," I greeted, she rolled her eyes but all I could focus on was how stunning she looked, bundled up in an oversized coat and knitted scarf. "Another oat milk latte with a shot of pistachio for you." I offered. I'd never actually seen her drink coffee in all the days we had spent together but I had remembered the conversation we had had on the first day of set. At the time I had found it overwhelmingly boring, but I'd have given anything for her to be yammering on at me now.

As expected, she continued to disregard my gift and beeped her card to enter. "Oh and Verity, I got a synonym swirl too." She stopped in her tracks before whipping her head round to shoot me a look. I braced myself, ready for the inevitable backlash. To my surprise she snatched the bag out of my hand, without a word and disappeared into the studio. "Same time tomorrow then, Doll!" I called after her. So, still no verbal communication but that was progress, nonetheless.

I continued this routine for the next few days until the Christmas break. Never receiving more than a piercing look and the odd acceptance of a pastry but I was determined to crack this shell. Though, every morning she went into work and left me in the cold.

There was a time when we would have arrived at the studio together and spent our evenings at home, wrapped up in one another. I felt like a fool for not appreciating those moments more. I should have been more present and acknowledged my feelings sooner, to have soaked the goodness out of every second since January, but instead my selfishness and ignorance left me waiting outside on the street, like a homeless dog. Yet, those few precious minutes every morning, when I saw her on her way into set, temporarily mended my heart only to be shattered again when she closed the gate behind her.

Ordinarily, I would have travelled back home to New York for Christmas and New Year, no matter where I had been in the world. It was always the one time of the year that I would see my family regardless of how busy I was especially as Mom's birthday fell on the 30th too, but this year, I had more important affairs to attend to.

I settled onto my sofa, ready to turn on some shitty Christmas film in a bid to feel more festive, seeing as though it was the 23rd of December, when my phone rang.

"What's up Scar?" I greeted my cousin.

"Hey, Axel, just wanted to check in since we won't be seeing you over Christmas." She explained, growing up as an only child, I grew close to my two cousins on my mom's side, Scarlett and Jackson. This marked the first holiday season in near enough thirty years that I wouldn't be spending with them.

"Yeah, sorry about that," I rubbed the back of my neck feeling slightly guilty for deprioritising my family. "There's just something I need to do in London."

"Yeah, I was going to talk to you about that actually." Scarlett began, her usually bubbly voice coated with a serious tone. "Why are you hanging around Verity's new work like a loser?"

"Why do you think?" I asked blankly. I forgotten that paparazzi would have been documenting my stalker activities for all the world to see.

"Yeah, I know *who* it's for, I asked *why*."

"Cos I need her to know I'm sorry." I coughed trying to hide the emotion in my voice, although I knew it was pointless when talking to Scarlett.

"Totally and you should be begging on your fucking knees for forgiveness after losing her."

"How did you know it was my fault?" I asked, confident that she didn't know the full truth behind our breakup.

"No offence, but it's always your fault." I could practically hear her eyes rolling.

"None taken." *If only you knew.* It was much worse than she could ever imagine. We sat in silence for a moment, my mind whirring with the memory of hurting Verity. "I don't know what to do, I just need her back, Scar." Silent tears rolled down my cheek as I pictured Verity's perfect doll-like face.

"You're Axel fucking Ford, you can do this. She needs grand gestures, not a glorified fangirl," she implored, "so pull yourself together and prove to her how much she means to you."

Snippets of our time together, the good times, the laughs, the passion and the heartbreak ran at lightning speed in my head. Finally, I allowed my emotions to consume me.

"She's the best thing that's ever happened to me." I sobbed, my body shaking with anguish.

"I know," Scarlett responded sympathetically, "get her back."

44

VERITY

I opened my eyes, awoken by the sound of my niece screaming her head off in the room next door. Although this was not my idea of an ideal wake-up call, it was nice not to be the only one crying for once.

I had been staying at my sister Charlotte's house for the past two days, to lend a hand in the pre-Christmas rush and be settled in for the festive period. Plus, it wasn't awful to have some company. Especially when a third of that company was a squishy baby.

Rolling out of bed, I changed into a fresh set of pyjamas - my uniform at the moment - and traipsed downstairs to get some breakfast.

"Morning Dom, long night?" I asked, grabbing myself a bowl from the cupboard and reaching for the cereal.

"Hey, yeah Zoe's dealing with colic and not feeding well on Charlotte right now. Poor thing." He rubbed a hand over his tired eyes.

"Bless her, she's lucky her dads a doctor!" I laughed, sitting down at the breakfast bar before shovelling in a mouthful of cornflakes.

"Ha, most days that is a blessing but my expertise runs out in the milk department unfortunately." He laughed, offering me a cup of coffee. "Feeling festive?" He pointed to my gaudy Christmas pyjamas.

"Just call me Buddy the Elf." I said sarcastically. Whatever the total opposite of Christmas cheer was, was how I felt currently. He chuckled slightly, taking a sip from the Rudolph mug he was holding. "What time are my parents due to arrive?" This was the first time I would be seeing them both since my mum walked out of my apartment. I had spoken to Dad now and again via text message but was yet to discuss matters with Mum.

My sister walking into the kitchen, carrying her babbling daughter, brought me back into the present.

"Around 5pm." He offered me a kind smile, fully aware of the situation. I nodded in reply. As Charlotte reached him, he wrapped his arm around her shoulder and placed a kiss on the side of her head.

"Morning Angel." He whispered to her.

"Morning," Charlotte yawned, "Can you take her for a minute please?"

"I'll have her!" I interjected, holding my hands out for Zoe, nothing soothed the heart like baby cuddles.

She smiled a gummy grin as I bounced her softly on my knee. Warmth filling my chest for the first time in a while. I could tell Charlotte was looking at me but holding something back. "Spit it out," I chuckled, giving my sister the go ahead to speak her mind.

"I really don't want to be that person and usually I wouldn't care, but with Mum and Dad coming over, you might want to actually get dressed today." She looked awkward at giving me an instruction, the bossy Mum trait was obviously not passed down to her.

"Yeah, I was going to, just give me a bit longer with this one and then I'll force myself into a shower." I pleaded. Charlotte was right, I'd been living in comfies since the premiere but that wasn't going to fly with my mother and I didn't need to add any more fuel to that fire.

A few hours later, I was dressed in clothes without a stretchy waistband and had washed and styled my hair. Fixing a red bow to my ponytail for ultimate Christmas vibes.

"Look you match!" Charlotte said to me, holding up Zoe like Simba to show me her matching ribbon that was tied into her surprisingly thick head of hair for a two-month-old.

"Aww twins!" I gave her a soft kiss on her forehead and squeezed her cheeks, before taking a seat.

The doorbell rang not too long after I had settled in the chair. As Dominic stood to let my parents in, Charlotte shot me an encouraging look. *Let's do this.*

Mum and Dad walked into the room. Dad immediately approached, wrapping me into a warm hug. "Merry Christmas, Bug." He said as he embraced me. "You look well. How's the film going?"

"Merry Christmas, Dad. Yeah, good thanks, everyone's lovely." I smiled, trying to hide the hurt I was still very much feeling.

"There are some very famous people in it, I saw online. That must be exciting!" He beamed proudly at me and it made me want to break down in tears.

"Yeah, nerve wracking too but no egos just yet which is encouraging." I laughed slightly, trying to ease the emotion in my chest.

"That's great to hear." He held me at arm's length, giving my elbows a squeeze before letting me go.

"There's my little princess." My mother's shrill voice filled the room. Before greeting Charlotte, she swept Zoe out of her arms and began rocking her. "What's this silly thing Mummy has put in your hair?" She said in a sing-songy voice, subtly making a dig at my sister. Charlotte and I locked eyes as I could tell she was trying her best not to bite our Mum's head off. *Not worth it*, I communicated telepathically. It was funny to see that since Zoe's birth, Charlotte was no longer the apple of my mother's eye. I also made a mental note, not to turn my back to her so she wouldn't spot my hair bow either.

"Zo-bow!" My dad exclaimed. "You're matching Bug!" *Cover blown, thanks Dad.*

The five (and a half) of us sat on the plush sofas in Dominic and Charlotte's large living room making small talk whilst we waited for dinner to be ready.

I managed to stay hidden in the corner for the next forty-five minutes and my mother made no attempt to include me in the conversation, which I was glad of.

"Oh, that'll be the alarm going off. The party food is ready. I'll be back in a second, just going to dish it all up." Charlotte announced to the room, as the distant sound of an alert tone rang from the kitchen.

"I'll come and help darling." My dad offered, heading out with my sister.

"I think Zoe has just made herself empty for dinner." Dominic joked, taking a sniff of his daughter's behind. "I'll get her changed quickly." I watched in horror as each of my family members left the room one by one, leaving me trapped with Mum.

"So, how are things?" I asked, breaking the silence, playing with my nails uncomfortably.

"Wonderful." She replied, matter of factly, "good to see you have pulled yourself together since the last time I saw you." I tensed my jaw, unable to respond to her callous attitude. Unsurprisingly, my mother didn't have the common decency to check up on her clearly heartbroken daughter. "Have you spoken to Axel recently? How's he doing?" She pried.

"Of course you care more about Axel's feelings than mine!" I blurted, unable to keep up appearances any longer. "I bet you think it was my fault it ended too. Well for your information, Axel broke *my* heart!" My voice wobbled but I managed to keep my tears at bay.

"Don't say I didn't warn you." She laughed bitterly.

"I don't need you to rub it in my face, is it too much to ask for a mother to check in on their child?!" I countered, feeling the rage begin to boil in my veins.

"You're an adult Verity, time to act like one. I'm not going to pick up the pieces here." She said, "this is classic Verity, expecting other people to fight her battles for her." She tutted and I saw red.

"When have you ever? Everything I've earned, I've done on my own, with only negative comments and digs from you. You can't take any credit for my successes." I stood up from my seat, spotting that the remaining members of the family were now huddled in the doorway, awkwardly, unsure whether to step in or stay quiet. My mother opened her mouth to speak before slamming it shut again, resembling a goldfish. All my life, people had told me I needed to stand up for myself and it was time I finally did it to my biggest oppressor. "You constantly treat everyone around you as if they are worthless unless they fit exactly into the specific box you have for them! I'm done with being pushed around and made to feel small."

I walked towards the door, unable to look at my mother for another second as the anger burned off me.

"If you leave this house, Verity, don't expect to hear from me again." She spoke sternly, not a hint of emotion in her voice.

"Until you apologise and start treating me like an actual human being I don't want you in my life." I left the room, my family parting slightly to allow me space.

"I'm so sorry," Charlotte said quietly as I passed by them to get to the front door.

"I'm sorry too." I responded, giving a quick kiss to my baby niece as I headed up the stairs to quickly pack my belongings.

"Text me later." She implored. I nodded with a half-smile. I reached the top of the stairs and heard muffled voices of Charlotte and my dad discussing what had just happened with my mum but couldn't make out what they were saying.

Quickly, I bundled back downstairs and threw on my coat, grabbing my keys from my side table.

Slamming the door on my family, I headed out into the cold December night, got into my car and drove to Lilah and Zane's to spend Christmas in a more welcoming environment.

45

VERITY

"Happy Birthday!"

My friends all sang in my tiny kitchen, reminiscent of my previous birthday when I first moved into the apartment. It was weird to think just how much of a roller coaster my life had been on, since I last blew out these candles.

"Twenty-eight is going to be your year, babe!" Jacob declared, clinking my glass of bubbles with his. "I can feel it."

"I bloody hope so after the disaster last year was." I sighed.

"Don't say that. Sure, you met a stupid arsehole boy but look what you achieved. You moved to London on your own, filmed your first ever hit movie and booked a second! That's amazing, you should be so proud of yourself!" Lilah reassured, giving me a squeeze.

"Thanks, Lils." I melted into her touch. "So anyway, how were all your Christmases?" I asked, remembering this was the first time we had all been together since the festive period.

"It was nice. I spent it with my mum and dad, unfortunately Josh couldn't make it last minute, but I'm learning not to set my expectations too high with him." She shrugged, taking a sip of her prosecco.

"Girl, you need to cut him loose. He's dead weight." Jake exclaimed, finally not holding his tongue and saying what all of us had been thinking in regard to Amelia and Josh's on-off relationship.

"He's a busy guy. I can't get too annoyed with him having the drive to succeed." She waved her hand brushing him off, although I could see in her face that his words rang true.

"He day trades Mils, he's hardly Alan Sugar." He rolled his eyes, not hiding his disdain for her boyfriend.

"Okay, okay that's enough, Amelia's a smart girl, she doesn't need a lecture from you today." Lilah interjected.

"It's no problem, it's why I love you Jake, you just enjoy the sound of your own voice, don't you?" She winked. If she had been upset by the comment, it didn't show. "As you've got so much to say, what did you do last week?"

"Chilled one with Mum, Noah popped round in the evening with a special gift." He smirked.

"If it's to do with his penis, we don't need to know!" I joked.

"Or *your* penis for that matter!" Lilah butted in, laughing.

"Calm down ladies, it's not dick related. Although the sex afterwards was pretty great." He giggled, "he gave me a key to his apartment!"

The three of us girls squealed - well Lilah and I did, Amelia had a much better handle over her excitement, ever the poised woman! Instead, she smiled widely and clapped for our bestie.

"That's amazing!"

"How exciting!"

"Congratulations Jacob." We chorused.

"Yeah it's pretty fab but enough about me, what did you two get up to?" He said with fake modesty.

"You're so demure, Jake. Mine was amazing thanks, given our special guest!" Lilah said, turning to me. "It was so fab having you to stay V."

"Thanks again, Lils."

"It was my pleasure. Zane and Theo can be so boring when they're together doing boy-stuff!" She laughed.

"Ahh yeah Theo mentioned you joined them." Amelia said nonchalantly. The three of us turned to look at her with confusion.

"I didn't realise you two were so close?" I asked, surprised.

"Yeah, we're friends, ever since you mentioned my blog to the sound guys, we've connected." She shrugged.

"Oooh! A replacement for Josh!" Jacob exclaimed, clapping his hands together. I looked at him gobsmacked that he went there.

"Oh God, the thought of you with my brother, I would feel awful for you." Lilah chuckled sarcastically.

"Whoa-whoa-whoa, I have a boyfriend remember and I'm not even interested in him like that. We both just like music and get on. Simple as."

"Damn, I see you two as very different people, to be honest!" I mused.

Knock knock knock!

"I'll get it!" Lilah said, heading to my front door. "What are you doing here? You can fuck right off."

At Lilah's fighting talk, I looked towards the entrance already dreading who I was about to see. As expected, Axel stood in the doorway, I felt the colour drain from my cheeks and my heart beat increased.

"How did you even get in the building? You don't still have a key do you?!" Lilah shouted.

"The door was open." I heard him reply, I walked over to the pair.

I touched Lilah's arm when I reached her, in fear she was going to hit him. She'd never been violent to anyone before, but the look in her eye indicated anything was possible, "I'll handle this, Lils." She backed away cautiously, like she was scared to leave me. I put a hand on the door, taking Lilah's place.

I'd never seen him like this; he had deep purple bags under his eyes, his stubble was longer than usual and his hair was dishevelled from fingers running through it.

"What do you want?" I demanded looking into his smoky bloodshot eyes.

"Happy birthday." He greeted, with less confidence than he had exuded at the gates of the studio.

"Cut to the chase, Axel." I said sternly, unable to deal with his bullshit today.

"Words can't express how sorry I am for hurting you."

"I've heard this all before," I interrupted, feeling the urge to slam the door in his face.

"Please let me finish," he begged, I raised my eyebrows for him to continue. "I was stupid for what I said at the premiere. It wasn't true. It *was* real to me. All of it. I was scared to open myself up fully when Sarah told me the news. You were right, I was gaining something from our arrangement. At first, I thought it was just the prospect of booking the movie role, but I was actually gaining something far greater." He reached out towards me, I flinched away, crossing my arms over my chest, he dropped his hands in defeat.

"But why was the film a secret? I just don't understand." My voice broke, emotion clogging my throat.

"I foolishly trusted Sarah's judgment on that one." I rolled my eyes. "I know, I know, she's gone. She no longer represents me and I turned down the Kensington role." His eyes shone with unshed tears as he drivelled on.

"Great, so it was all for nothing then. It was all in vain," I laughed, bitterly.

"I couldn't, not in good conscience."

"I've seen you've already moved on too. You must have a thing for blondes."

"What?" He interrupted me, pausing for a moment, as if wracking his brain, "that's my new agent. There's no one else."

A whisper of relief washed over me before I felt the usual rage bubble up inside me again, I was sick and fucking tired of people walking all over me. "You propositioned me, used me and threw me out when I no longer served your agenda. How dare you come here and apologise. Do you even realize how stupid you made me feel, Axel? Do you have any idea how much you took advantage of me? I was new to this industry, something you never let me forget. You belittled me, you manipulated me." I counted on my fingers, "all for your own selfish gain! And now, you expect me to believe a single word that comes out of your mouth? For all I know, this is just another one of your pathetic publicity stunts!" He blinked back at me, dumbfounded by my outburst. "You always told me to stand up for myself. So here I am. Leave me the fuck alone Axel." I went to slam the door in his face, but his foot stopped me.

"Verity, I'm so sorry." Tears fell from his eyes. I fought the urge to comfort him, seeing him so upset caused my heart to splinter, but I held strong. "Please, take this." He held out a box I hadn't noticed, towards me.

I wanted to ignore his request but curiosity got the better of me. "What's this?" I asked, unbothered.

"It's a birthday gift, please just take it." He pleaded. Tentatively I took the gift. And slammed the door in his face.

Just as the devastation started to set in, I heard the chorus of a round of applause from behind me.

"Yes V!" Jake called, "you sure put him in his place."

"I'm very proud of you." Amelia praised.

"Lucky you stepped in, cos I was close to decking him." Lilah threatened.

"Thanks, I guess!" I said, with a poor attempt at laughter. I'd never been so thankful to have my friends by my side.

"What's in the box?" Jake asked, tapping a seat on the sofa next to him.

"Don't be nosy!" Amelia smacked him on the arm.

"It's fine. I wouldn't want to open it alone anyway." I sat beside him. Amelia and Lilah joined us as I cautiously unwrapped the box.

"Cookies?" Jake questioned, bemused as to why a multi-millionaire actor had given me baked goods instead of Cartier for my birthday.

"Prick." I muttered under my breath. "Inside joke of sorts." I told my friends when I was met with their curious eyes.

"There's a card too." Lilah said, untapping it from the side of the box and handing it to me. I opened the envelope and slid out a card with '28' emblazoned on the front with a red balloon.

Doll, you deserve to live your dreams. A. x

I looked back inside the envelope and found a ticket to the Oscars ceremony in March.

"Oh my fucking God." Jake shrieked.

"Don't get too excited, I'm obviously not going." I burst his bubble. There is no way that I would be travelling to LA, alone, in close proximity with Axel. No matter how much I had dreamed of attending.

"Verity, be for real. I'm furious at Axel but bleed him dry! You don't have to see him and hey you might meet another fit actor to heal your heartbreak." Lilah winked.

She was right in a way. I'd been dreaming of the Oscars since I was a little girl but the last thing on my mind right now was another man.

"I'll think about it."

The next morning when I arrived to set, I braced myself, expecting to see Axel standing by the gate, in his usual spot, which he had taken to occupying for the past week before the Christmas break.

Each day, I stepped out of the car, filled with dread that he would be waiting. However, as I rounded the corner today, his spot was unusually empty.

I shouldn't have expected him to be there after our run in last night and the bollocking that I gave him. Yet, seeing his post vacant, left a surprisingly odd feeling in my chest, one that I couldn't quite comprehend - or shake for the remainder of the day.

46

AXEL

Fastening the cufflinks of my pitch-black shirt, I took a look in the mirror and straightened my red tie.

I'd been nominated for many awards in the past, including several Oscars. Yet, nervous energy flowed through my body as I imagined walking into the building alone and praying for a glimpse of the real prize. Verity.

I hadn't spoken to her since her birthday and thought better than to keep badgering her at work so I kept my distance. Each day where I didn't see her was total agony. I honestly had no idea if she would be arriving or not tonight.

Although, I had to remind myself that even if she did show, it wasn't necessarily because she had forgiven me.

I pulled my blazer and my broken heart together and headed to the waiting car.

I flicked through good luck messages from Scarlett, Jackson and my mom but I couldn't get the blonde English woman off my mind.

Stepping out of the vehicle and onto the red carpet, the noise from the crowd was deafening. The LA sun beat down on all the celebrities, dressed in their best, as queues of A-listers waited to have their photo taken by the waiting paparazzi. I obliged, having a few nonplussed snaps, signed a few autographs, posed for some selfies with fans and made small talk with the industry elite. All the while keeping an eye out for Verity.

With every step closer to the Dolby Theatre, my heart weighed heavy as I resigned myself to the fact that she wasn't coming. I was naive to think that after everything she'd willingly accept my invitation.

"Axel, how are you?" A familiar voice asked. I turned around to see Gus Kensington and his wife greeting me.

"Gus, Sylvia, great to see you." I kissed her on the cheek and shook his hand. "Congratulations on your Best Director nomination, I'll be shocked if you don't win!"

"That's very kind of you. Congrats to you also. *The Quiet Reverie* was *my* film of the year and your performance was awe-inspiring." He gushed, referencing the indie film which won me the nomination.

"That means a lot, thank you." I acknowledged, truthfully.

"He's still devastated you can't join his latest project, Axel." Sylvia interjected, placing a hand on Gus' chest.

"There'll be another opportunity, I'm sure." Gus responded before I had a chance to.

"I hope so." A genuine smile pulled at my lips for the first time in months. "I'm going to head in and grab a drink before the show starts. Best of luck once again. See you later to celebrate hopefully!"

"You too, Axel." We parted ways and I headed through the throngs of people, into the auditorium. My heart almost stopped when I spotted Verity, radiating effortless beauty from the sixth row. With a renewed sense of confidence, I walked to my seat which was located on the end of the second row. I had requested that Verity's seat be separate from mine, so she wouldn't feel uncomfortable sitting next to me, if she decided to come. Although sitting on the opposite side, four rows ahead, as I tried to fight every fibre of my being from turning around to gawk at her, I selfishly regretted the distance between us.

47

VERITY

I'd made a stupid mistake; I was sure of it. Sitting here now, alone, surrounded by A-listers I didn't know. I couldn't have felt more out of place.

I had spent the past two months going back and forth on my decision to attend. On one hand, I didn't want to accept Axel's invitation and would have happily stayed on the opposite side of the world to him but on the other hand, I had always wanted to come to the Oscars. Admittedly I had hoped it wouldn't have been as a plus one to my lying fake ex-boyfriend, but here I was, in an elaborate red floor-length gown with lipstick to match, putting on a show as I had become so accustomed to doing.

My agent thought it could double as a networking event but as I stared around the room at the celebrities I had watched on screen for years, I was in no right mind to strike up spontaneous conversation.

That's when I saw *him*.

I hated to admit it, but he looked incredible. Black was certainly his colour. Although he was groomed and more preened than he looked in my doorway, the same gloominess that had surrounded him was still present. As he walked further into the room, the confident man I had met last year seemed more reserved and introverted. I couldn't help but notice he had arrived alone, which caused unsolicited butterflies to begin fluttering. However, as he took a seat on the opposite side, any stupid thoughts of civil conversation between us vanished.

I forced myself to look ahead, not daring to glance in his direction for fear that he would be looking at me. Or worse. He wouldn't be.

The show began and I did my best to stay in the moment and soak every second in as each award ticked past. Eventually, the award for Best Supporting Actor in a Drama was called. My ears inadvertently pricked up as they ran through the nominees, knowing Axel was already on the list. My heart pounded in my chest. Why was I nervous for him? Why did I want him to win?

I waited with bated breath as the announcer opened the gold envelope. The room fell silent.

"And the winner is," he read the white card, "Axel Ford for *The Quiet Reverie*." Raucous applause exploded in the room and before I was aware, I was on my feet, joining the celebrations. I paused for a moment, catching myself. Despite how it ended, I truly was proud of him.

I watched as various members of his team hugged and congratulated him until he broke away and looked directly at me. For a split second, the crowd disappeared, and it was just us. I flashed a shy smile, still unsure of my feelings towards him.

Axel made his way to the stage as the cheering continued only stopping once he reached the podium.

"Wow, thank you so much." He began, a solemn smile spread across his face. I retook my seat, stars in my eyes as I watched the man I once knew on stage. "I don't quite know where to begin. This isn't the speech I was planning on giving if I was to win tonight, but seeing someone in the crowd has inspired me."

My heart jumped to my throat, as the onlookers listened intently.

"Firstly, I want to thank everyone on *Reverie*, it was a joy to work on and something I'll always be proud of. You all know who you are." He nodded his head in the direction of the cast and crew, who cheered once again. "People always ask me what my plan is for the future. If you'd asked me over a year ago, I would have told you I would only be making more indie dramas and never stepping into anything new. That mindset would have prevented one of the best years of my life from occurring."

My mouth dried. "If you were to ask me now what my plan would be, I would say, I will only be following my heart and not my ego. As doing the opposite hurts the people I love most." His smoky gaze bored into me. I was frozen, unable to react or look away, as the tears welled in my eyes. "From now on, I'll be doing everything in my power to mend any bridges I have burned. So just know, my career might be quieter, and you might not see me on this stage for a while," the crowd chuckled in response to Axel, "but I'm chasing happiness." A small sob escaped my lips and I clasped my hand over my mouth trying to conceal my emotion.

Instrumental music began to play, subtly encouraging Axel to leave the stage. "They're playing me off now, so better wrap up. To conclude, thanks to the Academy, thanks to my team. See you all soon." As Axel finished his speech, an overwhelming desire to get out of here coursed through me. This was all too much.

I apologised to the guests as I stumbled over bags and legs to make my exit.

48

AXEL

If I thought the joy was immense at seeing Verity sitting in the room, the pain of watching her leave was tenfold.

I meant every word I had said in my speech, careful not to expose our relationship to the crowd. From now on, my priority was getting her back and nothing, not even my flourishing career would get in the way of that.

I stumbled through the post-win interview, smiling woodenly and doing my best to charm journalists who hounded me with questions, as I fought the urge to double over in agony. I should have followed her, I should have skipped this obligation and chased her down the street. Yet again, my ignorant actions had caused me to lose her once more.

"Thanks guys, enjoy the rest of your night." I said goodbye to the room of interviewers and photographers and headed backstage to drop off the award to the designated area. As I pulled back the curtain, to my disbelief, I was met with a pair of piercing blue eyes and red lips. Verity.

"Axel, a picture please!"

"Congrats Axel, how amazing!"

"How do you feel, Mr Ford?" A dozen people gathered beside her but all I could see was my beautiful girl.

"Sorry everyone, I've got something important to attend to." I nodded at Verity gesturing towards the door, still not totally convinced that she wasn't a figment of my imagination.

Silently, we made our way to a quiet corner to speak alone. The electricity between us was palpable.

"I thought you had left." I said breathlessly, fighting every urge to touch her.

"I thought I was going to." She giggled, tucking a strand of hair behind her ear, coyly. That sound was music to me.

"I-"

"It's my turn to talk." Verity hushed me, taking my hand in hers. I could have broken down at that moment. The feel of her soft hand against mine was like breathing after drowning. "You hurt me. More than anyone ever has before. And I shouldn't have come and I shouldn't forgive you. And I shouldn't love you," my breath caught in my throat. "But I am here, I do forgive you and I do love you." She looked up at me with adoration and I felt my knees threaten to buckle at her confession. I cupped her face in my hands.

"I fucking love you." I whispered, "I love you so much." I looked at her lips asking permission, wanting nothing more than to close the space between us and kiss her. She nodded ever so slightly. That was the sign I needed. I kissed her deeper than ever before, making up for every day that I had not been able to, every lie I had ever told and every mistake I had ever made. I wanted to bottle this feeling and live in this moment forever.

"Let's get out of here," she breathed against my lips. I led her out of the building to my waiting limo. The minute the car door shut and the partition closed, all bets were off.

Our lips stayed connected as I reached under her dress to remove her thong, her hands tangling in my hair.

"I need you, Ax." She whimpered as my fingers found the wetness between her thighs.

"I can tell, Doll. You've clearly been missing my cock." I purred, knowing the effect my dirty talk had on her. She moaned as I circled her clit with my thumb before removing my hand and finding the curve of her waist, pulling her onto my lap. She rocked her hips eagerly, grinding her bare pussy on the hardness in my suit trousers.

"I missed it so much." She mewled, "I missed *you* so much." My heart swelled, feeling choked up with emotion at her words.

"I missed you too, sweetheart." I kissed the side of her neck, licking and sucking a sensitive spot until she was putty in my arms.

"Please Ax…" She whined, as much as I loved playing with her, I was not in the mood to wait any longer than necessary.

"Okay, Doll, lay back on the seat." I commanded, she did as she was told and I felt my erection pulse at her obedience. I stood above her, drinking her in, I wanted nothing more than to see her naked and ready for me, but I knew the journey wouldn't last long enough.

I began unbuckling my belt, watching her pupils dilated with arousal as I released my cock from its prison, she licked her lips hungrily. "I'm not going to tease you, Doll, as we have both waited long enough for this. But just know…" I leant down, lining up my dick with her sopping pussy, she bucked her hips eagerly. I pressed a kiss to her ear, prolonging the tension, "I'm not done with you when we get to the hotel." I felt her body quiver beneath me at my promise before plunging my cock inside her. She cried out in ecstasy and I moaned at the feeling of her cunt constricting around me. I thrusted into her with full force, holding her hips as I drove deeper inside her.

"God, you feel so good." She groaned. I reached down to resume my circles on her clit and she threw her head back, gripping onto the leather of the seat as the sensation consumed her. "How the fuck do you do this?!" She asked in disbelief as her first orgasm - of many, started to build.

"I know your body so well, Verity." I smirked, quickening my movements, "look at me while you come, Sweet." I directed, she grabbed my face with both hands and stared into my eyes, I watched as she came undone beneath me, she was the most beautiful woman I had ever seen. "God, I'm so in love with you." I whispered in disbelief.

Her doe eyes shone with tears, overcome with emotion. "Ax, I need your cum inside me."

Fuck. That was all the encouragement I needed, I thrust into her faster, chasing my orgasm, as she begged for my load in hushed whispers. Her nails dug into my back and her breathing increased, the knowledge that we were both on the brink spurred me on, I felt her pussy flutter around me. With one final pump I released inside her at the same moment she came on my cock once again.

I rested my forehead against hers, our laboured breaths mixing together before I pressed a sweet kiss to her lips and pulled out of her. She whimpered slightly at the feeling, her head falling back, feeling lethargic from the intensity of her climax.

She sighed contentedly as I stood up and began re-buckling my belt, taking in the vision of her before me. "That was so good."

"It's not over yet, Doll." I winked, the sight of her glazed eyes, smudged lipstick and dishevelled hair from our frantic sex sesh was enough to get me hard all over again.

I sat down beside Verity as she smoothed her dress, before pulling her against me and pressing a kiss to the top of her head, the sweet smell of her consuming me. She hummed blissfully. I found it difficult to believe

that this was my reality. Only an hour ago I thought I'd
lost the love of my life forever, but here we were
euphorically in each other's arms, ready to start again.

49

VERITY

The minutes passed by in a blur as Axel whisked me out of the car and into the lobby of the hotel. Dozens of fans waited outside to catch a glimpse of a celebrity, as this was one of the main spots that the nominees stayed in, post the Oscars ceremony. Their screams became background noise. All I could focus on was Axel. I was completely besotted with the image of him as he guided me through the crowd of well-wishers.

He was polite and civil to them on the outside, yet I could sense his frustration of how much he wanted to get me alone.

We made it into the lift and fell back into each other's embrace, picking up where we left off, kissing frantically once more. Just as the doors of the elevator were about to close, a hand stopped them. I heard Axel growl when he pulled away from me as an unknown man entered the lift. Axel and I smiled tactfully, trying to appear like we weren't ready to jump each other's bones. The stranger returned the expression before he turned his back to us, popped in AirPods and began to play music.

Axel snaked an arm around my waist, pulling me to him. His mouth grazed my ear as he whispered, "I'm done waiting."

My mouth dried at the meaning behind his words and my thighs clenched together, trying to relieve the tension building there.

Carefully, he scrunched up the hem of my dress, sliding his hand under the silk. I could feel my already wet pussy dripping down my thighs. It was at that moment I remembered I was no longer wearing underwear and that Axel had my discarded thong in his jacket pocket. His rough fingers found my naked skin and he began to play with my swollen clit. He dipped his thumb into my pussy as I did all I could not to moan out in ecstasy and give the game away to our friend in the box. "Good girl, keep nice and quiet for me, Doll." He whispered, I buried my face in the crook of his neck, holding in my whimpers as my legs began to shake at the impending orgasm.

The ding of the elevator sent a shock through my body and Axel stilled his movements. I tried to hold in my complaints as the man began to leave before he turned to face Axel.

"Congrats by the way." He said.

"Cheers buddy," Axel responded, nonchalantly as I stood like a deer in headlights, willing the doors to shut.

No sooner had the thick metal closed, Axel had removed his hand and pushed me against the reflective wall, repositioning, before slipping in two digits and relentlessly finger fucking me to my peak. He cupped the back of my head, kissing the side of my neck as he brought me closer to the edge.

"I can't wait to bury my cock inside you again." He purred, I groaned, my head falling against the mirror behind me as the sensation took over.

Just as we reached the penthouse floor, I came all over his hand. Axel could tell my legs threatened to give out and wrapped his arms around my waist lifting me up and carrying me through the opened lift doors.

"Ready for round three, Doll?" I could hear the cocky smirk in his voice and I fucking loved it. I nodded enthusiastically, unable to formulate words. As we moved through the large room, Axel freed a hand and swept up an ice bucket, with a large bottle of champagne in it.

I didn't have time to fully take in my surroundings before Axel chucked me on a plush, super-king-sized bed, all I was focused on was the man towering over me. "Remove your dress." He demanded, instantly I did as I was told, slowly lifting the crimson fabric over my body, his pupils dilated as I revealed my bare breasts before pulling it over my head. "You're so stunning." He breathed. I watched as he began undoing his tie.

"Red looks good on you, you should wear colour more often." I complemented, noting the unexpected tie he was wearing. I was too overwhelmed at the ceremony to notice before, but it was unusual for him not to be head to toe in black.

"You know, I wore this shade for you, Verity." He confessed as he removed the fabric from his neck. His words took me by surprise. There was no way he could have known I would be wearing the same colour. He really did know me well.

"Lay back." He instructed. Crawling over my body as I did what he asked. His breath ghosted over my nipples as he moved above me, my fingers found their way into his hair, trying to pull him closer. He chuckled darkly, reaching for my wrists. He held them in one hand and bound them together with the tie. "Red *always* looks good on you, Doll." Before I could register what he was doing he lifted my arms above my head, tying them to the bed frame.

My breath hitched at the feeling of being restrained, the fabric biting my skin deliciously. Arousal buzzed between my legs as I realised I was merciless to him. Axel placed a kiss to my lips before backing away, standing at the foot of the bed to admire his work.

"Where do you think you're going?" I asked in disbelief as he began to walk away, he shot me a wink, crossing the room towards the bottle of champagne. "Really?!" I questioned, "Is now the time for a drink Axel?" I knew I was being a brat, but all my usual manners escaped me as my clit pulsed needily and I had no way of relieving myself.

"I'm not getting the bottle, Doll." He smirked, as he picked up a large ice cube from the bucket with his finger and thumb and walked back to join me on the bed. He dropped the cube on my stomach, causing a gasp to escape me from the sub-zero temperature. Axel leant over and took the block into his mouth, sliding it up my torso until he reached my erect nipple on my left breast. My brain was scrambled, this was quite possibly the horniest I'd ever been in my life. The contrast of Axel's hot breath and the coldness of the ice was mind blowing.

I struggled against my restraints as he circled the bud, then mirroring his actions on my right side. A trail of melted water slicked my chest.

"Fucking hell, Axel." I panted. Torturously slowly he moved further down my body, dragging the half-melted cube with him. The river of freezing liquid formed a pathway to my begging core.

I jolted as his cold tongue made contact with my pussy and threw my head back in ecstasy. I heard him groan at the taste.

"God, I've waited so long for this." His breath ghosted over me as he spoke and I bucked up beneath him, desperate for a third orgasm.

He expertly manoeuvred the ice cube against my most sensitive area until it melted, causing my climax to approach rapidly. My legs quivered around his head and he held my thighs open, licking and sucking as the euphoric tsunami surged over, keeping up his movements until my pleasure was satiated.

Thoughts were incoherent, my vision blurred as he untied me and grabbed my bare hips. He flipped me over to my tummy effortlessly and pulled my body to the edge of the bed. Axel stood on the floor and positioned his dick behind me, holding on to the curve of my body as he slammed deep inside.

I gasped at the feeling of being stretched so completely by him.

"You take my cock so so well, Verity." He growled, thrusting harder into me each time. "Such a good girl." He wrapped my hair around his wrist and pulled hard, I screamed in pleasure as his other hand spanked my arse harshly.

"I'm gonna come again, Axel." I cried.

"I should hope so." He purred, driving himself into me with more force than I'd ever felt before. His grip deepened into my hip, each ruthless thrust causing fireworks to explode in my veins, pushing me closer to my fourth climax, "that's it Babydoll, come for me."

Instantly, blinding pleasure ripped through me. I screamed so loudly, I was certain we would get a noise complaint but at that moment I couldn't care less.

I felt Axel release inside with a moan, collapsing on top of me. We lay there as a sweaty pile of tangled limbs for an immeasurable amount of time before he pulled out and lay beside me on the bed. He cuddled me into his side, placing a kiss on my forehead.

"I don't deserve you, Verity." He whispered, his words made my heart swell and crack slightly. For all the hurt Axel had put me through, I had never felt as loved or understood as when I was with him.

I sat up on my elbow, looking him dead in the eyes. "Don't say that, Axel." He stared at me, confusion evident on his face. "You're the best thing that's ever happened to me. I don't know where I would be without you." I implored. He didn't say anything, simply cupped the back of my head and brought my lips to his in a kiss that said a thousand words.

"You're the love of my life, Doll."

As I laid there, basking in boundless euphoria, it was hard to imagine that we were once enemies. At one point, I would've given anything to be as far away from Axel Ford as humanly possible but looking forward I wanted him close for every decision, every milestone and every hurdle.

Despite the odds, the one person I once swore I couldn't stand, had become the one person I couldn't live without.

EPILOGUE

SIX MONTHS LATER

VERITY

It had been six months since Axel and I had reconciled at the Oscars and our connection had never been better.

I had wrapped filming for *Twelve Dates* a month ago and had been enjoying my unemployment. Or as I was calling it, 'unlimited time to be with Axel'.

The days with him were fun, heartwarming and filled with exploration into each other's interests and hobbies. The nights were hot and steamy, delving into our deepest fantasies and culminating in earth shattering orgasms and declarations of love. God, I never wanted this to be over.

However, as with all good things, this limitless time was due to come to an end soon as Axel was about to begin working on a new highly anticipated project. Although Axel had declined the offer of working on

Requiem after the events that caused the breakdown of our relationship, Gus Kensington was relentless in his pursuit of working with the superstar. As Axel had declared in his winning speech, he had taken a step back from the limelight, jumping in with two feet to build and strengthen the bond between us. Yet, I had always been aware of the fact that working with Gus was his ultimate career goal.

"Another email from Gus." Axel informed me, as he began typing out a reply, on his MacBook. "God I'm starting to feel guilty having to keep turning this guy down."

"Then why don't you accept his offer for once?" I shrugged, taking a sip of my pistachio latte.

"I made a promise that I would put us and most importantly, you, first. I'm not going to break that just for another movie. I'm sure they'll be more in the future and if not, then I'm more than happy with what I've achieved already." He insisted, stirring his own mug of coffee.

"Axel." I moved his laptop to the side, meeting his eyeline to ensure I had his full attention. "You have wanted to work with this guy your whole career and already missed out on one chance. Opportunities like this won't be around forever. But I will." I assured him, reaching out to intertwine my fingers with his. "You should take it. I want you to take it, Ax." He rubbed his thumb on the back of my hand, mulling over my words.

After another week of convincing, Axel finally decided to take Gus up on his offer of working on his next film, post *Requiem*. He wasn't one to show hyper excitement, but I could tell he was positively bubbling with anticipation to begin working alongside his hero.

Axel and I weren't the only happy ones in our home, Misto had been loving Axel's apartment and enjoyed watching the birds from eye level in the high-rise building however, we thought it was about time that the fluffy member of our family had adequate outdoor space to explore, hunt and sunbathe.

We spent weeks mulling over where to live. London or New York. Both of the cities had their pros: London was near my loved ones, New York was closer to his and each had their cons: NY was busy and the seasons were extreme, yet London was rainy the majority of the time. I suggested flipping a coin but Axel said that was too spontaneous even for him. Ultimately, we chose to stay in England as it held so many memories for us and was the place that we met and our love story began.

Once we had locked the location, the next tough decision was what house we were going to make our home. We viewed properties across the city, but all of them left something to be desired until we stumbled upon the baroque style house in Hampstead Heath. The luxury detached white building was decorated on the exterior with intricate designs and tall arched windows, with a set of steps in the centre leading up to an obscenely large wooden door. Everything about it was perfect and the fact that Lilah lived around the corner was a bonus!

I had never dreamed that I would live in a house like this, let alone with my teen crush: Teddy from *Sunset High*. We got the keys a couple of weeks before Axel was due to start filming and we immediately headed to the property to celebrate with a bottle of bubbles before moving all our belongings in.

"Welcome home, Doll," Axel smiled, unlocking the door. The wood creaked open to reveal the large empty entryway. Before I had the chance to take a step inside I squealed as Axel scooped me into his arms and carried me over the threshold.

After a few steps, he returned me to solid ground and laid a tartan blanket down on the dark wooden floor before taking out two glasses and champagne from the bag he was carrying.

"Take a seat," Axel instructed as he popped the cork off the bottle.

"Woo!" I called as he poured the liquid into the flutes and I sat down, crossing my legs.

Axel began sitting down beside me when a knock at the door disrupted him. He opened it and took a large bouquet of flowers from a delivery man.

"Oh, you shouldn't have, I didn't get you anything!" I gushed, they truly were beautiful. A bunch of red carnations and green foliage. My favourite flower and colour.

"Yeah, they're not from me, sorry Doll." Axel responded, laughing as he handed me the gift and sat beside me.

Puzzled, I opened the envelope that had been attached and slipped out the card.

Dear Verity, congratulations on the purchase of your home. I hope you and Axel will be very happy there and I would love to come and visit once you're settled. Love, Mum x

A cocktail of emotions swirled inside of me as I processed the words. This was the first time I had heard from my mother since Christmas Eve, so Charlotte or my dad must have updated her on my news as well as my address.

"If these are from Niall from *Twelve Dates* he's going to have an unexpected visitor later." Axel laughed, running a hand through his shaggy hair.

"They're from my mum." I said blankly. He sobered at the information.

"What did she say?" He placed a comforting hand on the small of my back. I suddenly felt my eyes water with unshed tears. "You don't have to let her upset you anymore."

"No," I sniffed, turning to look at him, "they're happy tears." My voice wobbled and a smile pulled at my lips. For the first time in my life, I knew she was proud of me.

Axel wrapped his arm around me, pulling me towards him and pressing a kiss to my cheek. We sat there, I wasn't sure for how long, watching the golden September sun illuminate the room in comfortable silence, until Axel finally broke it.

"Actually, there is something I wanted to show you." He shifted his weight and I slid off him, curiosity flickering in my mind. He began lifting the hem of his shirt.

"Yeah, impressive Axel, but I've seen your abs before." I giggled.

"Ha. Ha." He deadpanned though his lips curled with amusement. I watched as he removed his top completely, my eyes instantly falling on the plethora of tattoos decorating his pecs. My eyeline trailed the vines until they snagged on a tattoo I didn't recognise. "I haven't shown you the piece I got for *Accidentally in Love*."

I sat up on my knees to get a better look at the fresh ink, reaching out to touch it, "a bow?" I asked, confusion coating my words.

"A bow." He repeated, simply.

"It's lovely… but what has it got to do with coffee shops and Americanos?" I asked cautiously, I didn't want to offend Axel but I truly couldn't get my head around the inspiration for the design.

He chuckled faintly, amusement glinting in his smoky eyes, before reaching behind my head to tug gently on the red ribbon fastened in my hair. I tried to swallow past the sudden dryness in my throat, as the meaning behind the artwork sunk in. I stared at the delicate bow, tied into the leaves on the left side of his ribs, my throat constricting with emotion.

"It's for me?" My vision blurred. Tears welling in my eyes, as I asked the question, I suspected I already knew the answer to and I felt my heart double in size at the gesture.

"Of course, Doll." Axel's answering smile warmed my whole body and I couldn't do anything other than beam back before throwing myself at him and wrapping my arms around his neck. "The best thing I took from that set was you." He whispered, pressing a kiss to the top of my head, his hands snaking around my waist.

"I'd hope so." I laughed, basking in the intimacy of the moment.

I'd never felt happier, secure in my home, career and relationships. It's true what they say about expecting the unexpected, sitting here now soaking in the earthy scent of Axel's cologne, reflecting over the past eighteen months, I couldn't be more thankful that we had fallen completely and utterly, accidentally in love.

ABOUT THE AUTHORS

Ria Alice and Jessica May are two friends from the UK with a shared love of steamy romance novels. Their books contain pop culture references galore, fun, supportive friendships and a spicy relationship to top it all off!

When they're not writing, you can find them at a 2000's emo night, a karaoke bar or marathoning cheesy rom-coms over a charcuterie board.

Keep up to date with their latest projects on social media:
Instagram: @authorriaaliceandjessicamay
TikTok: @riaaliceandjessicamay

BY THE AUTHORS

THE HIDDEN SERIES
A series of interconnected standalones

Hidden Gem

ACKNOWLEDGEMENTS

Getting to know another couple in the *Hidden* universe was so much fun! It was daunting to write a guy who was total arsehole as we were worried we wouldn't fall in love with him and wouldn't want our girl to end up with him but God, did Axel give Zane a run for his money. We were giggling and kicking our feet like schoolgirls writing some of these scenes and we hope you felt the same way reading them!

As sad as were to finish book one, it's been a joy to see snippets of our OGs happy relationship progress through *Agenda* and look out for all four of main characters popping up in Book Three. Any guesses on whose story will be next?

Thanks again for our fabulous beta readers, the reaction to this story was electrifying and completely blew us away!

Lastly, thanks to you for reading our SECOND novel – that sounds insane to write – it means everything to know that some of you have been excited and waiting for this next instalment and we're hoping you love V & A!

P.S. We owe TikTok for the countless hours we spent scrolling through edits of fit male celebrities to visualise Axel! That was a very enjoyable part of the research process!

www.ingramcontent.com/pod-product-compliance
Lightning Source LLC
Chambersburg PA
CBHW030926120726
47906CB00002B/502